THE ONE THAT I WANT

THE ONE THAT SERIES

J. KEELY THRALL

Cover design: Sweet 'N Spicy Designs (https://sweetnspicydesigns.com)

Chapter header images designed using Canva Pro

Edited by: Jessica Snyder of HEA Author Services and Darlene Gardner

ISBN: 978-1-962258-00-5 (ebook)

ISBN: 978-1-962258-01-2 (paperback)

❀ Formatted with Vellum

To all the circles in my life.
Family, friends, colleagues.
Colleagues who are friends.
Friends who are family.
I am not me without you.

One circle in particular has lifted my boat since May 2020 and deserves a special shout out. Thank you, Morning Crew peeps. Your steadfast inspiration, encouragement, dedication, practicality, joy, skill, wisdom, and all around awesomeness make getting out of bed each morning totally worth it. Elated to be on this journey with you.

THE ONE THAT I WANT
BY J. KEELY THRALL

This summer, the sexy nice-guy risk she swore she'd never take is melting her defenses one smoking-hot kiss at a time.

GRUMPY-GAL Keira doesn't do emotional entanglements—until her favorite spicy hookup, sunshine-boy Connor Mack, asks for more than just her body. When wedding planning duties throw them together for the summer, their no-strings fling starts looking dangerously like love. With her manipulative parents back in play, Keira must choose: protect her heart, or take a chance on the one man who makes her feel safe, seen, and wildly wanted.

CHAPTER 1

CONNOR MACK

Sully's Tavern is a sardine can packed in tight with the after-work crowd, glugging its way to a well-oiled Friday night buzz. I pause by the untended hostess station, letting the babble roll over me, a boozy sonic wave.

After weeks of nose-to-the-grindstone, burn-the-midnight-oil work, I put the finishing touches on the Winstonian Hotel renovation proposal late this afternoon and hit send. All I have to do now is wait for Dad to greenlight my vision. A vision that, when I turn it into reality, will further burnish the reputation of Mack Family Architects and firmly establish me as the go-to project lead on future renovation projects.

Waiting isn't my strong suit.

I launch into the crowd. Normally, when any of us have a major, minor, or even mediocre life event to celebrate, my two older brothers and I get together. But tonight David, the oldest, is with his wife as they test yet another bone broth recipe in an attempt to find a food that won't set off her all-day morning sickness. Felix, our middle brother, is with his long-term girlfriend, possibly, finally, getting around to asking her to move in.

We'll catch up later in the weekend. Right now, I have a different way in mind to pass the time without going crazy. And a very different person.

Keira Tanner.

Five months ago, she offered me a one-fuck, once-a-month deal. No strings sex with an intelligent, ambitious, funny, beautiful woman? Not being a dummy, and having my own reasons for not wanting strings, I agreed. The sex has been kinked-up and smoking hot. Any guy's wet dream of a no-pressure arrangement.

I should be content. But lately, I've been wanting more.

More sex. More Keira. More often.

Will she accept a change to our agreement?

Slipping around a knot of people, I smooth my new tie and shrug off a whisper of doubt. She's smart. Strategic. She'll see the benefits that come from enhancing our no-strings deal. No need to worry.

"Connor, you do the deed?" My closest friend, Mateo, asks with a grin from his command center at the end of the bar. These monthly networking happy hours are his brainchild. He exchanges a nod with Sully, who starts preparing our drinks.

"The countdown clock is officially on. Now all I need is to find a way to keep from checking my inbox every few seconds while I wait for Dad to review the proposal."

"You're not really worried, are you?"

I tip the flat of my hand back and forth. "Something's up. He's been acting funny lately. Who knows? He could be looking to recruit new talent into the firm with the promise of a high profile project."

"Bah. He'd be a fool to pass you over. And Johnny Mack is no fool."

We accept our drinks, and my usual scotch on the rocks is halfway to my mouth before Keira, a sleek shark in a sea of lesser predators, weaves her way in our direction.

Her hips roll, a subtle side-to-side rhythm that has me thirsty. Thirsty for something far more primal than the drink I hold.

This month she sports short black hair with electric-blue stripes. My fingers itch, eager for another chance to slide through the thick silk.

Headed toward the facilities, she passes by without a hint of acknowledgement. Such a cool customer she shows the world.

The truth behind her facade is so much more compelling.

I force myself to take a slow sip before I hand my precious Johnnie Walker Black back to Mateo. "Keep this safe. Nature calls."

"I guess that's one way to stay out of your inbox."

"No idea what you're talking about."

"Fine, keep pretending nobody knows. But don't take too long, all right? You need to be back in time for the announcements. I'm counting on you."

Acknowledging his demand with a wave, I retrace my steps to the front of the restaurant and Sully's infamous coed bathroom. My oldest brother is the architectural engineering genius behind the stalls that come complete with individual sinks and sturdy counters. Perfect for hookup sex.

Thank you, David.

I head for the corner stall—our stall—eager to sell Keira on the high points of coming to a new arrangement.

Perched on the counter, she's ditched her suit jacket, leaving her dressed in a white blouse and a black skirt. Pleated. "For easy access," she whispered in my ear our first time. The skirt's hem rides high on her toned, bare thighs, and she's playing a game of cat's cradle with a scrap of black lace.

Her thong.

A hit of anticipation goes straight south, making the fit of my slacks uncomfortably tight.

My heart pumps faster as I slide the door latch home. She fidgets, as though the sound of metal gliding into place gives her ideas. Lock and key, pussy and cock.

Guess it gives me ideas too. But before we explore them, I need to make my second proposal of the day.

"Keira." I lean against the opposite wall instead of pressing between her thighs.

"Connor." Her husky voice trickles like a butterfly kiss over my skin, featherlight and distracting.

Must not give in to her siren call. Not yet, anyway. I shift my weight. *Come on, dude, you can do this.*

"The Bane Jazz Trio is playing at the Rio on Thursday. Come with me."

"I'm sorry, what?"

"Good music. Some dinner. A little conversation, a few laughs. A hint of will we or won't we that ultimately ends in a rousing round of naked entertainment."

Her face scrunches in confusion.

"A date, Keira. I'm asking you on a date. It's not an original concept."

"Crap." She drags a hand through her black-and-blue hair. "Is the sex not good enough?"

"Are you kidding?" It's my turn to frown. "You know the sex is off the charts."

"Then what's this about a date?"

"You're cute, funny, feisty, odd, I like you, and the sex is phenomenal. Is it really so bizarre I'd want to get to know you better?"

"Balls." She slumps. "I didn't expect this."

"What?"

"You. Going all girly on me."

"Excuse me?" A pulse of *uh-oh* shoots through me. I straighten from the wall.

"You said you were cool with no strings."

"I'm not asking for your hand in marriage. What's the big deal?"

"I thought the deal was we're using each other for mutual pleasure. Now you're pushing for new terms."

"And that's a problem, how?" I shave the distance between us to mere inches. "Anyone with half a brain nails down more favorable terms when they see the chance."

"Nope. No sale." She chops her panty-wielding hand through the air in an unmistakable *no way*. "Stick to the original understanding. Once-a-month, straight-up sex. No entanglements."

Disappointment hollows out my chest, surprising me with its strength. It's not like this is the first time I've ever been shot down.

Still, I thought we had a connection, the fizz that comes when two people see beneath each other's surface.

My mistake. I pull back.

"Don't go." The clasp of her hand burns my wrist. "What we have is good. Simple. Can't we keep it that way? No messy emotions?"

Her plea is a timely wake-up call.

What the hell am I doing, angling for complicated? Sherry cured me of that impulse years ago. I should be glad for Keira's reminder. Simple is best.

"You're right." I manage a grin. Not my suavest, but it'll do. "Blame it on temporary insanity. I turned in the proposal for the Winstonian Hotel today. Must have shorted out my wires."

"Hey, congratulations." She holds her fist out for a bump, genuine delight for me giving her smile an extra kick.

"Thanks." I shrug and bump, trying to play it casual. As though I'm not wincing from my dip into forbidden relationship waters.

"How about a round of celebratory sex?" She snaps her thong against my chest like a rubber band.

Choking on a laugh, I catch the thong and stow the black lace in my suit coat's inner pocket.

"Too soon? That was too soon, wasn't it? Damn. See? Emotions are stupid. Here I am, beyond ready to get busy with you and forget a shitty few days, but instead I've managed to hurt your feelings. That sucks."

My hard-on stirs back to life at the renewed prospect of sex with Keira. It doesn't care about dates and messy emotions. It likes hard work and achievable goals.

I shove the last of my inconvenient, unexpected *feelings* aside and throw myself into retrieving our easy, breezy setup.

"Depends." I draw the word out.

"On?"

"You said no strings, but there's one string we both seem to like." I pull my tie free and dangle it between us.

Eyes lighting up, she snatches her prize from my hand. "You're sure?"

"I was born sure." I offer my forearms, side by side. "Tie me up, use me for your pleasure. I guarantee it will be mutual as fuck."

"What's your safe word?" She secures the silk around my wrists, checking the tension.

"Crocodile." I step between her thighs and lower my voice. "What's yours?"

"I keep telling you that's not how this works."

"Don't care." I trace her hairline with my lips, taking in her scent. Something relaxes deep inside me. This. I've been waiting all month for this. I could kick my own ass for almost losing it, trying to make things complicated. "Mutual pleasure, mutual safe words. No safe word, no pleasure."

"Fine. My word is alligator. Happy?"

"Ecstatic."

"Ready for tonight's agenda?" Her dark brown eyes mesmerize me, the iris almost indistinguishable from the pupil. I could drown in their clear depths.

"Bring it."

"I'm going to place your hands behind my back. Touch you through and under your clothes to ensure you are prepared for the job ahead. Only when I'm satisfied that you're truly ready will I guide you into position. Then, on my command, you're going to fuck me, hard and dirty. Do you consent to this course of action?"

"Fuck yes. Condom's in my pants, left pocket. Jacket me up, and I'll jack you off good."

"You are such a bad submissive."

"Probably because I'm not submissive."

"Then why do you let me tie you up and boss you around?"

"Because it's hot as hell. Now get to touching, woman." I summon my brief career as a college stripper and rock a bump and grind. "I have a promotion going to waste."

"That's no good." She guides my arms over her head, wriggling to the edge of the counter. At the same time, I close the gap to block her from any danger of falling.

Touching from groin to chest, fully clothed, we breathe, adjusting to the enforced intimacy that comes from my cuffed embrace. I cuddle her closer, and after a moment, she softens against me with a sigh.

"Hard week?" I ask.

"Pretty hateful."

"I'm sorry." I kiss her cheek then her jaw then the corner of her mouth. "Boss again? Or did you run into another couple demanding that you score them a two-million-dollar penthouse on their five-hundred-k budget?"

"Boss. I don't know what's eating him, but his rat-bastard quotient is through the roof lately." She arches into me as I explore her face with soft nuzzles—nose, brow, temple.

I come back to her mouth and lick her lower lip then linger because she tastes good.

"Kissing wasn't on the agenda," she murmurs but meets my tongue with hers. I have no idea how long we spend reacquainting ourselves after a month apart, one slow, drugging kiss after the next, before she disengages, glassy-eyed and breathless.

"Think of it as a friendly amendment to the agenda."

"W-what?"

"The kissing." I give her a quick get-with-the-program jostle. "Good leadership is about staying agile, open to new ideas."

"You—"

"Need to be touched. Agenda item two. That's next, right?"

She shakes her head, possibly to get hair off her face or maybe because she can't believe my cheek. Either way, it tempts me to start kissing again. I aim low, teasing her collarbones.

Final destination—the sensitive tendon that runs behind her ear.

In retaliation, she spreads her legs wider, drags me closer. The new position complicates my mission, but I'm no quitter.

I double down, savoring her soft skin and the tiny shivers she can't control.

In the hidden space between my suit coat and shirt, she explores the muscles of my back. Her touch is light, a whirl of curious inquiry quickening my pulse. She dances further afield, dropping below my beltline to trace the curves of my ass, purgatory and bliss build with each tantalizing glide of her clever fingers.

"Sweetheart, you play back there, this is gonna be over long before we hit the rest of the line items on our agenda."

"Would serve you right." Her chuckle rumbles against me, low, a little evil, a lot pleased.

"So, it's like that, eh?" In retaliation, I set about upping the intensity of her shivers.

She unzips my slacks and wraps her hands around my cock.

Not, damn it, my bare cock.

Her lingering appraisal of my state of readiness through the thin barrier of my shorts soon has me pressing my forehead into her shoulder. She croons in sympathy but doesn't pause her inspection.

With each teasing touch, I sink deeper into the warm current she creates, weirdly freed by the improvised cuffs restricting my movement.

Keira's the team leader during these encounters. The temporary surrender of having to be the driver is still new for me and seductive as hell. I don't have to worry if I'm going too fast or too slow. If she's wet enough or wants more foreplay. With her, like this, there are no guessing games. She tells me what she wants.

Sometimes we negotiate. Mostly I simply say yes. And not too long after we agree on terms, we have a lot of fun working toward mutually satisfying results.

"Agenda item three commencing in T minus two, one—" She shoves both hands under the waistband of my boxers and grabs hold of my hard and very ready cock.

"Condom. Now. Please." I thrust forward, searching for more. More pressure, more stroking.

Finally, I'm gloved. This is the moment when I struggle most against my confinement. I can't lift her thigh for better access or use my fingers to spread wetness over her clit. Can't make any of my standard sex moves.

Instead, I'm controlled by her will, and it only makes me harder.

She lines me up, the tip of my cock nudging the lips of her pussy. Her heat licks over me. From my tied-up position, I can only imagine how pink she is, how swollen and ready. The not knowing for sure heightens my awareness of everything else. Her scent, the sound of her shallow panting, the tickle of her warm breath as it reaches my face.

"Command me, baby. Tell me we're at go time."

"Go," she gasps.

Hips flexing, thighs straining, I push inside and pull back, searching until I find the angle that makes her shudder and gasp again. Then I get busy.

She kneads my shoulders, eyes closed, lips parted, a frown of concentration digging between her brows. I speed up the pace of my thrusts, wanting to please her.

She jerks, a whole-body spasm, so fast I'm almost not quick enough to protect her from smacking her head against the tile. I cradle the base of her skull in my bound hands and take over her mouth as she shakes through her climax.

Electric shocks zap through my body.

I'm so ready, I ache. But I'm too wound up, and my release remains just out of reach.

Keira snakes her arms around my waist, forcing me even closer, compelling me to shift to shallow thrusts, and oh, fuck. She goes there. Her finger slides down to my crack, and boom, I'm done, shaking and weak-kneed from the power of my climax.

When I'm myself again, we're plastered together. Once we've cooled down and catch our breath, I peel back and discover two hooked arrows of blue hair standing at attention above her temples. The goat horns make me chuckle.

"What?" she asks, her husky voice rumbly with satisfaction.

"Sex hair."

"Damn it." She swipes at the short strands, making things worse. "My hairdresser promised this cut would stand up to the test."

"I think she underestimates your testing process. Ready?" She nods, and I retrieve my arms from behind her. She unknots the tie, revealing bright red marks on my skin.

"Your wrists. I'm sorry."

"It's nothing permanent. Don't worry." Acknowledging the transience of Keira's marks washes away my post-orgasm glow. I flash her a tight smile, unhitching the rest of the way to clean up.

Shooting my cuffs, I cover the evidence of our tryst as she washes her hands and wrestles with her hair. In the mirror, her brown eyes swim with secrets.

Secrets I still want in on.

"Same time, same place next month?" I ask.

"Sure."

I wait for a moment to see if she'll say more. She doesn't.

"Right, see you out there." I exit the stall and head back to the networking happy hour, giving Keira's hidden thong a considering pat.

Her *sure* isn't a confidence builder, but after the overwhelming success of this particular session, I'm not too worried. I'll explain my error was in execution, not expectation. That I'm not interested in dating so much as in arranging more opportunities for excellent sex.

We'll move past this awkwardness and everything will be back to normal.

Normal, only with more sex.

CHAPTER 2

KEIRA TANNER

"**M**en." I swing onto a stool beside my bestie, Helena, and thump my purse on the polished bar top.

"What's it this time?" Her voice hovers between resigned and amused.

"It's just... Aren't they supposed to be simple organisms? The half of the species whose needs are straightforward and immutable?"

"Immutable? Looks who's talking fancy tonight."

"Food, sleep, shelter, sports, sex." I count off on my fingers, ignoring her dig with the ease of long practice. "The base level of Maslow's Hierarchy of Needs pyramid."

"According to Keira."

"Pretty sure I covered the major categories. And nowhere on the list does dating or getting to know someone better appear."

"Poor you." She tilts her head and flutters her eyelashes at me in faux sympathy. "Getting shafted by human nature again?"

"You laugh."

"It's either laugh, cry, or strangle you."

"From the gentleman at the end of the bar." The owner/bartender sets down a couple of French 75 cocktails with his signature flourish.

"Thanks, Sully." Helena salutes him with her flute then leans in and repeats the gesture with a bonus air kiss at Mateo, her lover, who's hanging out at the other end of the bar.

He pantomimes the kiss landing on his heart. *Lub-dub, lub-dub.*

"That's so sweet, it's a wonder you don't have diabetes."

"Better diabetes than a life lacking sweets."

"If you say so."

I take the first mouthful of my drink, savoring the nip of alcohol while doggedly ignoring the tall, sexy man beside Mateo with every fiber of my being.

It's unfair that Connor fills out a suit better than any other guy at this event. Stupid broad shoulders. Wretched muscular thighs. Rotten tight butt.

Or that he can make me laugh during sex. Delicious, thong-melting sex.

Or that he's up for any and all kinky adventures.

Or, while I'm at it, that he's such a genuinely nice man.

I should have listened to my head instead of my hoo-ha and never started this fling with Connor Mack. Should have stuck with what I know works instead of letting myself get swayed by a pretty face and amazing orgasms.

And I definitely shouldn't have pushed for sex tonight. What was I thinking?

Clearly the man short-circuits my good sense.

The sooner I break things off, the sooner I can go back to normal, maybe even begin looking for a replacement who won't tempt me into trying for things I'm not equipped to handle.

A low-level ache rumbles to life in my belly. Heartburn on an empty stomach. That's all it is. Not regret. Nope, not disappointment and regret.

I knock back more of my liquid resolve. Operation Cut the Guy Loose is on deck.

"What's really bugging you?" Helena asks.

"You mean human nature shafting me isn't enough?"

"Cough it up, girl." She levels a stare at me that says she knows I'm avoiding something.

"Rat Bastard has been jerkface-ier than usual at work." I roll the bottom edge of my flute in a circle against the bar tap. "And the latest quarterly report from my parents' company arrived today."

"Ah. Another edition of their real estate investment brag book, right on schedule. Gonna take a peek at what they've acquired lately?"

"No."

"How will you destroy this one?"

"Thinking old school. Over a flame while rocking out to an eighties hair band playlist."

"Solid." We touch the rims of our glasses. "It's rotten that they keep sending you shit when you've made it so clear you want no contact."

"Nobody's real to them, so why should they take anyone else's wishes into account?" I grew up with my former Army Ranger father and beauty-pageant-loving mother steamrolling past my boundaries. I moved across the country to escape their vortex, but the postal service finds me like clockwork every three months.

Laughter erupts from the circle of guys surrounding Mateo and Connor. Mateo catches Helena's eye and makes a sideways nod.

"Come on, it's time for the announcements." Helena's friendly shove distracts me from spiraling down a parental rabbit hole.

I catch hold of her hand and yank it an inch from my face. She tugs for freedom, but I hold tight.

Third finger. Left hand. Bigly huge honking diamond, sparkling like the Eiffel Tower at night.

"You're engaged? How did this happen? I thought you and Mateo weren't serious?"

"We weren't serious. Last year. When we first started dating?"

"Right. I'm with you." I'm not. I'm lost. But I wise-frown-nod, selling sincerity like a boss.

"Things progressed." A smile unfurls from her lips to inhabit her entire body. In all our years of friendship, I've never seen her so happy.

A happiness that has apparently been building right under my nose. For months.

"How did I miss this?" I demand of the shiny rock in front of me.

"You missed it because you duck romantic entanglements the way a second-grade boy avoids playground cooties—as though it's a matter of life and death. Don't worry. I love you anyway." She gives my fingers a little pump of reassurance.

"I'm a horrible BFF."

"Nah. Just an emotional scaredy-cat slash ostrich with your head stubbornly in the sand about a few things. Like the fact that for the past several months, you've been practicing Olympic-level gymnastics trying to ignore, suppress, and otherwise avoid acknowledging your own growing hierarchy of needs when it comes to a certain hunka-hunka burning hottie." She hops off her barstool and pulls me through the crowd in her wake. Over her shoulder, she shoots me an impish grin. "But don't think for a second I'm not going to use your guilt for my own ends. Guess who's Handmaiden Number One to my Bridezilla?"

A trumpet fanfare cascades over the sound system before I can manage a response. Everyone in the room rotates toward Mateo, who now stands on a low-rise stage. We all know the drill after a year of him emceeing these networking gigs. After a welcome and shout outs for anyone with a business success to cheer, he'll detail the rules of this month's networking fun and games.

Scavenger hunt, trivia night, conga line—the format changes, the end goal stays the same. Work the room. Mateo argues these joint exercises will build career-long connections.

Maybe tonight I'll work the room and connect with someone to replace Connor.

At the side of the stage, Helena lets go of her death grip on my wrist to make googly eyes at her new fiancé. He returns the vibe times a million billion. I shift until their goopy display is at the edge of my peripheral view.

Or maybe I'll sit this one out. Wouldn't want to test whether whatever they have is catching.

"They're damn cute," Connor murmurs as he slides in beside me, angling so he becomes my buffer to the ebb and flow of the crowd. He's near enough for his body heat to seep through my clothes, making my pulse leap with second thoughts.

"They are. But some things you don't want scorching your retinas, like the sun during a solar eclipse or another couple's love affair." I keep my voice cool, maybe a little dismissive. He hands me another champagne cocktail, totally unperturbed.

Totally clueless.

No way would he be so considerate if he knew about my plans to make him redundant. Turning my wince into a shrug, I raise my glass in thanks.

Why do I feel guilty about breaking things off, damn it? He's the one who tried an illegal trip into no-fly territory.

"Listen, we need to talk—" I begin.

"Shh, he's starting." The crush of boozed-up young professionals pushes Connor closer, and now I smell me on him.

I smell us together, soap and sweat and the lingering scent of desire.

I press my thighs together, hoo-ha tingling with ideas, aware anew that my thong nests against his strong heartbeat. The heartbeat my hoo-ha swears we could make race if I let my free hand wander south and a little west.

It's official.

My hoo-ha is a traitor.

I toss my drink back in one go. Maybe the icy bubbles will drown this unwelcome flash of need.

"Hey, folks, welcome to our July Networkpalooza." Mateo smiles at the fiftyish people present, a decent showing for a Friday at the start of summer. "Before we get to the main event, I have an important announcement to share. Helena?"

My friend climbs the two stairs to join him on the platform.

"So, they're finally going public with their news, eh? About time." Connor's voice tickles my ear.

I break out in a full body frisson that ends with my nipples pinched tight and me grateful for the cover of my suit jacket.

"You cold?" He sculpts my hip with an absentminded micro-chafe meant to warm. Even when he's not giving his full attention, the man can't help being nice. Cop a feel while he's at it, yeah, sure, but the basic impulse is pure shiny Knight with a capital K.

A moan escapes me, a husky, needy, confused sigh I stomp out of existence, but not quite soon enough.

"Seriously, are you okay?" His breath stirs the hair at my nape.

I clear the horny from my throat. "When did you learn about their engagement?"

"Come again?"

Don't say gladly. Don't say gladly.

Luckily, I'm saved from answering by Mateo's amateur theatrics.

"Friends," he says with a dramatic sweep of his arm to encompass the whole bar. "Last year, when Helena and I met at this very event, I vowed to lay siege to her heart until she accepted me as her one true love, no matter how long it took."

"Which is dreamy and romantic, but really, who's got time for a long, drawn-out sacking of Troy?" Helena cuts in to ask.

The room erupts with laughter. Connor's chuckle buzzes through me like a low-wattage vibrator teasing my clit—not enough oomph to climax from, powerful enough to keep me hanging on the edge.

"Yes, well, fast-forward to now," Mateo continues in a normal voice. "We're thrilled to announce that—"

"We decided to put a ring on it." Helena flashes her big-enough-to-blind diamond.

The crowd revs its full-throttled approval. Connor and I clank our empty glasses together in a toast dry of liquor but drenched in giddy goodwill.

Our gazes catch, lock, and the noise of the room recedes until we exist in a hushed, still bubble. The beat of my pulse drums in my ears. My palms tingle.

Maybe I should have hung out in the restroom after all, ordered drink service through the bar's app. Getting shitfaced in a toilet stall sounds tacky but way more appealing than dealing with the reemergence of this perplexing hunger to go exploring, skin on bare-naked skin.

I don't do naked. I've never done naked. So where the hell is this craving coming from, and why is it not responding to my cease and desist orders?

I worry my bottom lip between my teeth.

He zeroes in on my mouth. His breathing speeds up.

"Keira." My name, gritty and urgent on his lips, rasps my needy edges. He shifts subtly closer, intent, ready to pounce.

"I'm canceling our arrangement," I say before mutinous General Hoo-ha can stage a coup against my better judgment.

"What?" His head snaps back.

"No more sex. It was a good run while it lasted, but it's time to move on."

"The date," he says, grit turning to growl in the space of two brief words.

"I told you my conditions."

He doesn't reply, just ponders me with wolfy blue eyes. Eyes I can't look away from.

Eyes that burn me, melt me.

A curious moth drawn to a curiouser flame, I lean closer, beguiled by this glimpse of untamed Connor. A low rumbling within me whispers of adventure and roads not yet taken. The promise of endless possibilities fizzes through my veins, the mix of scary and exciting more intoxicating than any alcohol.

"King-Con, my man, and Ms. Keira Tanner, the very two people we want to talk to."

Mateo's hail crashes me back to a boisterous present, and I don't stick the landing. Connor keeps my stumble from becoming a pratfall. I suck in a breath at his touch, the heat of his hand scorching through the layers of my clothes.

"Please tell me you're not plastered yet. After you say yes, I fully support the tying on of the mother of all celebratory buzzes, but only after." Mateo's cheeky grin tells me he's already halfway gone himself.

"Yes to what?" Connor asks.

I step out of his embrace until we stand a few inches apart. Under the guise of straightening my jacket, I try to shrug off the sense that unfinished business connects us, a hidden thread, taut and tender and thrumming with tension.

"Yes to being the best peeps at our wedding," Mateo answers.

"Best man and maid of honor," Helena clarifies, snuggling into

Mateo as he wraps his arm around her waist. "We won't take no for an answer."

That my best friend trusts me in the wake of my extended ostrich impersonation is astonishing.

But through thick and thin, she's always been there for me. Even during the times when I've been missing in action for her. Of course I'm going to do whatever's necessary to make her Bridezilla dreams come true.

Take names. Kick asses. Bury bodies in unmarked graves.

I stand a little straighter, determination lending me another inch of height. I will be her bridal minion.

"You're adorable." The words bloop unedited from my mouth.

"I'll take that as a yes," Helena says, beaming.

"King-Con?" Mateo asks.

"Is it even a question? Of course."

"Excellent." Mateo rubs his hands together with a suspicious amount of glee. Helena's beam settles into cat-who-ate-the-canary mode.

"Why do I get the feeling we just agreed to something without having a chance to review the full terms and conditions?" I ask.

"Because you weren't born yesterday?" Connor replies.

"Cynics," Helena says. "We're not asking you to rent the moon for the ceremony or land Beyoncé as our wedding singer."

"Though if you have an angle on Bey, we wouldn't say no," Mateo says.

"I recognize this tactic." I squint at the butter-wouldn't-melt couple. "Mention something pie in the sky first so the real ask looks paltry and doable."

"An oldie but a goodie in the negotiator's playbook," Connor says.

"We wouldn't ask if we didn't think you'd have fun with it," Helena says with a sniff.

"Ooh." I bounce on my toes. "Now we segue to the dropping of mysterious hints."

"Soon to be followed by the sincere, no-obligation, guilt trip if we don't fall for the excitement of smoke and mirrors," Connor adds.

"Seriously, if you can't, we'll understand." Mateo blinks at us with big puppy eyes.

"Right on schedule," I say.

"You two are impossible," Helena says. "I swear, all we want is help with an engagement party. Sheesh."

"Party? No sweat," Connor says. "Why didn't you say so in the first place?"

"Yeah, a party is no biggie," I agree. "Talk about burying the lede."

"Great. We'll discuss the details over brunch Sunday. Eleven o'clock at Sage West." Helena's bird-eating smirk returns, bigger and more winsomely obnoxious-cute than before. She winks at me, and aw, bingo-fuck.

In all the excitement, I neglected to identify the threat that is a clever best friend with a mission of her own.

Now I'm stuck partnering with the guy I just canceled.

The guy who launches my body to new heights of longing simply by standing too close.

A guy looking for the more I can't—no, *won't*—give.

CHAPTER 3

CONNOR

On Sunday, the doorbell screams me awake, and I discover an undead bird has nested in my mouth overnight. Three loud raps on my condo's front door follow, making falling back asleep impossible. Fucking older brothers.

I stagger into the living room, aiming to bust a nose and mainline some coffee.

On the way to punching out the brother at the door, I swing wide and aim a hard flick at the forehead of the lazy ass racked out on my sofa.

"Thanks for getting the door, jerkface." I sound like I swallowed a stone quarry.

New plan. Water then coffee. Then maybe some toothpaste.

Felix, my younger older brother, shoots me a middle finger before burying his head under my sole throw pillow.

The doorbell yaps yet-a-fucking-gain.

Right, right. Nose punch, water, coffee, teeth.

"Make it stop." The pillow lands with a dull thud between my shoulder blades.

"Serves you right, Mr. Let's Shut Sully's Down." I whip open the door to find my older brother and hit him with a glare and a yawn.

"Jesus, what died?" David staggers back as my morning-after breath wafts into the space between us like a sour fart.

"You, in a minute." Suffering through my bad breath is the least he deserves for showing up looking way too rested, way too early, after way too late a night. "Why're you here? Why do you even exist?"

"To torment you, of course." He holds up a cardboard carrier filled with coffees and a box from Donut Queen. "I come bearing manna and magic elixirs."

I contemplate shutting the door in his face. He'd just restart the torture. Or keep all the caffeine and sugar for himself. Not happening. "Maple bacon?"

He nods.

"Enter."

I leave him to deal with the door. Now that I'm up and moving, the roadkill in my mouth has grown more nuanced, kind of a squirrel-moose combo. I snag my toothbrush and paste from the cupboard over the kitchen sink. No way am I letting zombie Rocky and Bullwinkle ruin my maple bacon high.

"I thought you were turning thirty soon, not fourteen." David sets the Donut Queen loot on my dining table.

"What?" I spit a mouthful of minty suds into the sink and rinse.

"Dental hygiene belongs in the bathroom."

"It's efficient to brush in the kitchen." I tap the brush against the sink edge to shake out the excess water and store it once more. "Coffee, teeth, go."

"He's got you there, Davey." Looking rougher than I feel, Felix collapses lengthwise onto the padded bench that takes up one side of the table.

David and I exchange glances. Lily. Felix didn't go into detail last night, but the conversation about the two of them moving in together does not appear to have gone as planned.

"I'm just saying it has that whiff of defeat, like our baby brother is one step away from adopting a dozen cats and hanging up a sign that reads 'Livin' La Vida Single For Keeps.'" The cheerful lilt in David's voice doesn't match the lingering concern in his eyes.

"Hey, I tried long-term. Didn't work." I fill three tall glasses with water from the fridge door.

"Sherry was the wrong partner. One bad apple shouldn't doom you to a life of hairball puke."

"Uh-huh. Well, until my match shows up to rescue me from that repulsive fate, I'll be over here, well caffeinated and with clean teeth." I parcel out water glasses and sit. "You get chocolate with sprinkles too?"

"Dad's going on a date next weekend." Felix pushes up on an elbow, bloodshot eyes blinking against the glare from the overhead light.

His words tilt the planet on its axis.

"Say what?" I ask.

"Dad has a date. Pretty sure it's not even his first one."

"That's not right."

"The man's fifty-five. Mom died three years ago. You really gonna tell me he should have buried his dick in the grave?" Felix asks.

"Of course not," I say. "That'd be ridiculous."

Without a word, David opens the Donut Queen box and hands me the chocolate with sprinkles. I rip into it, teeth sinking into dough and icing and crunchy bits, the concrete sensations easier to deal with than the odd weightlessness Felix's words fills me with.

Dad is a red-blooded adult. Of course, he'd get tired of making solo withdrawals from his spank bank.

But a date?

With someone not Mom?

Rolling a shoulder to shake off the weird, I chase my sugar hit with a slug of hot coffee. "What do we know about the woman?"

"Nothing." Felix bites into a cake donut sans icing.

"Nothing? Some snoop you are."

"I invited him to the game on Saturday," he says around a mouthful of dough. "He said he's spending the weekend in Paris with a friend. He had that twinkle in his eye."

"The sex twinkle," David clarifies, and Felix nods.

All three of us shudder.

The sex twinkle embarrassed the shit out of us as teenagers. Our parents flirting in public and in front of our friends and at home and pretty much everywhere. Even as kids we knew *date night* was code for getting some.

"I figured the sex twinkle told me all I needed to know." Felix pops the last of his plain, boring donut into his maw.

"I'd forgotten about it."

"Me too," David says, aligning the donut box by a half inch until it sits square with some internal grid.

Mom first got sick six years ago. Ovarian cancer. She fought so hard to keep things normal. We all bought into the game, pretending that the next round of chemo, the next specialist, the next medical indignity would do the trick.

Not a lot of time for twinkling when you're fighting for your life.

I retrieve the maple bacon. This is two-donut news.

I chew more slowly, savoring the combo of sweet and spice. Maybe the new woman explains Dad's distraction. All those times when he's sneaked out of the office for a few hours. He's not recruiting new talent. He's dating. Okay. Okay. I can handle this, however weird it feels.

Dad deserves whatever happiness he can get.

David finally settles in to eat his danish. With a fork because he was born an old man, poor guy.

"Speaking of dates, where's your brunch this morning?" he asks.

"Sage West. What, wait, date? We're not dating. I'm not dating. I told you, it's just brunch. Brunch to discuss planning Mateo's engagement party." I fight a wince as the words leave my mouth. Shit. Nearly thirty, and my brother can still bait me without breaking a sweat.

"Damn it." Felix pulls out his wallet and hands David a twenty. "I hate when you're right."

"Just a student of human nature, son." David pockets the cash with a smug smile. "So, what's her name?"

"Who's name?"

"The name of the woman you've been seeing the past, what, four or five months?" David says in his patient voice.

I fucking hate that voice.

"I've seen lots of women in that time frame. No dating has occurred."

They're both true statements as far as they go. Felix shakes his head, like I've sealed my fate by trying to put one past David.

"All the evidence is there," David says. "You stopped talking about chicks, stopped endlessly clubbing. Started getting regular haircuts. Seriously upped your tie game." He gestures to my face. "Hell, I think you're even moisturizing."

"You're barking up the wrong tree. Like I said, this is a working brunch." I clear the table, turning my moisturized face away from my brothers' amused gazes. "What time is it?"

Felix checks his watch. "Ten after ten."

"Shit. I need to get moving. Time for you to go. And don't even think about accidentally dropping by the restaurant. I will kill you."

"He sure has a lot of heat around this non-date," Felix says to David.

"Curious, isn't it?"

"Haha, very funny." I herd them to the front door.

"Hope the party planning goes well," David offers as they start down the hall. "Give Mateo and Helena our congratulations, and tell your lady we look forward to meeting her soon."

I don't bother with a middle finger. I just slam the door on their laughter.

CHAPTER 4

KEIRA

When your best friend texts to move up the start of brunch by half an hour, your sleepy, innocent, unsuspecting self texts back a thumbs-up and rolls into the shower.

When your best friend beckons you to a table for four with a bucket of champers chilling at her side, a pitcher of orange juice and a pot of coffee in front of her, but no fiancé, you begin to smell a rat.

Helena builds a pair of mimosas as I squeeze through the jungle of sun-washed humanity enjoying a rare un-muggy summer morning on the patio at Sage West at eleven on Sunday morning.

"Where's your better half?" I plop down in a cushioned rattan chair to her right, setting my computer bag between my feet and a small cookie tin on the table.

"Matty'll be along soon." Helena gives the tin a side-eye/frown combo, well aware of my penchant for stress baking. "I wanted a few minutes alone with you."

"I knew it. You're up to something. What gives?"

"Nothing. Sheesh. I just want to make sure you're okay with all this." She makes a vague circling gesture with her hand before pointing at the tin. "Whatever you have in there makes me think maybe not."

"All what?"

"Maid of honor, the engagement party planning." She pauses. "Working with Connor. Friday night, you were bemoaning men in general. Made me think you meant one man in particular. Do you think you can work with him?"

"He asked me on a date. I turned him down." I shrug like it's no biggie. Like my brain hasn't spent the last thirty-six hours bombarding me with replays and the fifty million ways I could have handled things differently. Like I didn't have to make an emergency run for more chocolate chips and vanilla extract in an attempt at counter-programming. "But I can work with him if he can work with me."

"I was afraid it was something like that. You and your sex-only dogma." Elbows planted on the table, she massages her temples. "You know what the definition of insanity is?"

"Lay it on me."

"Doing the same thing over and over again and expecting a different result."

"*Pth-thp.*" I adorn my raspberry with a time-honored. thumb-to-nose four-fingered wave. "Doesn't apply."

"How so?"

"I'm not searching for a different result. I'm on the hunt for a specific result."

"Do you even listen to you?" She pulls her hair, groaning, and I laugh.

"Yes. I'm a genius with a genius plan. Now, hook me up with that mimosa."

Since she's no fan of my separation of church and state policy, I hold off on telling her that I terminated our hookup arrangement too. And that it's landed me in a bit of a funk.

A purely momentary funk.

Instead, we exchange sneers as she hands me a glass. We toast and swig, our monthly go-around about my life choices, if not settled, at least completed on schedule.

"Seriously, honey, your no-strings quest is a little loco." My bestie can never resist one last jab. Normally, I admire that about her. This morning, I stick my fingers in my ears.

"Lalalalala, I can't hear you."

"Okay, okay. Uncle," she says. "You sure you two can work together?"

"Yes."

"I'm trusting you."

"Quit worrying." Sandal dangling from my toes, I start a lazy kick, selling self-confidence for all I'm worth. "Unless Connor can't hack it, everything will be fine."

That's my story, and I'll stick to it, even if my steamy early morning dreams over the last two days hint that it'll take a while to get the Connor habit out of my system.

For Helena, I'll make this awkward arrangement work, so help me.

"*Hola, mi amor.*" Mateo swoops in to land a smacking kiss on Helena's cheek. I'm bundled into his enthusiastic greeting, receiving a kiss and hug of my own. As I pull free from his infectious goodwill, I catch sight of Connor waiting patiently behind him.

Ruh-roh. Random nipple erection alert.

I've never seen him in civilian attire.

Wow.

An unapologetic suit gal, my definition of peak hunk is a man killing it in pinstripes and a power tie. Mm. But clearly, my men's clothing fetish lacked scope.

Connor's rocking a pair of buff khakis and a white linen shirt with sleeves rolled halfway up his muscled forearms. The contrast with his early summer tan is… I shift in my seat as General Hoo-ha informs me she'd like to extend an enthusiastic greeting of her own.

I make the mistake of meeting his gaze. He's smiling, but his bright blue eyes are speculative, like he's wondering if I'm on the menu for brunch.

I lift my chin in silent hello then go digging for my tablet in my bag, creating a mini event out of shifting the cookie tin from one side of my place setting to the other to free up space.

Anything to distract myself from the magnificence that is Connor out of uniform.

He takes the chair on my free side, and the temperature rises ten degrees. My nape breaks out in little sweat beads, and I can only hope my upper lip doesn't pull a sympathetic ditto. Or worse, my armpits.

Hard to sell low-key chill when your ladylike glow outpaces your deodorant.

"Morning, Keira." His voice sounds morning-sex husky, and I swear my hardened nipples pivot toward him, little pinky-brown magnets creeping on their North Star.

"Hey." Ex-North Star, I remind them, thankful I opted for the padded T-shirt bra. "Mimosa?"

"Coffee, please. Thanks." He grimaces, hand on his belly. A belly I know firsthand is protected on either side by those sexy diagonal muscles that lead to General Hoo-ha's most-favoritest topography. "Late-night boozing with my brothers. Think my liver could use a break."

"How're David and Felix?" Mateo pours himself straight champagne. "I haven't seen them in months."

"Celia's pregnant." Connor grins.

"Hey, that's great. Congratulations." Matty punches him in the arm. "I bet David's over the moon."

"He's been mother-henning Felix and me like there's no tomorrow." Smile lingering, Connor leans back in his chair. "Practice, I guess. Either that, or my sister-in-law's not letting him pull that crap on her."

I keep quiet as the three of them cover his other brother's girlfriend woes and his dad's venture back into the dating pool. It's... weird.

Weird to experience Connor outside the narrow framework of the monthly networking events and our even more circumscribed sexual encounters. I'd been so careful not to learn anything about my best friend's boyfriend's best friend.

What do I do with the fact that he's got brothers? A dad? That he's soon to be an uncle?

Nothing. I don't have to do a dang thing with that information. Our association has morphed from just sex to just business. There's no need for me to freak out about knowing the names of his brothers. Or how good he looks in white linen.

Damn it, why is he so hot?

I sip my mimosa to cool down, lose the nipples-at-the-ready tingle.

Keeping him compartmentalized, like I do in the rest of my life, will be no problem. I'm thirty. Prime of my life, with a career I excel at, a fantastic best friend, and, okay, a pretty sucky apartment for a real estate agent who handles high-end properties. It's on my list to upgrade.

The point is, I'm good at going after what I want.

Show me a mountain, I'll scale that sucker and own the shit out of its summit.

Surely the reverse is true too. I can refrain from climbing. I have the willpower.

The waiter sets a pastry basket down and tells us the specials. Connor and I order the eggs benedict topped with avocado. Maybe a helping of the healthy green fat will mollify my inconvenient hunger. Helena and Mateo do a quick consult and order entrees they'll end up splitting in half and sharing because they've become *that* couple.

Once the waiter leaves, I hand the cookie tin to Helena to pass around and unlock my tablet to bring up the bare-bones spreadsheet I pulled together yesterday. No point in dwelling in the weird when instead we can frolic with clean and tidy numbers.

"I did some preliminary research during a break yesterday, but without basics like head count, date, theme, budget, it was tricky coming up with any useful projections. Still, I played out three scenarios that we could scale according to new inputs." When no one responds, I look up. Three sets of eyes blink back, all reflecting varying degrees of dazed reverence. "What?"

Connor finishes chewing and swallows before letting out a long whistle. He's grinning again. Blinding me with the whiteness of his teeth. Someone needs to tell him to stop it. He's a public health hazard.

Mateo shakes with silent laughter.

"You are a beast." Helena air toasts me with her glass.

"Wha-a-at?" I ask again, not getting the funny. I hate when I don't get the funny.

"Woman, I wish I'd known you in high school. That group report in AP Bio would have gone so much better if you'd been in charge," Mateo says. "And you can bake?"

"What's the big deal?" I ask Connor out of the corner of my mouth.

"We're impressed," he says with an exaggerated stage whisper.

"It's nothing." I wipe a finger smudge off the tablet's screen.

I got a half-assed jump on the details and did some baking. Big whoop. No need to share that yesterday's break technically began at five-thirty on Saturday morning after I gave up trying to sleep through my X-rated dreams of Connor. Or that it was the first of several bake-and-prep breaks I took while I was supposed to be compiling a roster of crème de la crème properties for my boss's big whale mystery client to review next week.

"For you, maybe it's nothing. But these chocolate chip cookies are the best I've ever had. On top of that wonder, most mortals need something more tangible before they can start planning," Connor replies.

"This mortal is most definitely impressed with the cookies—and grateful for your pre-planning efforts." Helena threads her fingers through Mateo's where they rest on the table. "When we told our parents about our engagement, it became instantly clear we'd be fighting tooth and nail for control over the wedding details."

"We put our foot down about the engagement party," Mateo says.

"And now you're having two," Connor says with a nod of understanding.

"How'd you guess?" Mateo asks with a rueful shake of his head

Connor pulls a "bitch, please" face. "How long have I known your mother?"

"She's ferocious. So's mine." Helena mock shudders. "Good thing they're generally awesome in their ferocity, or they'd have to have a fatal accident."

"That would just delay the wedding. Hard nope on the dual matricide." Mateo rains smoochy kisses across my best friend's knuckles and up her wrist.

"Gag." I pop a hand over my mouth. "Sorry, autonomous reaction to PDA. It slipped out."

"You"—Helena points a laser straight finger at me—"can keep a lid on—"

"Moving on," Connor interrupts smoothly. "How about you pony up some details for what kind of engagement party you want so we can fill in Keira's spreadsheet and get on with the planning? Any more cookies left?"

With each word he speaks, Helena's feathers smooth back into place. Whew. Dodged that bullet. I need to do better. I can't go pissing my BFF off each time she and Mateo indulge just because the thought of true love gives me hives.

Maybe I need a bridal minion mantra. Something like *their bliss is not my bliss, and that's okay.*

"The parental vision is formal, more a dog and pony show for distant family and business acquaintances than a party for us," Mateo says. "Which I get. We're both the first in our generation within our families to get married. Our folks want to display us for the masses."

"Prove we aren't drug addicts or serial killers," Helena mutters into her mimosa.

"We can always rethink our life choices after the wedding gauntlet, mi amor. Start an ashram or kidnap an orphan for ransom. It's a free country, even if we are related to would-be dictators."

My heart turns over at Mateo's reassurance. They really are perfect for each other. Maybe proximity to their true love won't make me barf after all. I smile at my progress.

"So, you're looking for something informal and unstuffy?" Connor asks.

"And intimate," I add. "Say, no more than forty people, max?"

"Sounds right. Keeping the head count on the small side opens up a lot of interesting venues in the city." Connor shifts his chair closer to mine.

"I'm thinking evening, right? A little music, a small dance floor. Elegant but lively." I lean toward him and scroll through some of the visuals I pinned yesterday, pointing out possibilities.

"We could tap one of the up-and-coming mixologists in the city and a chocolatier I know," Connor adds. "Make the night about unique pairings."

"Unique pairings. We could work with that. What about—"

A feminine cough and a masculine chuckle interrupt our flow.

Still tipped toward each other, we turn our heads toward our friends. "What?"

"Twenty people. The Saturday night of Labor Day weekend. And as long as you don't go crazy, like give out diamonds as party favors, we can probably swing whatever you come up with, budget-wise," Helena says, in a tone that's drier than a P&L spreadsheet.

"Eggs benedict for the lady and you, sir. Careful, as the plates are hot." Our waiter sets our orders down. On the other side of the table, another server lays out Mateo and Helena's smorgasbord of a breakfast. "Anything else? No? Very good. Enjoy."

The interruption provides me cover to regroup. I flick my napkin and lay it over my lap. For a second there, I was so caught up in the moment, I forgot where I was. Who I was talking to. All that existed was the spark between Connor and me as we clicked into our brainstorming groove.

"You mentioned a theme for the party. Like trains or superheroes?" Mateo asks as he tops up my glass. The mimosa is now more blond than orange, a hue change I approve.

"What are you, eight?" Helena wrinkles her nose, half-fond, half-incredulous.

"I think Keira means, like, what are the colors of your wedding so we can make sure the napkins match," Connor says.

"Colors of the wedding?" Mateo's eyes grow wide. "Black and white, right? Black tux, white dress?"

"You poor, poor wedding virgin." Connor's smile comes out to play again.

A desire unrelated to food flares to life low in my belly. Well, poop. There's not enough avocado in the world to satisfy this inconvenient body hunger. Nonetheless, I shovel a forkful into my mouth and chew with extra care.

"Just wait until the topic of centerpieces rears up," he continues. "According to David, that's guaranteed no sex for a week. Maybe two."

"Ah, hell no. No centerpieces. Not if it means no sex." Mateo spoons fried potatoes onto Helena's plate. "Promise me, mi amor."

"No arguments about centerpieces, I promise," Helena replies.

"I see what you did there." Mateo points his spoon at her.

She responds by placing a cookie on his bread plate and patting his forearm. He grumbles about being handled but tucks into his food.

Conversation over the meal turns general. The kind that normal people have when they're dining out with friends. Jobs, city politics, the latest binge-worthy series. The guys catch up on their sports news while Helena and I debate the merits of the latest meal prep subscription service to hit the market.

"It sounds good in theory," I say, "but I'm pretty sure I'd still end up throwing out rotting food. Microwave dinners are more my line, quick and easy."

"And filled with sodium."

"You say that like it's a bad thing." I stuff a final bite of egg, ham, English muffin and Hollandaise sauce into my piehole and heroically refrain from moaning. In truth, I hate microwave meals, but apart from baking anything sweet, I loathe cooking more.

"The Bane Jazz Trio is playing at the Rio on Thursday. I've heard good things." Connor tosses his napkin onto his equally barren plate. "How about the four of us go for a listen? See if they're a good fit for the party."

"Sounds good," Mateo replies. "Helena?"

"Let me check." She scrolls through her phone as a tic begins to throb at the corner of my eye. "Yeah, I'm cool. What time?"

"How about seven? We'll eat and go into more depth about party plans." Connor taps shit into his phone while my involuntary muscle twitching shifts into overtime. "I'll make reservations."

"Could you excuse us for a second? Connor and I need a quick convo." My chair screeches as I push from the table and grab his wrist.

After shoving another cookie into his mouth, he follows readily enough as I march toward the restroom.

If we're going to be working together, it's time for a few home truths.

I slam open the door of the single-occupant women's room. He catches the bounce before it breaks my nose.

"Whoa there, slugger. Slow down." He shuffles us into the room, eases the lock into place and leans against the door, arms crossed. "Want to explain the bee in your bonnet?"

"I told you I don't date."

"Yes, I heard you on Friday."

"So now we're headed to a concert?" I poke his sternum.

"Research for the party." He catches my hand. "Call it a strategy session if the idea of listening to music with friends spooks you so much."

"I'm not spooked. I'm irritated."

"Why?"

"Because," I begin but quickly peter out as it occurs to me I might have overreacted, that his suggestion isn't some sneaky way to get a date in or cancel my cancellation but a practical first step to planning the party. I clear my throat. "Uh, never mind."

I try to regain control of my hand. He flattens my palm against his chest.

His very warm chest.

He traces the U-shaped path from my thumb to forefinger and back, light and easy.

But not soothing, according to every single hair on my body.

They stand on end, hundreds of follicles swaying with each swipe of his fingertip, like smartphone cigarette-lighter apps at a rock concert.

"Tell me more about this irritation you have." Somehow, I'm standing between his legs, hovering a crucial inch away from full body contact. "Does it itch? Tingle? Cause shortness of breath? I've had first aid training. Maybe I can help with a little mouth-to-mouth."

I want his mouth. But. We're done.

Over.

Right?

I know the kind of setup I need for a sexual relationship to work for me. Connor pushes those boundaries. He has since we first hooked up.

Ninety-nine percent of me is certain breaking things off was the right decision. That last percent contemplates his lower lip and says fuck that, we demand action.

I yank his shirt, pulling his face down to my level. I mash our mouths together, desperate and lacking all pretension to skill. He meets me full-on, bumping teeth, dueling tongues, tasting of chocolaty sweetness.

"New offer," he pants as I nibble on his collarbone.

"I'm listening." It's a blatant lie. I'm much more interested in killing him one tiny, sucking bite at a time.

"You say no dating. Message received. So how about we follow the same arrangement as before but we up the frequency from once a month to once a week?"

"Okay." I punctuate my acceptance with a sharper nip and revel in his full-body shiver. "And after the planning and the party are over, we'll shake hands and walk away, no harm, no foul, no strings."

He stills, and I hold my breath.

It's the one condition I can't bend. The one boundary that keeps me sane.

The pause stretches to eternity, and suddenly I'm too aware of everything. The hubbub of the restaurant behind the locked door. The alien scent of cleaning products and the familiar one of Connor's sun-kissed skin. The blister rubbing into my foot from my too-new wedges. The soaking wet placket of my shapewear, sticky and confining.

"It's all right." I pat his shoulder. "I know it's asking too—"

"Yes," he says and launches an exploration of my neck.

"Yes? You're good with the restrictions? No dates? No touchy-feely?"

"Lots of touchy and feely, I hope, but no sloppy emotions and no dates. Got it." He murmurs into the shell of my ear, "Now, order me to make you come. To make my fingers make you climax."

My knees give way, and he spins us so my back is to the door. He slides his hand under mine and pushes until I clutch hold.

Tears prick the backs of my eyes.

He gets the thing I didn't say. That "same arrangement" means I still call the sexy times play-by-play.

I drop my head against his shoulder to regroup. Ordered thinking leads to ordered emotions, and ordered emotions are essential.

He waits, patient and hard and hot, agreeable and apparently ready to do my bidding.

I don't deserve it, but I am a lucky, lucky lady.

"In lieu of a tie, I want you to keep your free hand plastered to the door. No moving until we're done, hear me?" With a flutter of tingles, renewed anticipation surges inside me when he nods and obeys, his palm landing with a heavy thump above our heads. "I'm going to place your hand under my dress. Slide your fingers through my wetness until they're good and coated. Then I'm going to order you to finger fuck me until I come hard enough to bounce me into tomorrow. Are you okay with this course of action?"

"Hell yes. Let's get to fingering."

With a firm grip, I lead our hands to their destination.

"You're so fucking hot." His groans make me breathless as slowly, methodically, I slick his hand with my arousal. He gives me more and more of his weight until I'm a Keira-sandwich between his hard, heated body and the unforgiving door. "Please tell me it's time for agenda item three. I'm begging here."

"Roger that," I pant. "Three is a go."

He curls two big fingers inside me, massaging the heel of his palm over my clit, and in less than a minute, I detonate.

He presses an impossible third finger within, rotates his wrist, and I explode again, comets of sensation rocketing through my body.

I'm sure I'm done, but he proves me wrong, coaxing a sparkling series of smaller climaxes from me until he's chased every blessed ounce of pleasure into the light.

"That's it." I aim for his shoulder but wind up patting somewhere vaguely near his waist. "Give me a minute to recover, then we'll see about you."

"I'm good."

"Fair's fair." I struggle to surface from my post-climax daze. "You scratched my itch. Now it's my turn—"

"Honest. I'm all set."

I blink until his face comes into focus.

He's biting his lips, eyes dancing.

"What?"

A shit-eating grin escapes him. He leans into me until his lips caress my ear. "You were so sexy, I came in my pants."

Sunday, 1:18 p.m.

Connor: All clean now, in case you were worried.

Keira: I wasn't.

Sunday, 11:23 p.m.

Connor: Check your email.

Keira: We're not holding the engagement party at Chuck E. Cheese.

Monday, 5:32 a.m.

Keira: Helena added Lucas and Beth to the head count.

Connor: Why are you awake? Go back to bed.

Keira: 'k

Monday, 10:44 a.m.

Connor: Mateo added Chris and Gwynne. Did you dream of me?

Keira: Hahaha, no. 24 people? Sniff, sniff, I smell scope creep.

Monday, 2:30 p.m.

Keira: Make that 26. Keith and Ken.

Connor: Wanna bet on the final head count?

Keira: Stakes?

Connor: Something creative. Maybe sex with two ties?

Keira: We don't have to bet to make that one come true, cowboy.

Monday, 7:11 p.m.

Connor: I was worried for a while there, but it's been five hours with no additions. Think we're safe.

Tuesday, 8:57 a.m.

Connor: Andrew, Michael, Steph, Recca, Bob, Mohan, in. How many people do they know...???

Tuesday, 9:38 a.m.

Connor: Hey. You there? Everything okay?

.   .   .

Tuesday, 5:55 p.m.

Keira: Busy. Rat Bastard is having an attack of conniptions. So, we're at 32? No sweat.

Tuesday, 11:37 p.m.

Connor: I've got a couple venues on tap that can easily scale from 25 to 60. I can line them up to check out Friday late afternoon if you care to join me?

Wednesday, 5:29 a.m.

Keira: None of them is another pizza palace for kids, right?

Connor: What? Never.

Keira: I'm on to you, buddy.

Wednesday, 9:49 a.m.

Keira: Do H&M need a wedding slogan? Like...

Keira: Love + balance sheets = forever?

Keira: The bottom line is we love each other?

Keira: 1 + 1 = love?

Keira: Only, you know, snappier...

Connor: Where did this come from?

Keira: Googled wedding planning ideas to take my mind off staff meeting hell.

Connor: Oh, you need a distraction? How about a few good dick pics?

Keira: NO! [barfing emoji]

Connor: [three pictures of celebrity Dicks]

Keira: I got Clark and Van Dyke. Who's the third?

Connor: You wound me with your pop culture ignorance.

Keira: Excuse me for not rotting my brain on a steady diet of boob tube.

Connor: Though admittedly there exists an abundance of celebrity boobs, I'm disheartened by the lack of celebrities *named* Boob to lighten the misery that is your staff meeting purgatory.

Keira: So thoughtful, so kind. Third Dick?

Connor: Butkus. Footballer turned actor.

Keira: Oh, a sports Dick. Meh.

Connor: Sporting Dicks have good stamina, versatility, range. They are the best in Dicks.

Keira: ...

Wednesday, 3:16 p.m.

Keira: 33!!!!!

Connor: True love looks not with the wallet but with the heart.

Keira: Shakespeare posted that, right?

Wednesday, 6:20 p.m.

Connor: Business dinner with cranky-pants client ahead. Shoot me something sexy for counter-programming.

Keira: [Link to wiki page on the blue-footed booby]

Keira: [image of blue-footed booby in profile]
Side boob. Get it? Haha.

Connor: Well played.

CHAPTER 5

CONNOR

Thursday evening, I'm a strange mixture of anticipation and chagrin at the prospect of seeing Keira for the first time since my Quick Draw McGraw impersonation Sunday.

Blowing too soon after a little heavy petty, no thought, no control. I wince, not for the first time, at the scenario no guy wants to experience. Yet in the beat after my confession, Keira and I were holding each other up, sweaty and breathless, laughing like a couple of loons.

Maybe like… a couple of friends.

Cheerful resolve overtakes my doubts, lending a lightness to my gait as I jog up the steps to the jazz club where the Bane Trio is playing. Keira doesn't want our hookups to lead to anything permanent. She's out of luck on that score.

I'm not looking for love. Neither is she. We're agreed on that.

But now I have a new chance, and I'm going all in. There's no reason we can't do this thing—and each other—and not come out on the other side as friends.

We'll fuck.

We'll knock this burgeoning scope-overrun-a-palooza of an engagement party out of the ballpark.

And we'll end the summer as friends with world class, A-1, platinum-status benefits.

Ending those bennies just because we've arrived at an arbitrary date on the calendar? No dice. Our joint venture into party planning will give me plenty of opportunities to convince her I'm right and this is a good investment. All I'll have to do is win her over on the new-new deal.

I check the knot of my new tie and smooth it against my shirt as I check the club to see if she's here already despite my arriving fifteen minutes early.

Black with electric-blue duck profiles, the tie's the closest I could get to a booby print at Brooks Brothers over lunch.

"Connor, over here." Leaning against the padded bar rail, Felix gives me a chin lift as he speed types on his phone.

What the—? My steps slow at the little whoosh sound when he hits Send, and he stows his phone in the inner pocket of his suit jacket.

"What are you doing here?" I search the club as though the answer is hiding behind one of the potted fig trees.

"You invited me."

"I did?"

"Saturday night? Somewhere between the fourth and fifth shot, when you confessed your woman shot you down and you begged for company?" He slaps my shoulder. "David's on his way. Dad's with him."

Oh no. Oh, fucking no.

"You need to leave."

He quirks an eyebrow, pulls on his microbrew IPL.

Settles onto his stool.

Doesn't leave.

"Now. Leave now, and divert Dad and David." I rap my knuckles against his chest, and I'm not gentle. "I mean it."

"Connie, why in the world would I do that?" Gleeful speculation settles onto my middle brother's features as he takes another sip and stays put. "How'd brunch go?"

Shit. I know better than to drink with my brothers when I'm chewing on something private.

They always worm it out of me then hound me until the issue is resolved or we punch each other stupid. To be fair, we all pull this when called for, but fair can go jump in the East River tonight.

"I'm serious. Plans have changed, and I need you all not to be here—"

"Mateo, my man, it's been an age." Felix hails my friend over as he and Helena enter, nudging me aside to do the ritual back-smack man greeting. "I hear congratulations are in order."

"Luckiest guy in the world," Mateo says, sliding an arm around his bride-to-be's waist. "You've met Helena, right?"

The three dive into catching up while I speed through—and reject —options to save the night from becoming a cluster.

Pulling the fire alarm would only lead to more problems. Finding an invisibility cloak seems unlikely. I take out my phone to call David, get him and Dad to stay away. I can get Felix to make some kind of excuse to leave.

Everything will be all right.

And no. Too late. I freeze into a six-foot column of fuck-my-life. Because Dad is ushering Keira into the club ahead of him, his arm hovering in a protective curve behind her, his face beaming with delight.

David follows, eyes dancing like it's all he can do not to chortle.

I am so screwed.

Keira is reminding me of a shark again. With laser beams implanted in her brown eyes instead of attached to her head. Under neon rainbow-colored bangs, those lasers are squarely aimed at me.

Fuck.

I cover the distance between the bar and entry in a record-breaking leap, rueing my wardrobe choices for the evening. Instead of a booby tie, I should have worn safety pads and a jockstrap.

"Son, look at this lovely young woman we found all alone outside."

Of course.

Of course, my brothers would blab about Keira to Dad, the tattle-tales. Of course, out of a city of millions, Dad would manage to pluck

Keira, with her characteristically distinctive dyed hair, off the sidewalk before I had time to intervene.

And of course, he somehow makes Keira's solo arrival sound like I've failed to provide her with a proper escort, so he's happy to see me but disappointed in my behavior.

Still, he hugs me and ninja-dad shuffles her into my orbit. "Let me offer my felicitations to the happy couple. I look forward to talking with you over dinner."

"Me too, Mr. Mack," Keira says, using the upbeat, confident tone she must deploy with clients. Large, in charge, and as if nothing could phase her. She's close enough, though, that I can make out the tiny vibrations of a tightly wound frame.

"Johnny, please." Dad nods to her, pats my arm, and leaves us facing my eldest brother. The meddling puppet master of the family whose teeth I'd smash if I didn't fear my sister-in-law's wrath.

"David."

"Connor."

"You're a sneaky, scheming bastard."

"I'll alert the media." He smiles at Keira, pats my arm in the same exact place Dad did, and leaves us, a couple of outlier satellites hovering beside the gravitational pull that is a newly engaged couple. If I could just borrow her laser beam eyes for a minute.

A champagne cork pops, eliciting a wave of laughter from our entirely too-large party. As though the pop were the starter's gun at a track meet, the jazz club is off to the races. Lights shift to sophisticated murk, music to a languorous bass line, and conversation buzzes, freestyle.

"I didn't plan this," I say, turning toward Keira. "Apparently, I invited them while I was under the influence of vodka shots Saturday night."

"Ah. Vodka. Enough said." She sighs, and as the breath leaves her body, it takes that taut coil of tension too. "You know, if I'd had the smallest warning I'd be meeting Silver Fox Block and two more of his crazy-hot Chips, I'd have bailed."

"I wouldn't have blamed you."

"But on second thought"—she walks her fingers in a slow climb up my tie, and all the blood in my head rushes south—"now I'm glad I came. It's going to be so much fun driving you insane in front of your family, seeing if I can get a repeat of Sunday brunch." She smiles a shark smile. All teeth. "This time on purpose."

"Grrk."

"Cat got your tongue?" Her husky gurgle of a laugh charms my cock into full-on wood. "Oh yeah. I'm going to enjoy the hell out of this."

Dropping her arm, she turns toward the group, and in a sneaky-delicious move, dances a warning tattoo over my zipper.

Connor Jr. and I whimper at the too-brief touch.

We cover a shudder of anticipation by adjusting our cuffs, clearing our throat. Then we growl as the circle widens to welcome her, and she accepts a flute of bubbly from Felix.

Our brother better not have any ideas. She's ours.

Shock jolts me out of my pleasure haze. Since when did Junior and I go pure caveman?

I grab the scotch on the rocks David holds out and concentrate on the burn as it slides down my throat.

Anything to distract us from the all too couple-y mental image of tossing Keira over my shoulder and carrying her off to our caveman lair.

CHAPTER 6

KEIRA

onnor's dad is a charming rogue. The interplay between him and his sons is a revelation. Arguing, soapboxing, joking. Finishing each other's sentences. All with this bedrock vein of *I've got your back, bonehead* threading through each tease. It's clear they think of Mateo as a part of the family. They have zero reservations about extending to Helena and me that same easy inclusion.

It's the opposite of my family's dynamics growing up, with my father doing his best to mold me into an obedient little soldier and my mother dead set on grooming me to be her pretty pet. They each had a vision for who I was supposed to be, the perfect, pliant heir to their real estate empire, and it never occurred to them I might have my own vision. My own life.

It wasn't until I met Helena in college that I experienced healthy family ties up close. But even years of interacting with her boisterous relatives hasn't prepared me for tonight's peek into the lifestyles of the well-adjusted.

The only way I'm keeping my equilibrium is with some teasing of my own, guerilla style, because it's exponentially more satisfying to focus on steering Connor's slow burn than on the stark shortcomings of my upbringing.

"Then there's the time Connor wussed out of a full leg wax halfway in." Mateo begins another roast in an evening littered with them. Connor pitches his balled-up napkin across the table. Mateo dodges and continues, "Ended up patchy as shit in the weirdest places. All I'm saying is some things you can't unsee." He turns his patented puppy dog eyes on Helena and me. "His tips went down. The ladies voted with their pocketbooks."

"Shows that crowd had discerning taste," Connor's oldest brother, David, says. "I've always wondered about his stripping career. What if he'd really applied himself? Could he have become Chippendale-worthy?"

"Not a chance. Too scrawny," Felix says.

"Connor has plenty of muscle," Mr. Mack says, patting my hand in reassurance. "It's just lean."

"I'll take that under advisement," I say with a straight face. Catching Connor's eye, I leisurely stroke my forefinger up and down the stem of my water glass, just one of the seductive moves I've deployed this evening to make him suffer in the best way and keep his attention right where I want it.

He smooths his tie, Adam's apple bobbing. Good. Message received, sexy torment proceeding on schedule.

"Now, speaking of scrawny—" David begins.

"We weren't," Connor says firmly.

"Remember the spring you were convinced Mrs. Klein had a crush on you?"

"I was fourteen and clueless. She was hot and kind." The tips of Connor's ears turn red, but he's grinning, not mad. "A few years later, she was kinder and hotter."

The table breaks out in howls. Mr. Mack tries to frown but can't quite manage before he gives up, shaking his head.

"I think that's my cue to leave," he says to the table at large before turning to me. "A father shouldn't learn too much about his kids' secret lives." He taps a finger to his chest. "Bad for the heart."

"Sage advice," I say.

We share a companionable smile, two near strangers brought together in a moment of humor and understanding. It's suddenly too much, too… intimate somehow, despite it not being one iota sexual.

"Ladies, boys, you've been kind to put up with an old man horning in on your night out." Mr. Mack grabs Felix by the scruff of the neck for an affectionate little shake. "Alas, this old ticker needs its eight hours if I'm going to function in the morning. David, Connor, let's brief before the Attarian team arrives. Seven thirty, my office."

"I'll bring donuts." David stuffs his phone away and rises. "Celia's ladies' night is over. Time for me to hit the road too. Dad, we can share a cab."

"It was a pleasure to meet you, Mr. Mack," I say, stuffing my unease down to make way for good manners. "You've given me great material on—I mean, insight into—Connor."

"Johnny." His gentle correction comes with another smile. "The pleasure was all mine. Have Connor bring you to the annual family barbeque in a few weeks. He'll give you the details."

"I'll check my calendar and let him know."

Connor's wolf gaze alights on me, sharp and curious, as though something in my voice clued him in to the hedge in my answer.

His dad squeezes his shoulder, provoking an eye roll from Connor and another grin from Mr. Mack. What mysterious dad-code message is Mr. Mack transmitting through those four fingers and thumb? That quirk of lips?

This next glimpse into the Mack family's inner workings refires the heavy, restless ache building in my chest. The sense that I'm standing all alone on the outside of something special, looking in.

"Don't worry about the tab. I've taken care of it. Enjoy the rest of your night. Mateo, Helena, congratulations again. Keira, boys." Mr. Mack nods at each of us in turn before he and David head out.

The jazz trio comes back to the small stag and launches into "Blues in the Night." Felix distributes the last of the wine among our glasses.

I'm itchy, and my skin's too tight. Between my campaign to keep Connor on edge all evening and the unexpected front-row view of a family that genuinely likes each other, I'm a jumping bean of excess energy.

"Dance with me," I demand of Connor.

He bugs his eyes at me, possibly a reminder that, under the cover of the table, he has something interesting hidden.

Sucks to be him. I shake my hand insistently, and he caves.

On the dance floor, he spins me out then reels me back until we're as close as two people can be with clothes on.

"Hands stay where I can see 'em, or I walk," he says, hot and growly.

"Having a crisis, are we? Was it something I said?" I arch an eyebrow. "Or something I did."

"Like there's any question." His lips brush the curve of my ear. "Junior's so huge, he could fill his own zip code."

"Sounds painful. And promising." I walk my fingers from his shoulder to his chest.

"Oh, no. Uh-uh. I like this place. I'd like to return. That won't happen if they ban me on account of because I flooded the joint with fucktons of jizz juice." He captures my wandering hand and returns it to his shoulder, leading us through a few fancy steps. "Go easy on me, girlie."

"You wish."

"Just think," he says. "With a boner this big, if I come now, not only are we talking hundred-year flood, but I'll probably go into a coma. Coma patients don't generally help plan engagement parties."

"You're not getting out of helping that easily."

"All I'm saying is, can we risk it?"

"Not sure how I missed the fact that you're a goof." I try to hide a smile behind a stern frown and fail utterly.

"A goof with an enormous dick," he says before whirling me out and back again. "Tell me that doesn't balance things out."

I snort—because how do you answer that?—and we dance through a few songs, staying quiet, our bodies falling into sync. Our slow, easy rhythm does nothing to relieve Junior, saluting me through Connor's suit pants. But something about swaying cheek to cheek and hip to hip is soothing, like the pressures of the day and this evening are drifting away with each shuffle, glide, and turn. I don't relax easily or often, but the combo of music and man calms my hypervigilance, and I'm content for Connor to guide us over the floor, creating time and space for the two of us to chill.

"I like the trio," I say, my voice sleepy and warm in my ears. "We should definitely ask if they're available."

"Noah and Theo Bane are friends of a pal. Noah said the group's free that night. I'll text him later with the go-ahead." He leads me through a couple of fast twirls, making me laugh before pulling me in close once more. "Just think. One party planning task down."

"Five million to go." I blow my rainbow bangs off my face.

"Courage," he says. "Speaking of… Before we sit back down, we should probably talk."

"Whoa." I stop mid-sway. "I never realized how ominous 'we should talk' sounds on the receiving end."

"Yeah, well." He nudges me back into motion. "You like rules."

"I live by them."

"At brunch, we, ah, renewed our arrangement. Made a new deal."

"I was there." My heart starts in with a heavy bass thud. I'm still not sure I made the right decision, no matter the cheers from General Hoo-ha.

"Right." He swallows around a strangled laugh. "This is simultaneously more important and more difficult to ask than I'd imagined."

"I'm listening. Take your time," I say, but wish, just a little, that we could go back to dancing in a snow globe of quiet contentment.

"Guess I'm wondering what this iteration looks like? Are we having sex tonight? Is that it for this week? What if we score a location for the party tomorrow, would sex tonight preclude celebratory sex tomorrow?"

"I haven't thought that far ahead, to be honest."

I take a cleansing breath. "Listen, no sex tonight. And no more teasing—on either side. I-I need to think."

"Sure. Understood. Junior doesn't understand, but he's a hundred and fifty percent Cro-Magnon. At some point, he'll settle down." He crosses his eyes, making me chuckle. "Back to the happy couple?"

"Ten to one Helena will shoot knowing looks my way, thinking this dance proves something hinky and emotional about us."

"It is a well-known fact that people getting married transform into amateur matchmakers overnight. I've lived through this once with one brother, so"—he sends me on one last twirl and catches me in a dip, grinning—"no bet."

"Spoilsport," I say as he lifts me out of the dip, both of us ignoring the muted catcalls about our performance wafting from a certain table.

"Chin up," he urges with a cheerio British accent. "We'll stand united against their machinations."

CHAPTER 7

KEIRA

"How many guests are we up to?" I ask Helena and Mateo as Connor and I retake our seats and the trio begins a bluesy version of "Dream a Little Dream." "Fifty-eleven?"

"Smartass." Helena unrolls her middle finger my way, but it lacks commitment, more reflex than true irritation. "We're at an even thirty-four."

"Thirty-seven," Mateo corrects.

"Thirty-seven?" Disbelief turns my voice to a high-pitched croak. "What happened to small, intimate, and, well, small?"

"Adding people isn't a deal breaker. It's our party after all, right?" Helena squints at me with glinty eyes.

"Yup. Absolutely your party. No argument." I say, aiming to sooth. Anything to keep an Incipient Bridezilla Breakdown at bay so early in the process. Sure, we'll have some of those—my research this week tells me that—but research also tells me one of my prime duties is to make sure Helena comes out of this gauntlet with friends and family intact. I'm on it.

"There's no way we can throw a party without all of the Macks. I can't believe I left them off the list to begin with." Mateo exchanges chin nods with Felix, guy apology and forgiveness in live action bobblehead form.

"What about their plus ones?" Helena asks.

Mateo winces. "Okay, make that forty."

"Thirty-nine. I'm flying solo these days." Felix scoots his chair back and stands. "Right, I'm out. Keira, good to meet you. Helena, Mateo, congrats again. I'll look for that invite."

He barely waits through our chorus of goodbyes before he makes tracks for the exit.

"Felix, hold up." Connor catches up to his brother, and they dive into a spirited round of fast talking and manly frowning.

"Shit," Mateo says.

"What's wrong?" I rub little circles into the knot developing at the base of my sternum. Surely a food-related discomfort, not disquiet that Connor and his brother are having some kind of a tiff.

"Reading between the lines, I'd guess Felix and Lily, his longtime girlfriend, broke up." Worry digs into Mateo's brow. "I always figured they'd get married eventually. They'd been together since before Merida's death. "

"Merida?" Helena asks.

"Mama Mack. She died about three years ago. Ovarian cancer." He shakes his head. "She was such a sweetheart. It devastated the Macks when she passed. They revered her. Man, I revered her too. Everyone did."

"That sucks." Helena squeezes his hand. The knot in my sternum grows spikes.

"Yeah. That last year, when it became apparent that further treatment wouldn't help, the family made her the center of their universe, made sure she knew how much she was cherished every single day." Mateo's mouth flattens with remembered grief. "Celia and Lily became the daughters Merida always wanted. Sherry, not so much."

"Who's Sherry?" I ask.

Mateo gets a deer-in-the-headlights look on his face. "Uh—"

"Cough it up, honey," Helena says. "You can't leave us hanging now."

"Connor's ex-fiancée. Sherry did not like competing with a dying woman for his attention. Put my boy through hell. Silent treatments, guilt trips. You name it."

"She sounds like an asshole." I rattle the ice at the bottom of my glass, wishing it was something else, some*one* else. "What happened? He come to his senses and boot her out the door?"

"I wish, but no. She bailed about a week before Merida died. Stopped answering his calls. Wouldn't talk to him to try to work things out. In my book, he dodged a bullet, but I think he still carries guilt, believing his drama was the final tipping point for his mom."

"Bullshit." I indulge in more violent ice rattling. "He knows that's bullshit, right?"

"I don't disagree," he says. "But the heart is a weird organ, yeah? Not very logic based."

It's too far away to hear the words, but Connor appears to win the argument, screwing a grimace, a shrug, and a nod out of his brother. Felix leaves, Connor returns, and I'm left coping with the kind of swirling emotional hangover my anti-feelz policy is supposed to defend against.

For the rest of the night, I make sure we stick to the shallows. We swap business disasters and speculate on potential wedding day snafus. Note to self, issue a hard no if someone suggests making a dog the ring bearer. At one point, Connor gives me a long speculative look, like he knows what I'm up to, maybe even why. I stare back, daring him to make something of it.

Instead, he adjusts the knot of his tie and winks.

And leaves me alone like I asked. No head shrinking. But also no touching, no innuendo. No play. He just shares a winding, shaggy-dog story about the time his great-uncle Aloysius brought pot brownies to the company holiday party.

Nice guy Connor, killing me softly with kindness, consideration, and humor.

Later, as the taxi takes me home, I chew on what I learned tonight.

When I first contemplated negotiating a monthly bump and grind with Connor, I wondered why no woman had branded him as hers.

Now I have my answer.

Getting shivved in the heart by the person you wanted to make life-long vows with would make anyone twice shy. Add in the trauma of losing a beloved parent after a horrific illness?

All that has to affect your love life in major ways.

That wink, though.

I let myself into my crappy apartment and head to the bedroom, shedding clothes as I go. Slinking my panties off, I'm sucker punched by the scent of my arousal.

Once I'm stretched out between cool sheets, I reach for my trusty Sergeant Vibe, flicking him from parade rest to attention. His battery-operated motor revs, and my thighs clench in anticipation.

I trace the vibrator slowly down my front, drawing out the moment, building layers of tension.

That wink was pure wolfy promise. Like he'll be ready to play the minute I'm ready again too. Likewise, the byplay with the tie was his reminder that I hold the strings.

Can he possibly know how big a turn-on that is?

I dip Sergeant Vibe between my thighs and work the bulbous head over my clit, imagining it's Connor, ministering to my desires.

"Harder, more, there," I whisper to my phantom lover.

Each order makes me wetter. Needier.

I break into a light sweat, breath choppy and shallow. My hips start to buck, chasing each tingle, each thrill. I thrust two fingers into my channel, searching, searching for that fullness that will thrust me over the edge.

"That's it," I urge Phantom Connor. "Right there, right... there."

I pull in tight the instant before I climax then fly apart. Time stops as bliss overwhelms me. I shudder and quake and chase every last scrap of sensation until it's too much. I power down Sergeant Vibe, and Phantom Connor disappears.

For the first time in my life, I'm not okay with that.

My phone buzzes with an incoming text.

Friday, 12:07 a.m.

Connor: Poor Junior, RIP. Estimated time of
death, 11:57 p.m. He did not blow gently into
that good night.

> Keira: General Hoo-ha sends condolences.
> However, she is confident that Junior will rise
> from the ashes, phoenix strong.

Connor: And how is the General? Safely
bunkered for the night?

> Keira: The General made it home without
> issue. Her favorite battery-powered non-com
> performed other duties as assigned in
> exemplary fashion and now everyone is ready
> for sleep, like you should be.

Connor: If the General should need more or
different "other duties" seen to in your foxhole,
remember I'm just a text away.

> Keira: Good. Night. Connor.

Connor: Sweet dreams.

Ignoring the dopey smile that sprouts up during our exchange, I turn
over and hug my stuffed camel tight.

Cookies and pastries will star in any sweet dreams I have tonight.

Confusion-inducing hot guys needn't bother auditioning for a part.

CHAPTER 8

CONNOR

After my quick shower—the scene of Junior's recent demise—I pad to the kitchen, resting a naked hip against the counter while I take care of my teeth.

Keira shouldn't have insisted we dance.

Not if she wanted to keep me from getting ideas.

She let down her guard tonight, relaxed into my lead, laughing and joking, allowing me another peek at the woman she is when she forgets about being all buttoned up and suspicious of life. Though the topic needed to be dealt with, I could have eaten my own foot at breaking the vibe when my one-track cock pushed me to ask about sex. She pulled away, went back into hiding.

It's been a solid three years and counting since I was interested for any length of time in any particular woman. But I'm done letting Sherry fuck with my head, and I'm not going to walk away from the potential between Keira and me without trying everything I can to convince her to give whatever this is unfolding between us an honest shot.

I spit, rinse, and tidy up, shutting off the light as I make my way to bed.

We're good together. I don't know what her hang-up is around dating and relationships, why she's so adamant about keeping things temporary, but tonight I had a taste of us as a couple.

Even with the memory of my hellish experience with Sherry seared into my psyche, I can't dodge the fact that I want more, a lot more, with Keira.

How can I get her thinking about playing for keeps, not just playing around? How will I make sure I don't scare her away?

I cross my hands under my head and contemplate the long shadows on my bedroom ceiling.

Something light and fun. Something that will tweak her competitive spirit.

That, plus phenomenal sex.

Updated plan in place, I roll over and close my eyes, eager for the dawn.

Friday, 3:32 p.m.

Keira: Have to bail on our walk-throughs tonight. SRY

Connor: ?

Keira: Rat Bastard is foisting client babysitting duty on me.

Connor: Pulled the short straw, eh?

Keira: [eye-roll emoji] Yeah. Not an assignment I can refuse, alas.

Keira: Can you handle things on your own?

Connor: Of course. I promise to pick out the very best game emporium in the city.

Keira: You try pulling that, cowboy, and next time I tie you up, I tan your hide too.

Connor: Please clarify. Was that a threat or a promise? Junior wants to know.

Keira: [three eye-roll emojis] Send pictures. I'll do my best to weigh in.

Connor: [sends three more celebrity Dick pics]

Keira: Fuuuunny. I meant of the event spaces.

Keira: And by the way.

Keira: No political Dicks.

Connor: Roger that. No elephant or donkey dicks. I don't blame you. They sound hideous.

Friday, 10:04 p.m.

Connor: So, we're agreed?

Keira: Keep looking, yeah.

Saturday, 7:25 a.m.

Connor: Can't make Sunday's site visits. SIL battling both morning sickness and sniffles. David's pretending not to panic, but he's asked me to sub for him on trip to LV with Dad. Should be back in time to make the meeting with the chocolate peeps on Wednesday.

Keira: Got it. No worries. Hope she feels better soon.

Connor: No worries? Junior is worried. So worried, he's a little stiff and tender. Must be dread from the whole extended waiting period before he can receive his next set of instructions.

Lounging in my empty king-sized bed, I wait for her response, Junior tenting the sheets. Nothing new in the morning, but I figure he's especially pointy today because we're texting with Keira.

I missed her last night. Missed setting out lures for the updated plan. Missed annoying her, making her laugh. Missed her sharky laser-beam eyes, her multicolored bangs, and her giving me shit for just how awful the prospective party locations turned out to be. Missed the sex.

Missed that click I'm starting to equate with seeing her, like something off-kilter inside me snaps back into place whenever we're breathing the same air.

On impulse, I call her cell.

"What?"

As though she's petting us good-boy style, my cock reacts to her bad-tempered snarl by getting impossibly harder.

"Junior is awake and feeling restive."

"Restive?"

"Jumpy, if you will." I toss the sheet, and Junior sproings back and forth like an X-rated Jack in the Box. "Ready for some cardio."

"Ah." I shudder as her throaty understanding tickles its way down to my balls. "And are you looking for a coach to help you through this early morning workout?"

"I wouldn't say no, if you're offering."

"All right." Her tone turns brisk, a little stern. Keira's getting-down-to-sexy-business voice. "What's your safe word, Connor?"

"Crocodile. Yours?"

"Dude." She imbues the single, sighed word with full-on eye roll. "I've told you and told you… Gah, fine. You win, you stubborn mule. Alligator. Happy?"

"Delighted." I can't explain why it's so important that we each have safe words. But her *not* having one is bone-deep unacceptable. To the point where, when she first brought the subject up, I'd been willing to walk off the playing field if she hadn't agreed.

"Tyrant."

"You're the bossy one. Get to bossing, or I can't promise my hand won't start the festivities on its own." Because yet again, I'm so charged by this woman that it will take almost zero effort for me to reach orgasm.

"Oo, threats. Naughty. Tell me, do you still have any of the thongs you stole?"

"Surely they were gifts. Tokens of your deep fondness for our activities."

She makes a noise that sounds suspiciously berry-like. "Answer the question."

"Maybe."

"You are in such trouble." Her chuckle provokes a wave of tingles down the left side of my body. "Okay, here's what I need you to do. Get the green lace pair, some lube, and—do you have a headboard that you can tie things to?"

"Yes."

"I bet you have a drawerful of pervitude with all sorts of interesting things and my panties displayed in pride of place."

"No comment."

"You totally do."

"I totally do." Grinning that she knows me so well, I slide open my perv drawer, select the green thong from its velvet-lined box and grab the lube.

"Tell me," she says, a husky catch giving her away her interest in my answer. "When you're home alone, do you sniff 'em while you masturbate?"

"Red-blooded American male. 'Course I do."

"Too bad today isn't a sniff day."

"It's not? I'm bereft." Evil genius woman. Now all I want to do is shove her panties in my face and inhale the traces of her tangy, spicy scent.

"Connor, here's what's going to happen. You're going to put your phone on speaker. I'm going to walk you through tying your right hand to the headboard and lubing up Junior. Then your hand is my hand for the next twenty minutes. Are you okay with this course of action?"

"One hundred percent okay. Also, a hundred percent sure I won't last a full twenty."

I put my phone on speaker and nestle it on the pillow beside me. Her chuckles buzz through the connection, low and so full of promise my hands shake.

"All set," I say. "Start bossing."

"Connor Mack, loop the leg holes of my thong so that it's attached to the headboard, as close to the mattress as you can, a kind of slipknot."

"No problem. This is my grandparents' brass bed, lots of slats." I make the loop, the soft-rough texture of the lace catching slightly on my fingers and tickling my palms. I close my eyes and lean into the sensation, wanting more.

"Your grandparents' bed? Have you ever wondered—"

"About their naked, married-couple hijinks? I have indeed." I rub my thumb over the slight dent in the slat I tied the thong to. If I were looking at it, I'd see the faint pattern of scratches that first tipped me off to their possible nighttime proclivities. "This bed has a lot of interesting wear marks that one might call atypical of regular bed use."

"Wow."

"Yeah. A little weird to think they had sex more than four times. Once for my dad and once for each of his siblings." She can't see my grin, so I make sure it comes through in my voice. "Also kind of hot."

"One hundred percent perv."

"Admit you admire that."

"Maybe," she says with a chuckle. "Did you ever try waxing again?"

"Yeah. Even though I started stripping as a joke, I wanted to excel. Waxing was part of the deal." I pause. "Most physically painful decision I ever made."

"It's giving me ideas."

"I know that should terrify me, but say the word, and I'll figure out where to score some quality wax."

"You keep surprising me, Connor." Her pensive tone pulls me from the fantasy we're building.

"Is that a bad thing?"

"I— I don't know yet."

Seeing an opening, I make a pitch. "How about we play a game of As If?"

"What's that?"

"An exercise in pretend. It's simple. Until you know for sure whether you like one of my surprises, act as if you do. Take each surprise for a test drive, kick the wheels. Metaphorically, of course. I'm not sure my delicates, as manly as they are, would survive a real kick."

No "ready, smartass" reply issues from the phone. I check to see I haven't lost the connection. My dick is still hard, but the sun that was pouring through my window across my bed has disappeared, covered by a cloud.

I shiver, and it's not with happy anticipation.

"I could do as if," Keira says slowly. Like a wily salesman, I keep my mouth shut and let her do the heavy lifting on selling herself. "Not a blanket as if. We'd have to weigh the merits of each surprise on a case-by-case basis."

"A cost benefit analysis, yes. I completely agree. But the nature of surprises means that we may run high on the side of postmortems instead of pre-certifications. Doable?"

"Yes, okay. We can give your game a spin. As if."

"As if," I echo. Today, they rank as my favorite two words in the English language.

"As if and wax jobs tabled for the moment," she says, "we were in the middle of a hand job."

"Pretty sure we hadn't gotten to the hand-job part yet."

"Foreplay, sucker. You can pretend as if you like it." Her laugh infuses more blood into my erection, transforming Junior into rebar. Rigid and ready to put the stiff into concrete reinforcement.

"Touché. But just saying, I still have the use of my two hands."

"Pushy, pushy." She breathes in then lets the air out in a slow, centering exhale I only now realize I listen for each time we reach this point. The action that signals full immersion, no turning back, she's committed.

I miss feeling that breath against my cheek or stirring the hair over my forehead. Closing my eyes, I try to cut off the phantom-limb sensation.

I'm here. She's virtually here. Time to sink into the moment and let this be the sexy, dirty fun that kicks off the revised plan.

"Stick your right hand into the open leg hole. See if you can loop it around your wrist twice. If not, I want you to rotate your wrist a few times until it would be hard, but not impossible, to pull your hand out."

"Taken out of context, this would sound lewd."

"Taken in context, it is lewd. Now hush and listen. We're going for light bondage here, not cut-your-circulation-off tight, got it?"

My breathing deepens as I follow her instructions. I tug on the connection, and my stomach does a fast drop and rebound, kicking up my heart rate.

I'm caught and subject to Keira's will.

"All set." I settle more deeply into the bed.

"I hope this is your morning to do sheets, Connor, because we're about to make things very, very messy."

"Bring it."

"Squeeze some lube onto your belly. Be generous."

I comply. "Done."

"How does it feel?"

"Cold. Promising."

"Nice. Now, take a little of that promise and paint your balls. Two fingers only. Go slow. Be gentle. Think whisper-light touches. Remember, your hand is now my hand. That's me down there, exploring this soft, hidden terrain, this most personal space."

My breathing turns ragged as she continues to lead me through her remote inspection, as I slick lube in circles over heated, sensitive skin. The tingling at the base of my cock intensifies. I press my heels into the mattress and thrust with my hips, seeking friction, searching for more.

"Keira, I'm close, please…"

"Oh no. We can't have that." Her evil laugh flicks my ear, and I shiver. "I'm having too much fun for this to end so soon. Move your hand to your neck. Rest your big palm over your throat."

"Damn, you're killing me." I groan as I comply.

"That's the eventual plan. But before we get there, Connor, close your eyes and breathe for me. In. And out. That's it. Relax all that tension. Feel the weight of my hand on you, the warmth of my touch. I have you. Let's just be here and now until we're both ready."

I sink further under her spell, my breathing leveling out at the same time as every nerve ending in my body pulses with anticipation of what's next.

"How's your bound hand?"

The reminder of my captivity hollows me out the rest of the way until I'm boneless. I open and close the fist I have wrapped around the brass slat, testing my blood flow. The lace tickles, but there are no pins and needles.

"Good." My voice rumbles like a concrete mixer, heavy and bass. "All good."

"Great. Trace one of my fingers over your collarbones. Just kiss the skin, as if I were a feather."

My left hand, complete crap at fine motor control, trembles as I obey. In less than two seconds, I'm back to chugging air.

"Good man," she coos. "Pinch your nipples. Make it sting a little."

Groaning, I follow her command. My nipples have never been a source of pleasure before, but she lingers over them, first one then the other. Flicking, pinching, twisting.

My fingers, her control.

Finally, we make our way down my abs, dipping into my belly button for a quick tickle before tracking through the fine arrow of hair that leads south to my go zone.

"Let's check on your right hand again. Still doing okay? Fingers pink, not blue, no tingling?"

I flex my wrist, wriggle my fingers. "All good."

"Excellent," she purrs. "Good boys get treats. Rub your hand into the remaining lube on your belly. Get it good and coated."

The lube is warm from my skin so it doesn't take long. "Coated."

"Now wrap your cock in a firm grip near the base. Tug toward your crown. Slow now, keep it slow and draw it out. Squeeze like you're inside me deep and I'm making it hard for you to leave."

My hand follows her lead, again and again, up then down, as we build pressure and heat and slick friction one slow, drawn-out tug at a time.

Part of me floats above the bed, there but not there, an out-of-body voyeur observing as I'm drawn further and further into the richness of her voice, her attention, her care.

She tracks every breath I take, every grunt and groan, adjusting her seduction until she has me right where she promised, hanging between agony and ecstasy.

"Think you can last another two minutes?" She's doubtful. That only feeds my resolve not to disappoint.

"I can. Do anything. For. Two. Minutes." My lungs saw in my chest. I'm sprinting for the finish line of a race I will not lose.

"How do you like your blow jobs? Sweet, all tongue and kisses? Or spicy with a hint of teeth? I already know you're open to a little back-door action. Ever put a vibrator up there? I bet you have one in your perv drawer."

Sweat drips into my ears, my room smells like sex, and my sheets are a rat's nest at the foot of my bed. I'm an animal, no thought, no control, straining for more, for everything.

I'm clutching the headboard I'm tied to so hard it might snap.

My left hand pumps, brutal and urgent, pushing me closer and closer to the edge.

"Five, four, three, two—"

With a shout, I fly apart on one, brain zeroing out as sensation after sensation rockets through my body, finally leaving me a spent mess in the middle of my grandparents' brass bed.

CHAPTER 9

KEIRA

My thighs clench at Connor's gargle of pleasure. A flush of need rushes through me. Too bad there isn't a damn thing I can do to relieve the pressure. The clock on the wall ticks closer to eight o'clock, the start of what seems like my forty-seventh workday in a row.

But standing by the window in my office, all I picture is the fantasy in my mind's eye.

Connor, a sweaty, sticky mess tied to a big brass bed. At my mercy.

Ruddy cheeks, lips lush and biteable. The hint of a smile playing at the corners of his mouth, the dare in his eyes inviting me to begin round two. The vision almost makes me wish that I could join him there one day. Put a temporary cease and desist order on my no naked hookups rule and enjoy all he'd be more than happy to offer.

"Aren't you ready yet?" Brad Ratcliffe, aka Rat Bastard, aka my boss, asks from the doorway. "The team is assembling in the conference room."

Brad and I used to get along. Now nothing I do is right, like the test-fail-regroup/test-succeed-repeat strategy we ran to grow his business so fast has shifted into argue-play it safe-blame Keira for poor results.

I owe him my allegiance. He took me under his wing when I first came to New York City after I spent three miserable years trying to carve out a career in my parents' real estate investment company after college. But these days I mostly want to brain him for changing from a consummate professional into such a passive-aggressive dick.

"The staff meeting doesn't begin until eight. I'll be on time."

"I'll hold you to it," Brad says. His reflection in the window disappears as he walks down the hall.

"Wait, did I miss something?" Connor's voice is alert, aware, not post-orgasm fuzzy the way it should be.

"No. I gotta go. All-hands-on-deck meeting in five. Congrats on lasting the full twenty." I force some false cheer into my voice, but I'm pretty sure I just sound pissed. "I didn't think you could."

"Keira? Talk to me. What's wrong?"

"Fun's done. Back to business. I'll text you my impressions of the sites."

I disconnect on his "Just a sec—" after my second stab with a shaky finger and tuck the phone into my messenger bag. When I grab the portfolio of properties I researched for Brad's mystery project from my desk, it slips from my fingers and pages flutter to the floor.

"Damn." As I reach down, a sharp twinge shoots across my tight shoulders. I stop and do a neck roll. Try to calm myself the hell down as I make a tidy stack out of the chaos.

Why am I having a freak-out? Brad's needling this morning wasn't any different from most of our interactions nowadays.

I breathe in for a count of four, hold for seven, and exhale for eight, struggling to put the sensation into words.

With a whoosh, I deflate halfway through my next hold.

Oh.

I wanted to stay on the phone.

Continue playing As If. Lean on Connor as I indulge in a thoroughly unprofessional rant about my boss drama. Have him explain, in his cockeyed take on the world way, why Rat Bastard isn't worthy of my stress.

Well, shit. That came out of nowhere. But worrying now about the implications of wanting to lean on my just-sex partner for a squishy emotional assist won't help me power through what promises to be a grueling work session.

I tuck the revelation—and the lingering echo of Connor's pleasure—in a deep inner crevasse where they won't distract me today.

The wall mirror next to my door tells me my hair is behaving, my makeup a mask without cracks. My power suit could bench press three-fifty, it's such a badass.

Calm and confident. Professional. I set my intentions for the coming ordeal with one final breath cycle.

My yoga instructor would be so proud.

————

Keira

"You need to leave Ratcliffe and Associates, like, yesterday," Helena informs me as the bell on the door to my neighborhood coffee shop jangles behind us.

We take off down the sidewalk, heading for the first of the potential party sites before we're due to meet up with The Moms and some of Helena's extended family for our debut foray into wedding-dress shopping.

"You're not wrong." I suck down a third of my extra-large unsweetened iced tea. It's nine o'clock on Sunday morning and already ass-melting hot. "But I need a little more time to figure out my next step."

"Finances tight? You need me to float you something so you can make like a shepherd and get the fuck out of there?"

"Ha. Thanks, no. I've been pulling together some ideas, organizing my thoughts. I'm just not willing to let Rat Bastard push me into something rash."

"You'd plan all your minutes between now and the next millennium if you could."

"Again with the not wrong. But don't worry. I'll jump when I'm ready, swearsies." I kick a discarded cardboard cup toward a trash can. It's not as satisfying as I want it to be. I pluck the cup up and toss it into the bin. "I never figured Brad's ego would be so weenie that a woman outselling him would crush it."

"Really? Between the stuff you've shared over the years and the few times we've met, I'm not surprised. He always struck me as pretty controlling."

"Hey, I spring from the loins of two masters of emotional manipulation. I think I would have sniffed out a controlling SOB right under my own nose."

"Sweetie, you were an absolute wreck back when he scooped you up. It's no wonder he was able to take advantage. I don't think your nose rebooted for a good few years, and he kept you too busy for you to stop and think, let alone smell his bull. But it's not like he had it all his own way. From all you've shared, you became quite the expert on how to handle him to get what you wanted."

"Great. You're saying that instead of starting my life in New York with a fresh slate, I ended up in yet another manipulative power dynamic." My next mouthful of tea tastes like tin. "Awesome. Go, me."

"Listen." Helena bumps her shoulder into mine. "Don't start thinking loco. Brad, while a rat bastard, did a solid enough job of mentoring you, at least in the early days. You just outmatch him. Always have, so it's no surprise to me that he's getting shitty. He's sensed the launch of the countdown clock that'll end his cash cow."

"Hey, are you calling me a cow?"

"Moo."

"Smartass. I'll moo you," I say, shaking my fist at her with mock threat.

"Oo, I'm quivering."

"That's your caffeine overload. Three espresso shots? Really?"

"What? It's going to be a long, challenging day. A gal likes to be prepared."

"Can't argue that."

We settle into a block-eating stride in a companionable silence while she gives me space. Wise smartass bestie. Not sure where I'd be without her. On impulse, I link arms with her. She taps the bottom of her drink to mine and leaves me to my brood.

I've tried hard to move past my upbringing. To avoid being used as a pawn with no free will, no input into shaping my own life. It's why I'm so explicit with my sexual partners about my expectations. I want full-knowledge and full-consent buy-in of the rules from the get-go.

Helena thinks I go overboard, pushing prudent management of emotional boundaries to the extreme. But I say, better to be overly safe than an inch of sorry.

Could I really have been manipulating my boss all of these years and not even realize what I was up to?

"I can hear your brain cogs catching. Come on. Cough it up," Helena says after a while.

"I don't want to be a puppet. Or a puppet master."

"Oh, honey." She stops us in the middle of the sidewalk, sliding her hand down my arm to squeeze my fingers. "You aren't anything of the kind. You're a human being. Flesh and blood, filled with desires and needs and hopes. One who's not afraid of blowing up the status quo if it's not working. That's not manipulation. That's guts. It's not always comfortable. So what? It's not your job to make people comfortable."

I scrunch my face at her, not quite buying what she's selling.

"Can't wrap your head around that? Okay, let's try this instead. As my maid of honor, it actually is your job to see to my comfort. Well, it would make me super comfy if you'd take off that ugly, ridiculous hair shirt you're trying—and failing—to rock. It's unflattering, and I don't want it at my wedding."

"And here I thought scratchy lingerie was the latest in bridesmaid accessories."

"Hard pass." She jiggles our joined hands. "You have baggage. We all do. Maybe you feel like yours is over the weight limit. Welcome to the human race is all I'm saying."

"I don't promise not to brood on this more."

"You wouldn't be you if you didn't." She cocks a finger gun at me. "Work on accepting this bit, okay? Your self-perceived flaws are neither fatal nor contagious. Contact with you doesn't require immunity or a vaccination. Just a beating heart."

"There you go, ruining a perfectly good freak-out by hitting me square in the feelz. Why the hell do I put up with you?"

"My outsized, capital P positivity would be my guess."

"Your outsized something." I bestow a smacking kiss on her cheek and turn us to the entrance of our building containing our first stop. "Let's see if option one is up to snuff."

We easily knock both locations from the list of possibles, but I take photos to send Connor later. The first is soulless, closer to a mini-convention center than the intimate setting we have in mind. The second smells like disinfectant. A really ineffective one.

Despite the heat, we cab over to the boutique with the windows down.

"Do you think something died in the vents?" Helena asks after we pay the driver and climb out. She's a little green around the gills.

"Maybe a couple of generations worth of somethings." I suck up traffic fumes to cleanse my palette. "You'd think the review sites would be all over that stench."

"Must be a recent bunch of generations." She regards the bridal boutique in front of us then throws her shoulders back and straightens to her full height. "Okay. I got this."

"What's up?" I tug her to a halt.

"The Moms. They're really, really invested in the wedding."

"Competing for attention?"

"Worse. Colluding." She shakes her head. "I'm going to be lucky I don't end up in a Princess Di knockoff, complete with a twenty-five-yard train. They created a Pinterest board. It's fluffy, ruffly, and pink."

"Yikes."

"Yeah."

We plunge into chaos. A platoon of women of all ages, garbed in brightly patterned Sunday-go-to-brunch outfits, maneuver through racks of satin and lace. With the composed patience of seasoned campaigners, two well-coiffed generals oversee the madness from a loveseat in the center of the large room.

The Moms.

"Cousin! You're here!" One of Helena's teenage family members must have been set as a lookout. She hustles Helena into a fitting room. "We've already picked out the best options. Come on, come on. I can't wait for you to try on my choice. Can I be a bridesmaid? Pretty please?"

For the next hour and a half, Helena is coaxed into one gown after another. Some land in close-but-no-cigar territory. Most are duds. None captures the down-to-earth Bridezilla I know and love.

Worse, neither The Moms nor the aunties nor the cousins are listening to Helena's vision for her own damn day.

When they try to get her back into one of the first dresses she rejected, I blow a taxi-stopping whistle through my teeth, and all heads whip toward me. Enough with the bullying.

"Time's up. Thanks, everyone, for your suggestions. Helena will be sure to take them into consideration as she makes her decision about her wedding dress." I make sure to hit harder on the words *she* and *her* as I take out my phone and start tapping out a quick message to Mateo. "Hel, get dressed. We don't want to be late to the next appointment."

"On it," she says with a bounce to her voice that'd gone missing about half hour after our arrival.

There's grumbling, and The Moms shoot me a matched pair of we-are-not-amused stares. I hold my ground. Even well-intentioned peer pressure is a form of manipulation, and I'm not down with letting my best friend suffer when her search for a wedding gown should be a happy dress quest.

It takes another quarter hour for Helena to receive everyone's hugs, admonitions, and last-minute advice. Finally, I extricate her from a trio of aunts schooling her about all the sexual positions that guarantee conception.

Wide-eyed—and a little shell-shocked by the aunts—we bolt for the exit and toss ourselves into a cab.

"Where are we going?" Helena collapses into her corner of the back seat and starts massaging the arch of one foot.

"Does it matter?"

"No." She switches to the other foot and groans. "Anywhere but there is good."

"Let's see if we can make it better than good." I finish texting Mateo. "Your man is going to meet us at Blaylock in twenty. A few adult bevies and some ribs will wash away the nightmare."

"And you wonder why we're friends." She tilts into me, resting her head on my shoulder. "Thanks."

"You're welcome."

I slip on a pair of sunglasses while Helena takes a combat nap on my shoulder and the cabbie muscles through a snarl of Sunday lookie-loo traffic. Maybe, just maybe, this friendship isn't as one-way as I've always feared. My crises. My neuroses. My flailing around for a life-saver. Her throwing me one over and over and over. Take, take, take.

Maybe, just maybe, I give too.

The cabbie sees an opening and stomps on the gas. As we speed toward sustenance, I tuck the idea that I might be halfway normal in the friendship department into the same hidey-hole where the memory of Connor's pleasure safely resides.

My precious tiny hoard of peopling triumphs.

CHAPTER 10

CONNOR

Dad and I kick back in first class for the flight to Las Vegas. He's engrossed in an important magazine—code for the celebrity gossip rag he inexplicably subscribes to—and I have my avoiding-deep-thoughts playlist running through my noise-canceling headphones, drenching me in thumping drums. Our scotches perch on the seatback trays in front of us, and every so often, Dad roots through a bag of mixed nuts for the cashews.

Normally, I'd take this one-on-one time to shake the old man down about when he'll make a decision on who he'll tap to lead the Winstonian Hotel restoration.

But I have other concerns on my mind. Female concerns.

Female with whom I'm having sex concerns.

They might even be worries.

Worries that have only grown in the hours since Keira's abrupt brush-off yesterday.

Dad leans over and plucks my headphones off one ear. "You'll get an ulcer if you keep that up."

"What?" I sling my cans around my neck and pause the music.

"The gerbil wheel brain grind." He taps my temple. "Work, woman, brother, or other?"

"Dad. I'm twenty-nine. I can handle my own gerbil wheel."

"Never said you couldn't. Regardless, I have two ears and some decent life experience. Give me a try. Maybe I'll surprise you."

"You constantly surprise me."

"Means I'm doing my job. Also, I've lived long enough to recognize that snarky tone means you're trying to change the subject." He takes a sip of scotch while pinning me with the Dad-eye. I manfully refrain from squirming. "You're my least moody child, but that doesn't mean you don't have it in you to brood. My vote is woman trouble."

"Why do you say that? This—and I'm not admitting there's a this, mind you—could totally be a work thing."

"Work challenges tend to light a glint of mischief in your eye. Your brothers dial up your stubborn to eleven, but usually you deal with that by pounding on each other."

"I could be stressing about my squash game."

"If you were serious about your squash game, I'd give you that." He takes another quick sip before setting his drink down. "Spill. You'll feel better getting it off your chest. Troubles with Keira?"

"I don't know." I roll the bottom edge of my drink circles on the white napkin. "We were, uh, concentrating on something—"

"Is that the code the younger generation uses for sex nowadays?"

"Dad." I pinch the bridge of my nose. "Not helping."

"Sorry," he says, unrepentant. "Continue."

"We'd, uh, concluded discussion about the most urgent item on the agenda. I thought we were moving on to the next one when poof. She was gone."

"You lost the connection?"

"No. I mean she tells me she has a meeting to get to, and hangs up."

"Burst your post-discussion high, did she, with her lack of tender mercies? I wouldn't read too much into it. Busy woman slotted you into her busy schedule." He squeezes the back of my neck, giving me a dad-shake. "Focus on the attention, not the exit."

"Hm, when you put it like that…" I knock back a slug of my scotch.

Talking in veiled metaphor about sex brings back those birds and bees lectures Dad gave my brothers and me growing up. Funny how that tension between *reassuring* and *gross, my dad knows about sex*, still exists.

What he's implying makes sense, maybe even gives me a little insight into why Keira insists on no strings. Hell, at least half of why I've never tried for a long-term relationship after Sherry is because I made my job my first priority.

But…

I can't let it go.

Her change from start to finish yesterday morning keeps needling me as Dad returns to his glossy celebrities, and I catch the sun setting fire to the sky among the clouds.

She switched off.

The dirty talk, the razzing, the keen focus on my every breath, my well-being, on how to lead me to the outer limits of pleasure. That's what poofed into thin air.

No, it's more than that. I'm not such a pig to think I'm owed these things from a sexual partner. But when that partner retreats behind a wall with no seeming reason, it… I laugh.

Well, damn. My feelings are hurt.

What is it with this woman? She's making me crazy.

Poking at it, sore-tooth style, isn't going to help.

Better to turn this forced butt-in-chair time to something with more immediate potential for success.

I launch into another sales pitch for me heading the Winstonian reno. Dad gives me an amused look, waves for a refill of our drinks, then settles in to listen.

"We have a deep bench of work that extends back to Great-Great-Granddaddy Winston. The casino we'll be staying at this week. All your skyscrapers. Celia's museum project. Over the decades, our family has put its aesthetic mark on an impressive chunk of real estate."

Dad opens his palm, acknowledging the truth of my intro.

"We've now been presented with the opportunity to bring one of our faded gems back to the glory of her heyday. To make the

Winstonian Hotel relevant and vital again. Since the summer I pulled my first internship at Mack Family Architects when I was fourteen, I've been preparing to take on a challenge with this kind of scope, this kind of importance. Not just to the city or the firm. But to our family legacy too. I want to bring new life to this forgotten beauty. She deserves it. I promise I'll do right by the Winstonian, and I'll do right by us. All I need is the chance."

I wind down, and he goes into inquisition mode, peppering me with nuanced, granular questions and what-if scenarios.

"I like your passion, Connor." He pats my arm. "I want you to think more on those contingency situations and take time to really dig into the potential problems. Write up how you would address each, and add your strategies as an appendix to your proposal. MFA will have one crack at getting this renovation right. Let's not rush our shot."

"Shall do."

The in-flight meal is served, and maybe it's the food in my stomach, but I'm hopeful on all fronts when I finish eating. I change up my playlist, ready to chill with some 1960s bossa nova.

Dad asking for more data means he's taking my proposal seriously.

And unexpected phone sex could throw a wrench into anyone's schedule. So, no dwelling on the abrupt conclusion to our phone call or some minor glitch in communication.

Keira agreed to play As If with me.

And that's huge.

CHAPTER 11

CONNOR

S unday 8:32 p.m. Las Vegas / 11:32 p.m. New York City

> Connor: Flight got in late. All I want is a shower and my bed, but our client insists on a nightcap in the bar. How'd yesterday's meeting go? And do we have a winning party location?

Dots bounce forever on my screen, indicating Keira's typing a reply. After a too-long wait without receiving a text, I toss the phone on the hotel bed and hit the shower for a quick reset before heading down to meet the Goldens.

For years, I haven't missed getting tied up in knots by a woman.

Now, I'm all sorts of grumpy at *not* getting tied up in knots by a woman.

My brothers would laugh at the irony. I tell myself—and Junior—that patience is a virtue. Neither of us is thankful for the reminder.

The following morning, while Dad and I are at a breakfast meetup with the eager team from a newly formed niche property-management company, the Do Not Disturb on my phone turns off for the day, and the cell vibrates with a slew of incoming alerts. It's as much excitement as my pants and I have seen since arriving in Sin City.

Admittedly, that was only yesterday, but the point stands, much like the usual waking chubby I manfully ignored earlier while getting ready for the day.

Since breakfast is pretty much over, I excuse myself from the table and head to the casino lobby. Dad'll linger a little longer, validating the team's vision, hearing their hopes, encouraging their enthusiasm. Not because he has to—Mack Family Architects will likely never partner directly with this crew—but because he's genuine. His integrity pushes him to care about people, about their projects, about the impact of architecture on communities.

He thinks I'm passionate?

I learned it all from him. I might not have followed directly in his footsteps as an architect, but he's the one who taught me how to be a professional.

With twenty or so minutes left before the start of our next meeting, I plop into a chair to do some email inbox weed whacking.

My heart pounds with a happy double thump at the sight of Keira's name on the lock screen.

Monday 7:34 a.m. Las Vegas / 10:34 a.m. New York City

Keira: Two more loser venues.

Nothing since Saturday, then she ignores my text for twelve hours, and now she tries to drop back into my DMs with a terse party-planning update?

Oh, I don't think so.

I examine the pictures. Neither option gives me a buzz. But they do give me an idea.

Connor: I see we're looking at long and skinny with an odd quirk to the left at the far end or stubby and squat with questionable landscaping.

Keira: Not one of those words is filthy. Not one. Yet somehow you managed to perfectly describe the [eggplant emoji eggplant emoji] of my first two boyfriends. Have you been reading my diary??

Connor: My condolences.

Connor: Also, where might one find a copy of said diary? I'm curious about what other intriguing content might exist between its covers.

Keira: Kidding about the diary.

Connor: [sad eye emoji] I am suddenly in deep mourning. Must remember to wear black.

Keira: As long as your tie is silk, I don't care what color you wear.

Connor: When did you know?

Keira: Know what?

Connor: That you like control during sex? Did you discover it gradually or were you always aware?

Keira: ...

I groan at the replay of the bubbling Dots of Limbo. Fuck. Too personal, too soon? Probably. Damn it, when will I learn when to stop pushing?

Resigned to another depressing nonresponse, I flip over to email when my phone vibrates.

Keira: A mix of both. A few books and movies at key points that made me… itchy to try things a different way.

This time my heart quadruple thumps. It takes a couple seconds for the tremor in my thumbs to settle down before I can tap out my reply. Patience, patience. Don't scare the woman away just as she's opening up a little.

Connor: I hear you. As squirmy as it made us boys, my parents were pretty you-be-you when it came to sex talks. Respect yourself and your partner, but if a fantasy lights you up, give it a whirl, see if you like it.

Keira: That's… not how my family worked.

Keira: In no universe can I imagine my parents sitting me down for a talk about something as basic as puberty, let alone dating. Sex was definitely off the table. No way would I have gone to them for validation of—or advice on—my kinky proclivities.

Keira: All I know is something clicked into place, pointed me in a particular direction, and ever since I've been really clear about what kind of sex I like.

Connor: The bossy kind.

Keira: You're totally going to be weird about this, aren't you?

Connor: Never.

Connor: I mean, maybe?

Keira: And Helena wonders why I don't share.
Keira: Listen, I have to run. Rat Bastard is unveiling our mystery client today. I need to do final prep.

> Connor: Understood. And even though I have a million follow-up questions, I promise not to be weird.

> Connor: Weirder.

> Connor: I mean, I'm the one out of us who likes being tied up, right?

Keira: Point.

Keira: About last Saturday. I wanted to

Keira: Damn, gotta go.

Why the hell don't we have Star Trek technology yet? Beam me east, Scottie. Stat.

David owes me, big time. I should be in New York, not trying to hold unexpectedly deep conversations via text message.

Pocketing my phone, I cross the lobby as Dad arrives, and we head toward the elevators that will take us to the conference room floor.

"You're thinking deep thoughts again, son."

"What gave me away?"

"You've got your mom's forehead. Same three lines would sketch along her skin whenever she entered full ponder mode." He smiles at an image only he can see. "More troubles with your lady friend?"

"No clue, honestly."

"Ah." A wealth of understanding resounds in that ah.

"How'd you know Mom was it for you?" I ask on impulse. "For real, not the fairy-tale version Mom always told us."

"Bunch of little things. They added up to a giant neon arrow flashing at Merida that read, 'She's the one.'"

"Give me a for instance."

"Her ponder lines. Her need to win at card games. The way she linked our pinkies together as we walked down the sidewalk whenever it was too hot to hold hands."

"Those sound just as whimsical as the stuff Mom peddled."

"Sorry, chump." He claps me on the back. "My list won't help you. You're going to have to figure the little things out for yourself, see if they build into your own personal arrow."

CHAPTER 12

KEIRA

W hy does the mention of left-leaning odd quirks and questionable landscaping make me hot? Why do I reply to Connor's inquiry into my kink origins? And what the hell was I thinking to go into that shit about my parents?

Typical of the man to get me headed in two directions at once. And untypical of me to prefer focusing on Connor than on Brad's drawn-out client reveal.

The flip in my priorities brings me up short. Maybe I don't understand all the whys behind my reactions to Connor, but hiding in the personal to avoid the professional?

Big stinking clue I need to accelerate my departure timeline. Fly this coop and flap my own business wings.

A fullness blooms inside me, muscling out the grind in my gut that's been dogging me since things started going south at work.

I'll help Rat Bastard on this last project. Then Operation Fly, Fly, Be Free is a go.

It's good to have a plan.

I perform a final inspection in my office mirror. My pretty rainbow bangs are gone, dyed a conservative jet black that matches my suit and blouse. Which makes the new burgundy tips stand out all the better. I sleek my hand down the jacket lapel and fasten the single matte black button. Good.

Battle armor in place, I collect the portfolio filled with crème-de-la-crème properties the other women on the team and I pulled together during our all-day work session on Saturday and hoof it to our conference room.

I'll need to take them with me when I leave.

What? I stumble to a stop just shy of my destination. Where did that come from? Yeah, we're all suffering under Rat Bastard's increasingly petty, petulant leadership. But is it really on me to help my colleagues? They're free to leave anytime, just like me.

Now that the idea is seeded, though, I can't shake it loose.

Okay. All right. I'll simply adjust the details of the plan, not the ultimate vision.

Placing further fine-tuning on the back burner for now, I push through the conference room door. And stop as though I've run smack into a large pane of glass.

Oh.

I'm wrong.

This isn't petty.

Brad's managed an epic power play. The ultimate, really.

My parents sit at the oval conference table, a pair of porcelain statues overmatched for their plebeian surroundings. They glow with the otherness that comes with true power, little-g gods condescending to breathe the same air as mere mortals.

I haven't seen them in over six years. Not since I rejected the future they had mapped out for me.

Not since I gave up my hope.

My coworkers slowly freeze mid-action as neither my parents nor I break the growing silence. The room churns with unshed storms, the fine hairs on my body prickling to electric attention.

"Keira, surely no introductions are necessary." Rat Bastard rests his hand between my shoulder blades. I shrug it off.

"What are you up to, Brad?" I barely move my lips.

"The Tanners are looking to expand their luxury rental property holdings on the east coast." He bows to them, a stupid, deferential, belly-showing gesture they accept as their due with near identical half nods. "What could be more logical than for them to come for help to where their daughter is employed? Keep it in the family."

I stuff down a sigh. Poor Brad. He invited my parents over the threshold. He has no idea his life is no longer his own. How much of his soul has he sold them so far?

And why the hell are they here?

Possibly I should have read those quarterly reports instead of burning them while performing a jig.

Doesn't matter, anyway. They don't own my future, not anymore and not ever again.

My parents pop up out of the blue and want to buy a raft of condos?

I will sell them that fleet of condos. I will count my fattened commission.

Then, once more, I will walk away from their toxic drama without a backward glance.

"Jessica, power up the projector, please. Jenny Kate, you be our scribe this morning." I nod to each as I approach the table. "Mother. Father. Based on what you shared with Brad, we've lined up several potentials we think will fulfill your requirements."

"What have you done with your hair? And your outfit." Mother shudders. "I've told you and told you, dresses are more appealing to—"

"We've put together a video overview," I say, cutting into her opening salvo, "emphasizing a variety of neighborhoods, square footage, age of property, architectural style, et cetera. Afterward, I'll walk you through some questions designed to clarify what we need to look for based on your investment goals. From that, we'll narrow down a prospect list to inspect this week."

"Acceptable," Father says. "Continue."

No contact between us for years, then my mother chastises me in front of my boss and colleagues, and dear old Father shows off his specialty—the judgment and command twofer.

Lazy, improve. Barely adequate, strive harder. Not our kind, kill the relationship.

As the video plays, I lock down every stray emotion, every hint of vulnerability until I'm a polished diamond of cool professionalism.

I captain the rest of the day, clipped, single-minded, steering us in the direction I want us to head. Anytime my mother gets personal, I reframe. Anytime Rat Bastard tries to bonhomie his way into the three-way lock going on with my parents and me, I shut him down.

Father's silence speaks the loudest, is the hardest to push past. But I manage, and we work through an enormous amount of material. By the end of the day, my whole body, head to toe, throbs but not in the good, Connor-induced way.

"Okay, let's wrap for today. I'll pull together the itinerary for tomorrow's site visits and share it with you later this evening," I say, shuffling my notes into a tidy stack. "We'll reconvene at ten a.m."

"You'll dine with us. Shall we say seven o'clock so you have time to change into something more suitable?" Mother punctuates her question with a familiar, patient smile. The one that's always implied there's a right answer, and she's sure I'll get it if I just work a little harder to please her.

"I'll have to decline. Work obligations trump family dinners, right?"

She prune faces but sucks down her rebuttal when Father stands. That simple action gains him control of the room.

"Exactly right." Despite myself, my heart leaps at his agreement, but the rest of me goes still, waiting for the judgment, the command. Instead he buttons his suit coat. "Ratcliffe, show us out."

Like the Pied Piper, when my father leads, others follow. He drains the conference room in his wake, Mother and Brad nipping at his heels. Jessica, Jenny Kate, and my other coworkers peel off in ones and twos, leaving me alone in a room reverberating with the loud and heavy silence of things unsaid. Things that have never been said.

Hello. We missed you. How are you? We love you.

We're sorry.

I tilt my head back and blink as fast as a hummingbird's wings.

No tears.

Professionals don't cry.

Monday 12:14 p.m. New York City / 9:14 p.m. Las Vegas

> Connor: Three meetings into the day, and it's only ten a.m. I think I need a sling for my hand. Poor thing is sprained from so much shaking. Send cookies, pretty please.
>
> Connor: ^chocolate chip cookies
>
> Connor: Lunch keynoter says it takes more than four walls to make a home. [eye roll emoji] Does he think this is a self-help convention?
>
> Connor: [photo of a shiny outdoor pool] Wish you were here. Wish I was too. No rest for the wicked. I wouldn't mind milk with the cookies. Just laying it out there.
>
> Connor: Dad booked us for dinner and a show with old friends. Kinda excited to see if there'll be any boobies (blue-footed or other) in the kick line. Will send evidence if yes.
>
> Connor: P.S. Still cookieless. I mean, this is America. You'd think there'd be cookies on every corner. Or at least on the menu of a five-star restaurant. [grumpy face emoji]
>
> Connor: Intermission. No kick line. No boobies. A total bust (haha, see what I did there?). I know it's getting late in NYC and you're an early riser so I'll say good night. Hope the meet-the-client went well. Let me know when you get a chance.

Finally home for the night after hours more prep for Tuesday, I hunker down on the couch, snuggling my stuffed camel under my chin, and debate whether to respond to the play-by-play thread of Connor's day.

I debate my life choices, the meaning of the universe, and whether we'll colonize Mars in my lifetime. If I could jump on the off-world shuttle tomorrow, would I escape my problems or would they follow me, like toilet paper stuck to the bottom of my cosmic shoe?

I debate whether to show up tomorrow morning for round two of my parents' hidden agenda.

The more I stew, the harder it gets to breathe. When I start to shake, I push my forehead into Camuel's belly to ride out the storm.

Damn, they're doing it again. Screwing with my head.

Cold and juddery, I gather my weighted chenille blanket around my shoulders and head into my bedroom. I'll work on figuring out why they're here tomorrow. For now, I need to turn off the scramble in my brain.

Which means I'm probably better off not texting with Connor.

Instead, I'll plan a chocolate chip cookie stealth drop for the man with a sweet tooth.

Cookies, I can handle.

CHAPTER 13

CONNOR

Tuesday 5:57 p.m. Las Vegas / 8:57 p.m. New York City

> Connor: Can you fit in a trip to another potential party location before we hit the chocolate peeps on Wednesday? I need to swing by the Winstonian Hotel. It has an event space that *might* fit our needs.

I don't hold out much hope Keira will respond. My phone says my messages from yesterday were read, but she hasn't replied.

She's busy. And still all kinds of cautious about how our new arrangement will play out.

Okay, fine. I can be patient.

"Stop tapping your foot," Dad says, racked out on a pool lounge chair beside me. "It's killing my vibe."

Okay, fine. Not so fucking patient.

She's a fan of open and clear communication when we're face-to-face and getting busy. That she doesn't seem to practice that value when we're apart is a little too reminiscent of some of the bull Sherry pulled for my peace of mind. Even if we're not a couple, not officially dating, we can still work together to improve how we… work together. Okay, okay, I need to fine-tune the pitch, but the idea is good.

If we're going to be long-term friends with benefits, we have to put in the work on reinforcing our foundation, or whatever we build will eventually collapse.

Bonus that this gives me another opportunity to negotiate more advantageous terms.

I'll sell her on a list of hows, whens, and whats for messaging. Woo her with rules. We can use the discussion as foreplay for our next hookup.

And hopefully, I'll avoid reliving the same mistakes of my past.

I take a page out of Dad's book and shift from a seat at a patio table to the lounge chair next to him. We're stealing a couple hours of downtime at the hotel pool before the awards dinner this evening. Might as well take advantage of the break to relax.

My fingers start a tattoo on my thigh. I shake my head and give in, keeping my busy digits out of Dad's line of sight.

No, not so fucking patient. But, hey, at least it's quiet.

CHAPTER 14

KEIRA

Wednesday 10:02 a.m. New York City / 7:02 a.m. Las Vegas

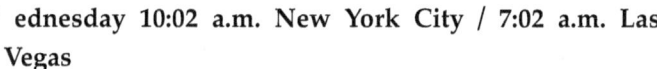

> Keira: The Winstonian? Yeah, I can make that site visit. Send me the deets, I'll meet you there.

Elbows propped on my office desk, head bowed, I rub my temples. Tension headache? Check. Exhaustion? Check. Gnawing pit in my stomach? Check, check, check.

How the hell am I going to muscle through to the chocolate tasting with Helena, Mateo, and Connor—and now fit in another location survey—on top of what promises to be day three of brinksmanship with my parents?

I've already taken the max dose of painkillers. Fat lot of good they're doing. I lean back in my chair to stare unseeing at the beige ceiling tiles.

Time to admit the issue isn't a headache. It's a people ache.

Multiple people aches.

Tuesday was a nightmare with a script I could recite in my sleep.

Obsequious butt-kissing from Brad. Scurrying, panic-induced semi-competence from my usually super-capable coworkers. Me, in human robot mode, struggling not to shrink back into the tight fit of my parents' expectations or smack face first into one of Mother's gotcha traps.

From the age of the HVAC systems to the bylaws of the co-ops and condo associations to the location of the quarry in Italy where the marble in the guest bathroom of one of the condos came from, she left no detail, petty or profound, unquestioned.

Just another test in a long line my parents have administered over the years.

Leaning an elbow on my desk, I massage my forehead. What will today's test include?

Rather than give myself a second headache—can you have two headaches at the same time?—I flip over my phone and bring up Connor's text thread, smiling as I scroll through his Dicks and boobs and infectious good cheer.

Oh, to walk the world with that effortless ease, that sense you'll be welcome just as you are in any room you enter.

Must be nice.

"Brad says to tell you your parents canceled for today." Jessica comes into my office and takes a seat in one of the visitor chairs. "They'll be here at noon tomorrow. He'll email you which properties they want to see."

"Thanks. He give a reason why they canceled?"

"Nope." She shrugs before tilting her head to stare at me with speculation in her narrowed gaze. "Can I ask you a question?"

"Shoot." I refrain from pointing out she just had. No need to share my churlish mood.

"Why the hell are you slaving away for Brad when you've got connections like your parents?"

"Wanted to see if I could make it on my own, I guess," I say, giving her an explanation scrubbed free of drama.

"If I were in your shoes, I'd have totally cashed in on the Tanner name."

"Call me stubborn."

"Call you something, at least. Maybe crazy."

"Haha. You and my bestie would get along great. She, too, thinks I'm crazy." I stand, stowing my phone into my bag. "Since we have this unexpected reprieve, I'm going to take advantage and squeeze in a couple of showings with Anita and Darington."

"All kidding aside, the other gals and I are here for you," Jessica says quietly as she gets to her feet. "We know how much you've pulled for us to get anything like a fair shake from Brad over the years. Let us do some of the heavy lifting every so often. One, because relationships aren't supposed to be a one-way deal, where you give and give and the other side only takes, okay? And two, well, we might just surprise you."

"I—" I open and close my mouth, doing a great impersonation of a fish choking on air. "You—"

"Hey, just, you know. Keep it in mind. We don't bite. Well, Jenny Kate might." She crinkles her nose before grinning. "We're going to happy hour tonight to slander and defame our evil overlord. For once, will you join us?"

"I can't." I catch her hand as her expression cools. "I swear. This isn't an it's not you, it's me thing. You've clearly caught on that I need remedial classes on the whole friendship thing, or you wouldn't have —" I flap my free hand between us to encompass this whole interaction. "But I legit have plans after work. Could we rain check? Say Friday or Monday?"

"Sure thing. I'll check with the gals and send you a calendar invite." Her smile returns, and I match it.

We exit my office, her heading toward Jenny Kate's cube, me to grab an iced tea and call my clients.

Or should I skip the clients and kidnap Helena to debrief my convo with Jessica?

Tempting, but no. I'll see her tonight, and maybe by then I'll have figured out how to process it on my own. My bestie doesn't need me to drop into her workday with an SOS that hardly counts as a life-threatening situation.

More like a life-unexpected situation.

Like, do I maybe have a bigger friend circle than I figured? Or the potential for one, at least?

Muddling over the friend-thing threatens to distract me when I should be leveraging this brief reprieve from my parents to benefit my other clients.

But there's one last T to cross before I put personal firmly on the back burner and turn up the heat on business.

Wednesday 10:28 a.m. New York City / 7:28 a.m. Las Vegas

> Keira: P.S. Sorry you ended the night sans boobies. Bummer. Play your cards right tonight and your luck might turn.

> Keira: P.P.S. Safe flight.

The prospect of a midweek booby call with Connor brightens the sunny day. I slip on my sunglasses and put a little English into my hip action as I own the sidewalk.

Headache? What headache?

CHAPTER 15

CONNOR

Las Vegas is well known for its wild and crazy. After hitting up a certain specialty shop my last morning there, I finally scored legit side boob, in the form of a 1940s-style pinup girl photo, silk screened onto a tie of hot-pink shiny satin.

It's loud, in your face, and one hundred percent NSFW.

Keira's gonna love it. Or groan. Either reaction works for me. I can't wait to tease her with sneak peeks while I show her the Winstonian's ballroom options. The hotel's old-world charm may just make up for the fact the property is in dire need of a facelift. And walking through the hospitality spaces another time may spark some new thoughts I can add to my proposal too. The sooner I get that puppy updated, the sooner Dad can make his decision.

My cab pulls up to the hotel. I exit and wince at the 1970s-era signage clashing with the classic brownstone façade. Poor, tired thing looks like she's close to giving up. I want to tell the old girl to hold on until I can shower her with a heavy dose of TLC.

To the left of the faded entrance canopy, Keira leans a hip against the large stone bricks, frowning into her phone, thumbs flying.

Her frown makes me frown, and that's two frowns too many on a gorgeous Wednesday summer afternoon in the city.

"What's your safe word?" I ask as I stroll up to her.

"What?" She surfaces from her distraction, blinking as though stepping into the light. She focuses on me, suspicion turning her brown eyes bright. "Alligator."

"Mine is crocodile. Now, Keira." Her mouth quirks in recognition as I mimic the slow and formal rhythm of her let's-get-down-to-pleasure phrase. Ha. Success. "Here's what's going to happen. You're going to order me to holster my hands in my pockets. Next, you'll tell me to kiss you hello. Full throttle, no brakes."

"I'm listening." She slides her phone away without giving it a last glance. A rush of heat pumps through me at this second victory. "Go on."

"You'll tell me I'll know when you're done with the kiss, and part of me will wonder, wonder the whole time I'm fogging your glasses just how you'll show me." I step closer, until only the space of a breath separates us, and lower my voice. "Will it be pain or pleasure? Subtle or overt? Wet or wetter?"

Gaze drifting over my shoulder, she scrapes her teeth along her bottom lip but remains quiet. She's wearing a navy-blue pantsuit today, not her usual style. Is the lack of her usual skirt a message of some kind? An implicit no?

Before I talk myself into what Mom used to call a man-panic, Keira reaches into her purse and pulls out a pair of sunglasses.

"You can hardly fog my glasses if I'm not wearing any." She winks as she slides the smoke-tinted aviators up the bridge of her nose.

"No, ma'am." I duck my head to hide a relieved grin while blood crowds the base of my dick. "Whatever you say, ma'am."

"Like I believe your meek act." She tsks, shaking her head. "Now, Connor Mack, you're going to lay a *From Here to Eternity* kiss on me, an all-in, roll-in-the-sand, don't-care-about-the grit-in-your-crack kind of kiss, a kiss like you invented sex sort of kiss, see?"

"Yes, ma'am."

"Here's the catch."

"Damn it, there's always a catch," I grumble, even though my dick stretches to fill the confines of my boxers with anticipation of what's coming.

"Poor baby." She takes that last step to close the gap between us and cups my jaw, roughing her thumb over my five-o'clock shadow.

I'm toast. A man-shaped vessel of craving, willing to do anything to keep her touching me. Groaning, I press my crazy-hard dick lightly against her belly to show her what she does to me.

"Nice." She gives my cheek a smart pat and steps back. "Now, place your hands in your pockets and keep them there until I say different."

I comply automatically, her confidence another shot of sexy heating the blood in my veins.

"Now, you're going to kiss me like a gentleman. A filthy-minded, gentleman pervert."

"On it." I begin my descent toward her luscious mouth, attention converging on her pretty, pouty lower lip.

"And you're going to do it on one leg."

"I'm what now?" I stop halfway to my target. She sucks her lips between her teeth, but she can't bite back her shit-eating grin.

"Serves you right for trying to top me from the bottom." She buffs her manicure against her lapel and examines the results. "Is there a problem? Surely your super-studly six-pack is up to the challenge of keeping you balanced. Need to cry uncle?"

"Not in this lifetime. I am painfully, ridiculously, up to your challenge."

"One last thing." She taps my breastbone, halting my renewed downward trajectory. "Since my mouth will be otherwise occupied, your cue to stop will be me nipping your bottom lip. Are you okay with this course of action?"

"Since I'm the one who suggested it, I'd take that as a given."

"Nuh-uh." She presses against my breastbone again, this time stopping me with her hand, not her index finger. "No taking things as given. Express consent. Always."

"Yes, then. Yes, I'm okay with the stated course of action." Despite my horny dick and hungry mouth, I nod my sober agreement. "And yes. Express consent. Always."

I wish she hadn't donned the sunglasses. I can't tell what she's thinking, feeling. Until a slow smile catches the corners of her mouth, tugging her lips into a curved bow.

My lips mirror hers. So does my soul until I'm one big, happy, cosmic grin.

"One leg, Connor Mack."

With a chuckle that feels like a high five, I balance on a single foot.

CHAPTER 16

KEIRA

His lips hover above mine, so close, so close, his soft, warm breath minty and enticing. I will him closer, but the tricksy so-and-so hesitates, drawing out the moment of first contact.

Part of me wants to knock him to the ground and jump his bones. The bone he calls Junior in particular.

The other part wants to schoolgirl giggle at the image we must project, with Connor about to kiss me, dress shoe kicked up behind him like he's halfway to being swept off his feet.

I lick my lips, accidentally on purpose painting along his bottom lip, following the sensitive line that demarks dry from wet, friendly from salacious.

My ploy works. He growls and chases my mouth as if he thinks I'll try to escape.

Ha. As though I'd run away from imminent dessert.

We kiss, and the sounds of traffic and pedestrians fade away, letting me tune into the quickening of our breath, the slick and sliding pressure of our mouths rediscovering the many ways we fit together.

I wriggle at the tickling path he trails along my palate, threatening our balance, a hungry mew catching in my throat. He steadies us—I don't know how—and deepens the kiss, his tongue inviting me to go exploring. He shudders when I accept, pushing into his mouth.

Pressed full length together, my hands are anchored in his hair, my back hard against the hotel's exterior, his erection burning a sigil on my belly. I surrender to the pleasure, pulling him closer, uncaring, unthinking of orders or who's teasing whom.

Unthinking of anything but the next shiver.

"Get a room," a heckling voice calls out.

"Nah, man, it's a nice show. *Muy caliente*," another voice replies, followed by a "hello, gorgeous" whistle.

Instead of stopping, Connor changes angles and begins a fresh round of teasing. As one luscious, breath-stealing moment ticks into the next and the next and the next, awareness dawns.

This man will kiss me until our lips dry up and fall off unless I intervene.

"Hubba, hubba, cute butt," a woman says.

Connor laughs in my mouth. The effect is like shooting champagne. Effervescence hits my bloodstream, and already tipsy, I'm now one-hundred-percent drunk on his delight.

Another whistle yanks me back to rude sobriety. With extreme reluctance, I deploy the end scene signal, giving a sweet, raking nip to his lower lip.

After a "no-not-yet" groan, he surfaces, resting his forehead against mine. The scrape of shoe leather hitting the pavement punctuates his return to a two-legged stance, but instead of pulling back, he leans more fully into me. Like he can't quite muscle up the will or desire to stand on his own.

Our lungs heave in tandem. Greedy as a thief, I sneak my hand under his suit coat to measure the racing thump of his heart.

"Where's Sully's when you need a good semiprivate stall to get your rocks off?" he asks after a minute.

"Half a city away, alas." I pat his chest. "We need to get moving. We don't want to keep Helena and Mateo waiting."

"Permission to free my hands?"

"Oh no. I don't think so. Not until your soldier is fully at ease. I'll manage the door."

"Too kind, General." His laugh into my hairline calls a parade of goose bumps to tickle down my neck.

"That's General Ma'am to you."

Sassing back feels natural, as though we'll never run out of grumbles and teasing. This man. Quick. Funny. Nice. A trifecta of characteristics I usually avoid when it comes to sex partners. I futz with storing my sunglasses to hide my sudden frown.

Why does *nice* scare the shit out of me?

"Hey, where'd you go?" he asks.

"What?"

"One minute you were here, the next, poof, gone. Guess my kiss wasn't all that after all."

"It's not you, it's me."

"That's usually my line."

"Does it get you out of trouble?"

"Not as often as I'd like."

"Yeah, same. Listen, I just stumbled over a stray thought. No biggie. Your kiss was killer. Five stars. Reassured?"

"Indeed, General Ma'am." He offers a crisp, shallow bow and a lazy, smug grin.

He's the one sporting sex-hair horns this time. It's adorable and feeds something deep down I don't want to examine, so I don't tell him he's wearing my mark. Instead, I fixate on his tie, which escaped its confines during our sidewalk interlude.

"What's this?"

"Side boob, Vegas-style."

"Classy." I tuck the vivid image away so it'll stay our secret then head to the entrance.

The assistant event manager greets us, and the next half hour passes like a peculiar version of Goldilocks and the three no good, very bad, frustrating event rooms. The biggest is a beauty but way too large. The medium is closed because of recent damage to its plaster ceiling.

Connor assesses every space we walk through with eagle-eyed attention, all the while charming our guide into pouring forth intel without her realizing her faucet is on full blast. His unshowy competence is an unexpected turn-on.

The assistant leaves us in the middle of the hotel's smallest ballroom so we can, quote, get the gestalt of its vintage New York charm.

"Usually I'm down with vintage, but what an eyesore."

"It's available," Connor says, revolving in a slow circle, hands in his pockets, where they've been this whole time. Another unexpected turn-on. "That's a point in its favor."

"It's fifty shades of ugly brown."

"Some of it might be rust."

"Brown, rust, orange. Harvest gold. I can see why you want this project so much. Lots of potential, great location. But this?" I rotate my hand to encompass the room. "This is hideous."

"I don't know, the corduroy curtains have a certain *je ne sais quoi*."

"Aren't the wedding colors pink and turquoise? Pink and turquoise will roll over and die in this environment."

"They'd be fighting out of their weight class, no question." He peers at the ceiling then inspects the parquet floor under our feet, rocking his weight back and forth on a few of the tiles.

"We could skip the decorations. Come up with a specialty-drink list from the seventies and pretend the retro is on purpose," I say, grasping at straws.

"Helena ribbed Mateo the other week because his suit lapel was too wide. I'm not sure she's a retro kind of gal, but you know her better than me."

"We're doomed. And time's a tickin'. We need to nail a location down so we can concentrate on the other billionty-million party planning things." I snag a chair from one of the naked table rounds. Would white tablecloths counterbalance the mud-colored chic? I sit and keep going, whoosh, until I'm wedged in the seat. "A little help here."

Connor pivots his inspection from the wall art—big, dun-colored peacocks, poor things—to me.

"Seems like you're in a predicament."

"I'm stuck." I wiggle my feet. Pathetic. The table's too far away and the chair too slippery for leverage, leaving me without enough purchase to pull myself out of my sinkhole.

"I see that." He cocks his head. "Very unfortunate."

"We can't hold the party here. Can you imagine this happening to either of The Moms?"

"Their bottoms wouldn't fit through the frame."

"Are you telling me I have a skinny ass?"

"You have a delectable ass, one I'd be glad to fawn over at length should you wish to issue an invitation."

"I see you're not helping."

"I'm in a dilemma. You said not to free my hands until Junior is safely sleeping. Apparently, my boy has a bad case of insomnia. Your current stuckness is distracting him from his sheep counting."

"You're blaming me for your hard-on?"

"Blame seems harsh. Let's go with responsible." He squats to get a closer look, and somehow I manage not to drool at this latest casual show of his ability to keep his balance while his hands are bound. "You're jammed in there, all right."

"We're not holding the party here."

"Nope."

"You could help anytime, you know."

Squirming for freedom, I level a glare his way. He just squats there, looking cute and innocent. Like butter wouldn't sizzle in his mouth.

"I think you know what to do to make that happen."

The low, husky timber of his voice melts my muscles into limp noodles.

"You really are the most scrumptious perv, aren't you?" I stretch to pat down one of his hair horns.

"And all yours to command, General Ma'am." He waddles forward to lean into my touch. I reward him by scratching lightly behind his ear, and he practically purrs. He widens the vee of his thighs until his knees hug my calves. "Tell me what you want."

My insides flutter, schoolgirl crushing on the smart, smartass hottie wide open and available in front of me.

"Drop your knees on the ground and place your hands on them."

He makes a slow tease out of obeying. First one knee then the other slides down the side of my leg to my ankle to the outside edge of my sandal, an unhurried pressure telling me without words he's right there.

The tug of fabric on fabric pulls my pant legs tight over my thighs, and now I desperately want time travel to be a thing so I can start the morning over and choose a different outfit.

Stupid pants.

He frees one hand to unbutton his suit coat before flattening his palm to roam over the planes of his chest. He hums with hungry anticipation as he follows the arrow of his hot-pink side-boob tie down the middle of his body, leaning back until the outline of his hard cock is on display beneath his slacks. He barely brushes a finger along the side of his penis, but his cock jolts, and I moan.

"I'm ruing my wardrobe choice," I admit. "If I had a skirt on, I'd tell you to—You know what?" I try unsuccessfully to unstick myself again. "Fuck it, I'd tell you to get me the hell out of this chair. Then I'd tell you to put your head under my damned skirt and eat me out."

"I could get you out of the chair, strip your pants to your ankles then eat you out." His thumbs brush circles onto said ankles, whisper-soft circles that intensify the fluttering in my belly. "Why should your poor wardrobe choice stop us from getting what we both want?"

Anticipating him face deep in General Hoo-ha territory elevates the flutters into a full-body shudder. I rub the seam of my pants against my clit, my fingers squeezing into a space made tight from the confines of the chair. The scent of my desire blooms in the air between us.

Connor inches closer and closer, focused on the subtle movement of my busy hand. His nostrils flare, drinking in the scent of my body preparing for sex. With him. On instinct, I press my hand to his mouth. He takes my index finger inside, and our eyes lock as he sucks.

"Excuse me? Connor? I'm sorry to interrupt. But, um, my boss is, well, he heard you were in the building, and he's on his way. I'm sorry!" The assistant events manager calls from the ballroom's entrance.

Even in a rush, he stands with that same smooth grace that characterizes his every move. My fingers, wet and exposed, curl into a protective fist, feeling awkward and abandoned.

Awkward and abandoned sums up my hoo-ha and the rest of me too.

"No worries, Penny. We were just talking about how quaint the room is." He frees me from the seat's clutches. "You'll want to pull this chair from the floor. The caning is toast."

"Oh no." Penny trots from her post at the edge of the room. "You're not hurt, are you?"

I'd have more respect if she'd directed the question at me, but I can't ding her for being mesmerized by Connor. Hair mussy, face flushed, leaking pheromones like he has them to spare.

What heterosexual woman wouldn't go a little gaga in his presence?

"No, Keira doesn't seem to have sustained any damage." He circles a solicitous arm around my waist, a protective boyfriend move that, any other day, I'd deflect. "You're good, right, honey?"

"I'm good."

Penny deflates. Strangely, I seem to grow an inch taller.

The hotel manager dashes in to gush over Connor. As they fanboy over the hotel's grand history, I come to understand better why landing this project is so important to Connor. Through his eyes, I see past the bad makeup job to the room's classic proportions, to what it once was and could be again with a healthy dose of TLC. Yeah, after a thorough facelift, this ballroom alone will be the envy of her peers.

But it's not simply prestige or climbing another ring on the career ladder that sparks his ambition.

It's the connection to his roots. The idea that, in some respects, he'll be working with his great-great-great-grandfather not only to restore the hotel but to ensure it thrives for generations. His enthusiasm is contagious, generous as he gets all of us revved about the future of the Winstonian.

The manager makes noises about treating us to dinner, but Connor redirects the man's eagerness by promising to bring Connor's dad with him for a lunch meeting next week. For a few moments, it's fifty-fifty whether we'll need a stretcher to carry the guy out, he's so hopped up on excitement, but finally he floats away, high with anticipation.

We escape onto the street. The wind has kicked up, easing the early evening air from sweltering beast breath into something almost refreshing. A stack of dark gray clouds is building in the distance, but the storm it promises is still hours away.

"Thought they'd never let us loose," Connor says with a glance at his watch. "Those shoes work for motating or should we cab it?"

In answer, I start walking. "You did a good job with the manager. He was tripping over himself, he was so geeked at having one of *the* Macks on site."

"It's always just a little weird to experience that reflected glory, but if I'm being honest, it fills me with pride too. Four generations of Mack architects have added their unique signatures to cities around the world. Now we're carrying on the tradition in the fifth. It's pretty cool."

"Did you always know you'd join the family business? Why'd you choose the project manager path instead of becoming an architect or engineer?"

"Always knew. My brothers and I started interning as kids, and coming into the office was like getting to eat dessert first every day. Though in retrospect, maybe those summers were Dad's way of getting us out of Mom's hair? At any rate, I learned early that, as much as I love figuring out how to turn an idea into reality, sewer pipes and staircases aren't my favorite kinds of puzzles."

"What are?"

"People. Endlessly fascinating people. Do they know what they want? Can I help them figure it out? Can I get a team of them pointed in the same direction and working toward the same goal? Project management seemed like a good fit, and turns out, to blow my own horn, I'm exceedingly good at it."

"I can see how you would be." We walk for half a block in silence. "Any word from your dad about when he'll decide on your proposal?"

"We talked in Vegas. He asked me to make some revisions. I figure he wouldn't have if it were hopeless, right?" He laughs, shakes his head. "The firm's done all manner of projects. Skyscrapers, municipal buildings, convention centers. Big, necessary, a little soulless. Slick co-op retrofits, industrial loft conversions. Splashy and hip. But we've never had the chance to revisit one of our early designs."

"And you want in."

"So bad I can taste it. Think of all we'll learn by digging into our history, restoring G-Daddy Winston's creation to its former glory." He shoots me a side-eye glance full of mischief. "That, plus it's an opportunity to go after another award for the firm's trophy chest."

"I see how it really is. You want a new pretty-shiny."

"I like to play. That's hardwired into my system. And I really like to win. That's the cherry on top."

"I like cherries too." I nudge him with my shoulder to show solidarity with his competitive streak.

"What about your family? Any siblings?" He cups my elbow as we cross an intersection. "You mentioned your parents are pretty uptight. Do they live in the area?"

"No siblings. My parents live in San Francisco. We're... not close."

"I'm sorry. " He slides his hand down to lace his fingers through mine and gives my hand a little pump. "That's gotta be tough."

Even a week ago, I'd have snatched my hand back and made a snarky remark. Today, I accept his compassion as Connor being Connor. And maybe I could use a little of his sympathy after the last few days. Maybe I can indulge. For a minute or two.

"It is what it is." My shrug is more of a jerk. "They haven't been a part of my life in a long time. I don't lie awake at night worrying too much about it."

But the amount of time isn't zero either.

Why couldn't my parents have stayed on their side of the country? Why the hell are they here?

I give my head a little shake. Mr. Sunshine here doesn't need to hear me wallow in my family's dirty laundry.

Time for a new topic.

"Tell me, Connor, are we walking toward a double date?"

"Nope." His immediate denial comes with a cross-body hand chop. "This is another party-planning strategy session. With chocolate, sure, but a date would include flowers of some sort. Maybe a buggy ride through Central Park. Ergo, this is definitely not a date."

"I think you might be protesting too much."

"Keira, one of us would have to ask, and the other person would have to consent. That's the deal, right? Full consent?" He jiggles our clasped hands. "If you want a date, I'm open to negotiations, but you're going to have to be the one who asks. Once burned and all that."

"That's some snappy patter ya got going there, but if it smells like a date and quacks like a date, the assumption must be that it's a date."

"We all know what happens when you assume. It makes an ass out of—"

"Haha, funny man."

"Tell you another thing, sweetheart," he says, managing to put a leer into his voice. "If this were a date, I'd make sure to cut the evening short and take you to a more suitable location."

"For sex?"

"For sure."

"But we're helping Helena and Mateo. So we can't duck out. So this isn't a date."

"See? Don't let anyone tell you you're no good at logic puzzles."

"I want sex."

"I've been a walking boner since I stepped out of the cab and into your sweet command."

"We can't ditch our friends."

"Sadly, no, given our wedding-attendant roles. And I've been to this place before. Their restroom leaves much to be desired."

"There goes the between-courses-quickie idea." I shove my sunglasses to the top of my head. "What are we going to tell them about our progress?"

"We'll focus on the positives. Good music."

"That's pretty much all we have."

"Maybe we can tell them that we'll have news at the barbeque a week from Sunday. Between now and then, we'll double down on securing a venue."

"Barbeque?"

"The one at my dad's? You remember, he invited you the night of our first non-date."

"Technically our second non-date. Remember brunch."

"Do we have to remember how I swung too early and fouled out?"

"And all this time I thought you'd hit a homer." I snicker as his cheekbones flash a lovely blush. "I wasn't planning on going, to be honest. Work has entered the fifth circle of hell."

"Mystery client woes?"

"Yeah. Until I get them off my plate, I'm gonna have a hard time scheduling all-day getaways." Not telling him the clients are my parents makes my nose wrinkle. There's no real reason to keep their presence in town a secret, but they've already taken my professional attention. I don't want them tainting my personal life too. Better all around to keep the info on lockdown.

"Sure thing." He gives my hand another quick squeeze. "We can play it by ear."

His easygoing nature is oddly electrifying. No hard line of questions. No trying to pin me down or coerce a commitment. So different from the usual assortment of guys I've tried playing with since coming to New York. Flutters ping around in my chest, giddy little zip-zaps juicing my heart rate.

"Do you think that brown ballroom will grow any more appealing?" I ask to distract myself from my body's jitterbug dance.

"It hurts me to say it, but no."

"All right. Tonight, we focus on chocolate and our happy couple, not the lack of a location or the fact that the restaurant's bathrooms are subpar. No orgasms. Worst Hump Day ever."

Except, somehow, it isn't.

"Cheer up. What this place lacks in bathroom design, it more than makes up for in its bar. Good booze and chocolate will anesthetize your existential pain."

As we walk, I practice surfing my flutters and not freaking out.

No matter what wig and lipstick we want to paint the evening with, I'm pretty sure this chocolate-covered pig is a date.

CHAPTER 17

CONNOR

" think I hate chocolate," Helena says as the four of us waddle from the Carleminster's private tasting room toward the exit. "At least a little."

Repressing a discreet, chocolate-martini-flavored burp, I steer Keira through a maze of tables, hand low on her back, and silently concur. Two hours of chocolate infused everything has cured me of my Vegas-induced jones for chocolate chip cookies.

"So, no chocolate fountain for the party?" Keira asks, rubbing soothing circles on her belly.

"Hell, yes, we're having a chocolate fountain," Mateo pipes in before Helena can answer. "Turn down another chance to drink ambrosia? It doesn't compute."

"Of course, we're having the fountain. But I'm calling a moratorium on chocolate until the party. The wait will make us want it more." Over her shoulder, Helena sends my buddy a flirty wink.

"So long as chocolate is the only thing included in this moratorium." Mateo cozies up to Helena for a round of sweet-nothing mutters.

Tonight's party reconnaissance has been a torture-pleasure mash-up. Watching Mateo walking tall and so damned proud, like he won the relationship version of the World Series, makes me want to high-five him, slap him on the ass, and pour champagne over his head while yelling "Dude, you da man!" in his face at top volume.

But the solidness of what he and Helena have built leaves me itchy with questions. They're tight. On the cusp of promising one another for better or for worse, in sickness and in health, with the kind of foundation I rolled my eyes at whenever Mom and Dad got mushy but somehow always assumed I'd form with my life partner. I crapped out hard with Sherry, but Keira, now. What would a lifetime construction project with her entail?

Quicksand? Doomed to sink before a lasting foundation can set? Or have we moved onto firmer ground? Am I still a simple negotiation to her, a walking, talking contract only good for delivering orgasms on command, or has working together on this party opened up a possibility for something more?

"They need to get a room," Keira says out of the corner of her mouth as the whispers morph into a mini-make-out session in the restaurant's vestibule.

That's the evening's other torture—roasting in our own slow burn while our friends spritz us with their high-octane sex vibes all night.

Feeding each other chocolate-covered strawberries. Exchanging sweet, messy kisses. Sending each other knowing looks.

It was like they were competing for the title of happiest, horniest couple in New York.

Keira pulled out her tablet full of spreadsheets, but trying to concentrate on party business did jack all to protect us from their potency. And if Keira's feeling anything like me, she's vibrating like a lust-filled tuning fork.

"All right, you two. Break it up before you get us all arrested," I say when Helena's hand disappears between their bodies while tracking south. "I'll see about a cab. In the meantime, try to keep your clothes on."

Keira's snort ringing in my ears, I step outside to find no valet on duty and a deluge.

Rain, rain, and more rain.

Rain so hard, it bounces off the pavement.

Rain so loud, it's a throbbing drumbeat against the canvas awning.

Rain so hot, it practically steams.

"Was this in the forecast?" Mateo asks as the three join me in Noah's city spa.

"They mentioned scattered showers," Keira replies. "Nothing like this."

The street is deserted but for a few smeary, red brake lights glowing in the distance. Luckily, one set of headlights turns onto the block, and I issue a taxi-whistle impressive enough to yank a proud-papa grin from my cranky doorman.

"You two catch this one," Keira says as the taxi pulls up. "Connor and I can fight over the next."

"You sure?" Helena asks.

"Yup, you two need to get to a room, pronto. You have to be what's causing the heat wave, you're so hot."

Helena swallows Keira in a voluminous, extravagant hug. Mateo and I perform our customary handshake and back thump. As we break apart, miraculously, I'm holding a condom.

I grin as he hustles his fiancée into the cab and it motors away, leaving us sheltering in place. Even with the awning as cover, the rain muscles its way in, water seeping into my loafers and creeping up my socks. I wiggle my toes, but there's no escaping the damp cotton.

"I have recently come into possession of a prophylactic." Keira displays a foil packet in the center of her palm.

"Funny, there seems to be a rash of that going around." I mirror her presentation.

"We can take this in one of two ways." She makes a fist around her condom. "First, our friends could be announcing their intention of making a baby."

"And second?" I slide nearer.

"Second, they could be reminding us to bang safely." With her free hand, she fiddles with my side-boob tie, bringing us a few inches closer and my dick from its semi-resting state back to fully online.

"I'm going to vote for option two."

"Here are two more options." Voice smoky, soft and low, she slips into her fun-times cadence. She tugs on my tie, and I lean until she can whisper in my ear. "First, we could call it a night, postpone our friends-endorsed bang since I don't do home visits and the bathroom inside is as inferior as you claimed."

"Or?"

"Second, we could disappear into the alley." She flicks my earlobe with her tongue then gives it a nip. "And fuck against the wall."

"Rain check versus rain screw?" I shudder as she expands her region of little bites. "Is there really a choice?"

"There's always a choice. Always."

"Message received and acknowledged."

"So?"

"Gotta go with option two, again. Consistency is key." I capture her wandering mouth for a kiss so hot it nearly dries my socks.

We're both panting when we break free.

"Connor Mack, I want you to put your hands in your pockets until and unless I say different. We're going to head down yonder alleyway, and I'm going to take full, filthy, and uninhibited advantage of you in a place where anyone could discover us. Are you okay with this course of action?"

To answer, I obey her command to self-shackle once more, throwing in a filthy, uninhibited leer to show my good faith.

"Lead on."

Taking me by the tie, she quick marches us toward the gap between buildings. The moment we leave the overhang, we're soaked. Rain snakes under my collar, plastering my hair against my forehead. Keira's suit melds to her body, revealing her curves. One of these days, I'll take a bite out of her ass—with her full consent, of course. Maybe then it won't star so frequently in my most prurient fantasies.

I snort. Who am I kidding? I'll simply have more fantasies.

Lucky me.

"What are you chuckling about?" she asks as she threads us deep into the narrow space.

"If I say your butt, will you get mad?"

"Depends. What about my butt?" She puts more sway into her prowl, confident her behind is a luscious handful.

"Let's just say, the rain likes you. A lot."

The rain follows us into this urban cavern, the height of the buildings no match for a Mother Nature determined to wash the city's nooks and crannies clean. The sound shifts from giant's roar to muffled murmur, the intimate pillow talk between lovers as they drift into a satisfied sleep.

We discover a lone bistro-style table hidden in the shadows between two dumpsters spaced about ten feet apart. Another twenty feet or so along, a single, caged bulb shines over a doorway, deepening the shadows while granting us a weak light.

She stops, and I accidentally-on-purpose stumble to a halt against her back so Junior can show her how much he, too, appreciates her ass. She leans into the pressure, gliding her bottom across my hungry erection.

"Of all days to wear pants." She faces me and slicks her hair back with both hands. "Skirts are honestly so much easier."

"You need me to invest in some business kilts? I could start a trend, like those fleece vests that swarm the financial district."

"Kind of you to offer, but I don't want you swinging out there when any stray wind could show your jewels off to the world's randos."

"I didn't know you cared."

"I don't care." Frowning, she lands her hands on her hips. "It's just—"

"Okay that you don't want me on display." I pop a kiss on her nose. "I'll take it as a compliment to my prowess."

"Big head."

"Big, swollen head. Big, swollen, tender, hot, hard head." Between words I lick rain off her jaw and along her throat, reveling each time her breath catches.

"That's it. Time for sex. Now." With impatient fingers, she unknots my tie and stuffs it in her purse before peeling me out of my jacket in a series of quick jerks. "Hands back in your pockets."

I comply as she blankets the small table with our jackets. Her white blouse gleams in the faint light for a moment before it's drenched, and every square inch of silk begins teasing me by playing peekaboo with her skin.

Satisfied, she deposits her purse on the covered surface and makes a quarter turn toward me. My view is her luscious ass, one pert, silk-coated tit, and her confident smirk. "Watch."

"Couldn't look away if you paid me."

She cups her breast, squeezing and kneading. Saliva pools in my mouth as she pinches her beaded nipple. Playing rough with herself, she makes me want to bite and taste, suck and soothe.

I take two steps forward. She stops, ticktocking no with her finger. "Uh-uh."

Groaning, I hold my position, hands curled and caged against my need.

"Good boy." As a reward, she widens her stance and hinges slightly from her hips, tilting her ass toward me. Nothing else in the universe exists. Just us.

Us and her round butt.

"Sweet General Ma'am, you are killing me."

"I think you have some life in you yet." Her purring voice strokes my cock. "But let's see if we can get you closer to the edge."

With one swift move, she drops trou, pants, and thong down to mid-thigh.

I whistle, long and low, my heart jerking around like it wants to burst out of my rib cage.

"That's the sweetest damn moon I ever did see. Please, General Ma'am, can I bite it? Just a little?"

"Not tonight. We've dillydallied long enough. Time for the main event." She hops on the table, spreading her legs and shoving her clothes to her ankles. Slowly, deliberately, she curls her pointer finger as if to reel me in. "Report for duty, soldier."

CHAPTER 18

KEIRA

want fast and hard. I want Connor deep inside me, riding me as though our orgasms are the only way of beating back the apocalypse. But that's not what I get.

No, I get rank insubordination.

Typical crafty Connor.

First issue? His massive erection. That mammoth practically demands a thorough inspection before getting into uniform.

"Is it possible Junior's put on a little weight since our last field exercises?" I measure for length and girth. Heat sears my fingers, but I can't stop touching the silken beast. "He seems a little extra tonight."

"Are you calling my cock fat?" Connor laugh-croaks as he endures my comprehensive pre-check.

"Just speculating, is all. You think it's from tonight's chocolate?" I pump him from balls to tip and back, punch drunk on his moans. "Seventy-eight percent special dark as cock enhancer?"

"Sure. Why not? More likely you're the cause, though." He kisses my throat before nestling his forehead in the crook of my neck and shoulder.

My belly flips. Not from heartburn or an overfull stomach.

No, it's the weight and warmth of his touch, his search for connection, even comfort, as I drive him to the brink while he honors the false restraint we agreed to by keeping his hands sheathed.

It's his words, sweet in my ears. It's his trust. Trust he shows me every time we play.

No, every time we interact.

I blink water out of my eyes and call it rain. Then proceed to run smack into insubordination issue number two.

Slowpoke Connor who likes to do things at his own pace.

Plucking the wrapped condom from my bra, I lose no more time girding his behemoth loin. I line him up and guide him in, the steady pressure of his penetration stealing my breath and speeding his until the air chuffs from his lungs.

"Showtime, cowboy." I squeeze him with my thighs.

"Sure thing, pardner."

Instead of taking off at a gallop, though, he moseys like a Sunday driver with all the time in the world.

"This is not what I had in mind when I called action." I frown at him.

His lips curl in an I-see-something-tasty smile as, obligingly, he rolls into a rhythm that works my clit with each long, yet somehow still languorous thrust.

I clutch his waist and sink into the moment. The cooling rain, the heat of our union, the friction that pushes me closer and closer to orgasm.

He stops abruptly. As I inhale to complain, he covers my mouth with a chaste kiss, his eyes wide and filled with silent warning.

"What?" My whisper is muffled against his lips.

"We've got company. Smoke break, maybe." The devil man punctuates his bombshell with a long, slow glide. I stifle my moan against his chest.

"We have two options," he speaks into my left ear, landing another home thrust.

Goose bumps break out along that side of my body.

"T-two?" I shudder and shake, the threat of discovery an exquisite thrill.

"One, we could admit defeat. Walk away off the field, dejected, horny, and humiliated by quitting." He switches ears, ensuring my goose bumps are evenly distributed. "Two, we can resist. Play to our strength of stealth fucking in semipublic. Go home satisfied and proud and worthy of playing again another day."

"When you put it like that." I inch forward on the table. "Option two is the only honorable course of action."

"Good girl."

"Watch it, buddy." I pinch his ass.

He jumps, reigniting what becomes the longest, slowest, quietest, most luxurious screw in the history of fucking, Connor melting my insides in a relentless, building tide.

The rain eases from its initial torrent, settling into a light shower that turns to a steam bath as water droplets hit us. Ozone and the scent of sex sting my nose. Each breath of air is a swallow of salty, musky ocean.

When I can no longer hold back my moans, Connor is there, hiding them inside his mouth in exchange for a taste of his chocolate-covered tongue.

Connor is there, building my climax layer by incremental layer.

Connor is there, groaning and straining, and finally, finally fast. Faster than sound, faster than light.

Connor is there, catching me against his chest as we come, first me then him, his hands somehow still tucked in his pants.

Connor is there.

He stays inside me, connecting us as we tumble down from our summit. His face is nestled in the crook of my neck again, but I turn mine outward, away, closing my eyes against the scary something surging in my depths.

"This just in, new Hump Day status report. Best one ever, am I right?" he asks.

"Can't think of a better one." My words paper over the swirl crashing around inside me.

"Permission to deal with the condom, General Ma'am?"

"Granted."

The rain has stopped, doing squat to lower the temperature, leaving me a sopping, sweaty mess. I reclad my bottom half and unstick my clammy blouse from my chest. Is it worth trying to put my jacket on to cover the transparent fabric? Easier to consider that practical question than investigate why my post-climax bubble is deflating so fast.

Connor disposes of our protection in one of the dumpsters and returns, properly if damply zipped and tucked, hands pocketed.

"You can free your hands now. Scene's done."

"And was it a good scene, would you say?"

"Searching for compliments?"

"Actually, searching for reassurance." The smile he offers blinks on then off, like he can't quite get it to stick.

A pulse of alarm jolts through me, adding to my unease. "Explain."

"The phone sex last Saturday. I'll be the first to admit it was a little one-sided, but I thought we were both into it?" Hands still sheathed, he scuffs his shoe against the pavement. "Until right at the end, at least. I gather you were at work?"

Bracing myself, I nod. Where is he going with this?

"I get it." He echoes my nod. "Things pop up."

"But?"

"I'm going to sound like a wuss, and I can't believe I'm saying this out loud, but here goes. I know we're still feeling our way into this more-sex, more-often deal." He pauses to brush a wet curl of hair from his forehead, his grimace saying he's having second thoughts about continuing.

"You can't stop now, not right in the middle like that."

"Fair enough." He clears his throat. "You, uh, you left me hanging. For two days. Your silence left me wondering if I'd done something wrong."

"I'm sorry. Work—"

"I understand about work. I do. Damn, I totally sound like a wuss." He groans. "Listen, it's me who's sorry. My ex loved to play silent-treatment games. Guess last weekend pressed some old buttons. My baggage, not yours. It's not fair of me to dump that old bullshit on you."

This time his smile lasts a little longer, even if it's more self-deprecating than happy. Careful to keep space between us, he reaches around me to pick up his suit coat.

"This is a good example of why I keep trying to have no-strings sex partners." I touch his hand, and he stills. "I suck at aftercare. I am sorry about tripping your triggers. It definitely wasn't intentional. I like head games but not the cruel kind."

"Did you say suck?" He captures my fingers. "Sucking during aftercare sounds promising. Like maybe it would loop into pre-care, which would set us up for play, which would lead to more sucking."

"Did you just turn my apology into a setup for a blow job?"

"Yes."

"Unbelievable."

"But it made you laugh."

"Do I look like I'm laughing?"

"On the inside. It's all right to let it out, you know. I won't tell."

I shake my head and release a tiny snort. Leave it to Connor to turn awkward into okay.

"Ha, knew you were holding back." He pulls his jacket on then helps as I struggle into mine. "We can practice the aftercare thing."

"Practice, huh? Like when you suggested we act As If?"

"Exactly." He cups my elbow and leads us from the alley. "We'll start tonight when I see you to your building, and you text me you've reached your apartment without being dismembered by monsters in the elevator."

Despite the downpour that chased every sane person home for an early-ish night, the city that never sleeps doesn't let us down. We flag a taxi in under a minute and settle into the back seat. Somehow—why am I not surprised?—my hand winds up clasped in his, resting on his warm, damp thigh.

As the taxi's wheels splash through puddles, I leave my hand where it is and debate whether to introduce another topic or if one heavy-duty convo per night is enough. In the end, I decide it's too important to let slide.

"While we're clearing the air and adding to our As If practice sheet... There was no smoke break, was there?"

Though he remains silent, the white teeth of his quick smile gleam in the shadows. It's confirmation enough.

"Listen, no more lies during a scene, okay? This one worked out. I do love to walk that edge of exhibitionism, and you played it perfectly. But manipulation, lies, they kill any hope that the sex is truly consensual."

"Got it. My turn to say I'm sorry. " He lays a kiss on my wrist before returning our hands to his thigh. "No lying is a good rule for real life too."

"Yeah, too bad more people aren't familiar with the concept."

"Speaking from experience?" he asks, drawing a half arc with his thumb over my skin.

"Can't we all?" I swivel toward him on the vinyl seat before he can ask a follow-up. "Look, this is new territory for me. Normally, I'd cut bait and run before ever getting near a discussion like this. But I'm weirdly up for this As If practice. I am. Just... can we agree to no lies and taking baby steps?"

"Yes, ma'am."

"Good, good. What will they look like?"

"The steps? Whatever we want." He bursts out laughing at my death glare. "Okay, okay. Why don't we start with texts? Your days are crazy. Mine are too. How about we give each other a pass on immediate responses to anything personal but commit to at least one text before going to bed each night to touch base. For party-planning messages, let's shoot for a two-hour turn time. Doable?"

"I can test run that, yes."

He gives my hand a gentle squeeze as I settle into my seat once more.

Now that we've defined deliverables and timelines of this... As If thing... we've got going, the churning within me flattens to a calm sea. I can handle one measly text an evening.

No sweat.
So why am I sweating?

CHAPTER 19

CONNOR

Wednesday, 11:57 p.m.

Keira: Home.

Connor: Good job on not getting eaten by monsters in the elevator. [monster face emoji]

Keira: Getting eaten in an elevator sounds like a #lifegoal, tbh.

Connor: Aaaand now you've woken Junior, after we've *just* put him to bed. He's hungry, and he wants more of your pie.

Keira: I've always heard it's good to go to bed hungry. Does wonders for your motivation in the morning. Nighty night! [snoring emoji]

Best Hump Day ever. An excellent dinner with friends as the starter, with a hot-as-fuck fuck in an alley for dessert. But the cherry on top has to be that Keira committed to texting and followed through.

I love that she loves courting the potential for exposure during our encounters. That kind of daring is its own turn-on. But those rare times when she exposes her needs, lets down her guard? That's when she's magnificent. Okay, she's always magnificent. But when she forgets to stay buttoned-up? When she tells me what she really wants? More, please.

Like bringing up the fake smoke break thing. I messed up. She called me on it. Ditto the phone sex. She apologized when I spoke up about what I needed, meeting me as an equal in a moment of shared vulnerability. After Sherry's master class in dancing around the truth and playing mind fuck games, it's more than a breath of fresh air to enter Keira's no bullshit zone. No lies, more communication, and practicing As If.

Works for me.

And I will work my ass off to make sure it works for Keira too.

Thursday, 8:08 p.m.

> Connor: Lunch with the Winstonian's manager ended with dinner. I'm beat. And hopeful. Dad sported his thinking-deep-thoughts look the whole time.

> Keira: Think he's getting closer to announcing a decision?

> Connor: Yeah. I think today may have sealed the deal.

> Keira: Good for you [high ten emoji]

> Connor: How was your day?

CHAPTER 20

KEIRA

Cuddled into the couch with Camuel, waiting for my hair color to set, I reply to Connor's question and ask him another. The TV burrs in the background, canned laugh track filling my small living room with peppy goodwill. A neglected glass of red wine sits on the side table, next to the leftovers of my Lebanese takeout.

A typical Thursday evening, doing typical Thursday evening things to unwind.

What's not typical? The domestic hominess of Connor and me swapping the flotsam of our days. The normality of sharing a peek into my peak pique about Brad is a whopping surprise.

Rat Bastard proved his name again today and as I pour that into my texts, I find myself laughing, able to see the funny through Connor's eyes.

It's... nice. Different. Only a little tiny bit scary.

My phone alarm beeps. Time to rinse out the dye. Shoot. I make a face at Camuel. "Guess I need to wrap this up, huh, buddy?'

Camuel gazes at me placidly, content I'll do the right thing and not let my hair fall out because I'm uncharacteristically gaga over a guy. My stuffed camel is sitting a little taller tonight, proud of the new side-boob tie gracing his long neck. I snap a pic and send it to Connor before I can think myself out of it.

Thursday, 8:12 p.m.

Connor: Is that my tie?

> Keira: It's our tie now. Possession is nine-tenths and all that. Gotta deal with my hair. TTYL. We're on for the Madagascar tomorrow, right?

Connor: The Mad and a couple of others. Look forward to seeing what kind of hair art you've created this week. I miss the rainbow bangs.

> Keira: Rainbows might make a reappearance. You never know.

Connor: Tell your camel to be careful with that tie. It could lead him down some dark alleys.

> Keira: I wouldn't worry. He doesn't get out much. More of a stay-at-home camel.

Connor: Well, he clearly appreciates side boob, so he's got that going for him.

> Keira: He's an awesome companion. Good listener. Never argues. Doesn't leave the toilet seat up.

Connor: Suddenly, I'm worried about the competition. [wink emoji]

> Keira: Good night, Connor.

Connor: Sweet dreams.

CHAPTER 21

CONNOR

The weekend doesn't go as planned.

Keira's clients derail our Friday night plans, so I take Felix and we drink our mopey way through each potential venue. Two not-so-happily solo guys pining into our liquor is a pitiful sight. Adding salt to the wound, none of the locations will work with a head count now hovering around seventy.

Saturday and Sunday, Felix, Dad, and I pull emergency crew duty for a family friend at a sailing regatta and get our asses handed to us by coming in dead last both days. At least the beer is cold. Keira sneaks in visits to another few possibilities between perplexing wedding-prep business—pretty sure my head would already have exploded if I had to navigate the geopolitics of choosing the right paper, font, and ink color for invitations. By the end of the weekend, we're able to nix seven more sites from contention.

Every night, we text.

Every night, I yearn a little harder for a time when our sleep-tight wishes are whispered under the covers of the same bed.

· · ·

Sunday 10:38 p.m.

Keira: At this rate, I think we need to hire a field
somewhere upstate. That's it. Any available
open field. A couple of outhouses. Some
small-town granny can cook hot dogs and
baked beans.

Connor: Mateo gets an asthma attack
whenever he's ten miles outside of a city.

Keira: And Helena would kill me the minute her
heel sunk into a cow patty. Damn. There goes
that million-dollar idea.

Connor: Back to the drawing board. Want to
regroup tomorrow over dinner?

Keira: Would this be another of your stealth
dates?

Connor: No idea what you mean by that.

Keira: [side-eye emoji] Uh-huh, yeah, right.
Doesn't matter anyway, I can't. Scheduled for
happy hour with some of the gals from the
office. Group bonding.

Connor: Group bondaging sounds fun. Can I
watch?

Keira: Dude.

CHAPTER 22

KEIRA

"Sorry I'm late. I had to sneak out via the service elevator," I say as Jessica makes room for me in the half-moon booth she and our coworkers have staked out. The cocktail bar they chose is close enough to the office to walk to, but far enough away we're not in danger of random Rat Bastard drop-ins.

"I swear, Brad's getting twitchier by the day," Jenny Kate says.

"And sweatier. Have you noticed his pits? It's like he has a glandular problem," Mildred says with a delicate shudder.

"You think he's having an affair? He's fifty-something. My vote is the sweat's from crushing guilt due to midlife shenanigans." Amanda nods in the wise way of the already tipsy.

Frozen peach sangria is pressed into my hands as speculation about our boss goes crazy epic. Secret love child, secret agent, secret blackmail. All three. Undetected brain tumor, undetected mad cow disease, undetected extraterrestrial parasite. All three. The less realistic, the louder we laugh.

"What do you think?" Jessica knocks her elbow into my side.

"You've known him the longest. Is he having Elvis's secret love spawn via alien surrogate?"

"If it's a surrogate pregnancy, why would he be the one sweating?" I ask.

"Because he's about to be a father twenty times over, and preschool is hella expensive." Jenny Kate's massive eye roll punctuates the southern *well, duh* infusing her voice.

"The truth behind the sweat"—I pause to collect everyone's gaze—"is he killed the butler in the pantry with a candlestick, and he's scared witless he'll be found out at any moment."

More cackling breaks up the final pieces of my lingering workday blues. Escape-and-evade tactics are a new low in my relationship with Brad. He's pushing for me to accept an invitation to meet one-on-one with my parents and not listening to my repeated no.

One more nail in the coffin of this freaking job.

The group descends into a new round of outrageous rumors, complete with colorful characters, deadly weapons, and increasingly unbelievable spots for stashing bodies. Soon, we devolve into chugging our fruity wine after each scenario. Someone orders all the fried food off the appetizer menu. Someone else suggests karaoke. We move venues, and the evening extends long past happy hour.

At the end of the night, Jessica and I linger on the sidewalk as the other women peel away in twos and threes. I'm buzzed, higher on all the girl-power anthems we belted out than from the wine.

"I'm happy," I confess in a loud whisper, as if I'd jinx the moment if too many people heard.

"Good for you." Jessica bumps her hip into mine, and we both reel for a second before regaining our balance. "I always figured you traded in happy for successful."

I'm quiet for a stretch as I turn over her words. Had I made time for happiness since escaping my parents' world and moving to New York?

"I think you call success what I might label survival." The truth lands funny in my greased-up, boozy belly. "Either way, you're right. I haven't prioritized happy."

"Nothing wrong with making that choice. But I admit, I was half expecting you to bail tonight. What changed? It's not your parents' arrival. You've been loosening up for a while."

"Growing up, I guess. Trying to leave old shit behind."

"Amen, sister."

She waves down a taxi and climbs in, promising to text once she's home safe. I snag another a moment later. With the window open to the late-night air, the aroma of nighttime New York takes up familiar residence in my nose.

Connor in my life is what changed.

His constant confidence is wearing away my shields, drip by drip, leaving me wide open to new experiences.

Sorta, kinda open. Let's not go crazy.

The new stuff hasn't killed me yet, so I guess this whole As If thing is working out okay.

I unlock my phone and let my thumbs loose, a semi-sloshed addict ready for my next fix.

Monday, 10:43 p.m.

Keira: Girls' Night Out kicked my ass.

Connor: Need me to kiss it better?

Keira: Tempting.

Keira: Maybe [lipstick kiss emoji] [peach emoji] [thumbs-up emoji] tomorrow after looking at Wendigo's event room...

Connor: About that... [crying buckets emoji]

Keira: What?

Connor: Taking David's place on another work trip. Won't be back until Saturday morning, then I'm headed straight to the beach house to help prep for Sunday's BBQ.

Keira: Oh. Disappointing. But, I mean, it's work, right? Work comes first.

Connor: TBH, in this case, family comes first. Celia's still dealing with heavy-duty morning sickness, and we all feel better with David sticking close to home. I'm pinch hitting where I can.

Keira: That's

I stop typing. What is it? Kind? Mystifying? Another example of his addictive sweetness?

Connor's willingness to step in for his brother is... not a revelation so much as a reconfirmation of his inherent kindness.

Prioritizing family over work. Inconceivable in my parents' world view. Discomfiting to see their work-first message bubble onto the screen from my fingers.

My insides do a loop-de-loop and settle into a new position. One that's a tad more welcoming and a hair less cautious of the good guy side of this man.

Monday, 10:45 p.m.

Keira: That's cool. We'll catch up when you're back.

Connor: Miss me?

Keira: Well, I'll miss something about you. [eggplant emoji] [single tear emoji]

Connor: More proof you need to come to the BBQ on Sunday. Pretty sure that's the exact shade of purple Junior will be sporting by then.

Keira: We'll have to see. Though I'll note that aubergine *is* General Hoo-ha's most-favoritist color.

CHAPTER 23

CONNOR

Dad and I fly to Chicago in the morning and plunge into a whirlwind of diplomacy. Our client blames the builder for cost overruns. The builder claims the client is acting in bad faith. What should have been a routine check-in descends into a blurry gauntlet of late-night brainstorming, early morning concessions, and afternoon headbutting. While Dad rolls up his sleeves to work his side of things on site, I spend most of my time stakeholder-whispering, diffusing threats of lawsuits and fistfights.

By the time my evening text sessions with Keira roll around, I'm drained. She is too. Neither of us has the juice for a visit to Planet Climaxalot, but we manage some *and how was your day, dear* back and forth until my eyes start crossing.

Friday, 9:52 p.m. Chicago/10:52 p.m. New York

Connor: I may not turn thirty for another couple weeks, but damn if I don't yearn for the days of afternoon naps, blankies, and a snack. It's official. I'm old.

Keira: I have a weighted chenille blanket. Great for making forts to block out the world.

Connor: Maybe you should bring it to the BBQ. We could escape into its cozy embrace, let Junior and the General get reacquainted then catch a post-o snoozefest.

Keira: Still not sure I can make it.

Disappointment lands a swift, breath-stealing punch. I flop into a loose-limbed sprawl across the bed of my hotel room.

"Stop pushing, dumbass," I tell the ceiling. "She's not Sherry. She's not playing you or expecting you to beg for scraps of attention. Give her room to breathe, you moron."

If Mom were here, she'd scold me for talking smack to myself, but she'd agree.

And if she flies away, then she's not the right queen bee for your honey and good riddance.

Bittersweet memories of Mom wash over me in waves. Her grin, the weight of her hand ruffling my hair, the comforting squish of her monster hugs. Even at the end of her life, she would try to wipe stray food off my cheek with thumb and mom spit. Those last, late-night talks we had in the weeks before she died where we solved all the world's problems.

We moved her into the boathouse at the beach to be closer to the water, the rhythm of the tide soothing her when the pain meds no longer could. Sheltered in the blue-gray shadows of her darkened room, she shared her wisdom, her love. Her hopes and dreams for her boys. All four of us, Dad included.

Fucking cancer.

Robbed her, Dad, all of us, of so many moments. Big, small, momentous, mundane.

I understand the lure of Keira's no-emotions mantra. In the year after the crash and burn with Sherry and the soul-crushing pain of Mom's passing, I shoved every stray wriggle of crappy-shaped emotion into deep freeze. Even now, it's a struggle to let this unexpected bout of grief tumble through me.

But half-alive is no way to live. I snort. Guess Dad's right. I am an optimist.

Meeting Keira was like being introduced to a tart-tongued, thong-wearing, kinky electric rainbow powered by Niagara Falls. A force of nature so palpable, how could I help but take notice—and work my fingers to the bone to win that rainbow's favor?

With the promise of all that potential on the line, hell yes, I'll accept the ups and the downs. Even when I have to act As If the moments of uncertainty don't flood me with a rank need to push for assurances.

Friday, 9:54 p.m. Chicago/10:52 p.m. New York

> Connor: Hey, no pressure. Listen, I'm snoring as I type. Time to hit the sack. Sleep well.

CHAPTER 24

KEIRA

As Saturday morning dawns, I wake up still kicking myself for causing Connor's abrupt retreat from our nightly texting. My wavering about attending the barbeque is not doing either of us any favors—and stretching out my indecision any longer is a coward's move.

As Iffing with Connor has kept me sane this week.

I'd like to As If some more.

I'd like to As If up close and in person again, preferably with a couple of orgasms as reward for progress made.

Two things have kept me from committing. The slow-moving hurricane that is my parents and the prospect of hanging out again with Connor's family.

Brad remains stubbornly asleep to the fact that my parents are making the office a living hell. Our receptionist has started hiding out in the bathroom whenever she sees them coming. The copier won't hold up to much more kicking and banging as the team uses it as a release valve. The phones have stopped ringing because we've stopped answering.

It kills me that I could resolve this by giving in. One little meeting with my parents. How hard could it be? I'm different now. Stronger. No longer dependent on them for anything.

But damned if I'll let the three of them manipulate me. I left my parents' world to escape that bullshit, and I won't let it smear the life I've built. No, instead I'm going to fast-track my exit strategy, expand it to include the rest of the team, provided they want to come with.

"Unlike Rat Bastard, I will protect my people." I turn to Camuel hanging out on the pillow beside me. "Will you look at that? All of a sudden, I have people. That's new."

Pretty sure he'd give me a thumbs-up if he could. If he had thumbs.

That dilemma solved for the moment, I focus on the other half of my hesitation.

With Connor's family, it isn't so much about wanting to keep my distance as fear I'll burn to a crisp getting a little too up close and personal to the beguiling, bright blaze of their family bonds.

Watching the interactions between Mr. Mack and his sons that night at the jazz club called up all my childhood yearning for a perfect 1950s sitcom family—complete with parents who want the best for their kid rather than more ways to use their kid to further their business empire.

"Not the Mack boys' fault I had a crappy childhood." I pet Camuel's soothing, soft belly. "And really, what is the barbeque but an opportunity to As If? I'll simply act as if hanging out with nondysfunctional families is a daily occurrence. Easy peasy."

After a quick kiss on my stuffed camel's nose for courage, I prop myself against the cushioned headboard of my bed and grab my phone off the charger.

Saturday, 7:02 a.m. New York/6:02 a.m. Chicago

> Keira: We still functioning under the As If compact?

Connor: Yes.

Keira: All right, all right. Deep breaths. I can do this.

Connor: [raised eyebrow emoji]

Keira: I'm flipping work the middle finger tomorrow and coming to the BBQ.

Connor: You sure?

Keira: Yup. Tired of perseverating.

Connor: My Mom would have loved you for your vocabulary alone. Why the need for the As If reassurance?

Keira: That.

Connor: What?

Keira: Your family. You like each other. You help each other without keeping score. You're friendly to strangers. The only way I'm going to fit with all you decent people tomorrow is to lean heavy on the As If.

Connor: Don't worry. I'll make sure we find a secluded spot for indecency so you don't spontaneously combust.

Keira: Gratitude. I'll hitch a ride with H&M. See you tomorrow.

My stomach flips and flops, second-guessing my As If Brave plans. The call to retreat pokes at me, urging me to flee.

Run away, regroup. Shore up my vulnerabilities.

Maybe this is the treadmill Helena tried to warn me about at Sully's the night she and Mateo announced their engagement.

For once, I see my approach-avoidance pattern clear as day.

Get close to the flame, feel the danger of its heat, bolt before I'm on fire.

But also for once? I'm not budging.

CHAPTER 25

CONNOR

S unday, 8:02 a.m.

Keira: My barista is kinky.

Connor: I'm listening.

Keira: Usually I get your standard-issue foam heart topping my latte. Today I get: [picture of foam trails that look like a stubby cock and balls]

Connor: If that's a come-on, I think you should pass. Dude lacks stature.

Keira: But ya gotta give him points for trying.

Connor: IDK. Seems presumptuous, asking you to drink his foam in public. Did he even spell your name right on the cup?

Keira: First, gross. Second, lemme check.

Keira: Keiko. I mean, that's close. He should get partial credit.

Connor: Think you should avoid that coffee shop from now on. First dicks in your coffee, next what? Boner biscotti?

Keira: How is this different from celebrity Dicks?

Connor: First, it just is. Second, because.

Keira: A compelling argument. Not.

Connor: You still coming today?

Keira: Planning on coming a few times today. That is, if you're up to the challenge.

Connor: Junior and I are exceedingly up for the challenge. In fact, we're about to have our morning spinach to ensure we're at peak strength.

Keira: Morning spinach better be code for bacon and eggs, or I'm gonna [barfing emoji]

Connor: Definitely code for bacon and eggs. Really, who eats spinach on purpose?

Keira: Weirdos and freaks.

Connor: And my brother David, who's both, so that fits. See you in a couple. Tell Mateo to drive safe.

A mosh pit of glistening bodies in all shapes, sizes, shades, and stages of undress fills the pool terrace at our beach house. From the banana hammock on our eighty-year-old neighbor that doesn't leave enough of his junk to the imagination to the matching floral muumuus shielding my childhood friend and her wife, our guests are coping with the blazing sun in their own unique ways. Everyone sports sunglasses and SPF and their cold beverage of choice.

Even in the shade of the vine-covered trellises edging the pool deck, the heat is smacking us around. A bead of sweat makes a suicide run down my spine, about the only thing today moving faster than a mosey.

Linda and Leslie natter on about little Lionel, who sounds like a budding tyrant. I make all the appropriate "I'm listening" noises, trying not to let my impatience for the arrival of a certain party keep me from enjoying the moment. It's not that they're late—we didn't set a time for them to get here—it's just that they're, okay, yeah. They're late.

Seven o'clock this morning was late according to Junior, though, so it's possible we're not sober judges of the situation.

"So, when Lionel reasoned he didn't have to clean his room, he had people to do that for him—"

"And backed up his argument with a slide show he created on his phone—"

"Well, we couldn't help but be impressed."

"Lionel's life coach says—"

A stir near the glass folding doors that mark inside from outside breaks my attention. Keira, Mateo, and Helena stand framed by the linen curtains, laughing at something Felix is saying.

I can't stop the grin that takes over my face as I absorb Keira's choice of proper barbeque attire. Pink-and-blue cotton candy hair caught up in pigtails matched with a floaty, filmy dress covered in Ferris wheels, big-top tents, and clowns. She fits right in. A breeze flattens the material over her thighs, a passing flirtation that whets my appetite.

She's here. She came.

Part of me doubted. Even after her reassurance this morning, I didn't have faith she'd go through with a playdate on what's essentially my home turf. From the crumbs she's dropped, I have a hint of how huge a concession this is for her. But no real intel on why.

Appeasing my curiosity can wait.

For today, basking is in order. Bask in the sun, bask in her presence, bask because she's here not for another engagement-party-planning session but because she wants to be with me.

"Lionel sounds like a peach," I cut in before L and L finish explaining how a four-year-old's tantrum is a harbinger of greatness. "I'm sure he'll grow up to be president."

"Either president or a psycho," Linda says, eyes rolling. "Sometimes I hear myself talk and think, what the actual fuck?"

We share a laugh, and I leave them debating whether Lionel needs a digital detox or a sibling.

"Have you seen the DiGregorios?" Felix asks as I edge into place beside Keira.

"Are they here?" Mateo swings around, lifting onto the balls of his feet in search of his target. "I've been trying to get a meet with their director of development."

"They're down on the beach." Felix waves toward the beach-access stairway at the far end of the terrace. "I'll introduce you after Davey hooks you up with some drinks."

"You knew the DiGregorios would be here and didn't tell me?" Mateo smacks my stomach.

"I didn't know you wanted to meet them." I rub where he hit, hoping to direct Keira's attention to the glory of my sweaty abs. "As penance, I humbly offer to remove myself from further party-planning duties. Clearly, I can't be trusted."

"Oh no, you don't." Keira backhands my poor belly on the same spot. "You're not leaving me holding the bag."

"Nice try, slugger." Helena leans in to give me a pair of air kisses. "But no go. You're stuck for the long haul. By the way, we're up to eighty-three guests as of this morning. Surprise!"

Keira and I groan.

"This is good news, I guarantee," Mateo says, dipping into a sales-pitch singsong. "We've identified all of the long-lost cousins of cousins within fifty miles. Should mean we hold at a steady figure."

"Unless we submit to The Moms' demands about inviting some of The Dads' former work colleagues." Helena tips her flat hand side to side like she's balancing a scale. "I don't give us good odds on holding out."

"Damn." Keira scrunches her nose. "That means the Winstonian's seventies revival ballroom just moved into the number one spot on the venue list."

"The Khaki Wonderland? Thought you nixed it as not the right kind of retro groovy," Mateo says. "What other places are on the list?"

"Define places," I say.

"Define current," Keira says.

"Define list," Felix chimes in. The four of us stare at him. "What? It was next in the logic tree."

"He isn't wrong," Keira says.

"When it comes to logic, I'm rarely off my feed." My brother herds us toward the bar where David's slinging drinks alongside the hired bartenders. "For instance, logic says the exact head count for this party keeps changing."

"Truth," Mateo says.

"So logic might dictate you choose a location that can grow or shrink to suit your needs, with no last-minute fuss if you suddenly add all your third cousins from Yonkers."

"They're already on the list," my friend says and sighs, "but I see what you're getting at."

"You need a private home. One that's fully equipped for hosting parties." Felix cocks a how-long-are-you-planning-to-be-a-dumbass eyebrow my way.

A horde of kids zigzag through the crowd, laughing and shouting their way to the beach-access steps. The air hums with the relaxed vibe of a party hanging loose and easy.

Felix's point hits me square between the eyes.

"Damn it," I say. "I hate it when you're right about something so obvious."

"What?" Mateo asks as we belly up to the bar.

David delivers a couple of margaritas to a neighbor then heads our way, wiping his hands on the towel hanging over his shoulder.

"This place." I wave broadly to encompass the terrace, house, beach. "What about holding the party here?"

"Lily could do the catering. Right, Felix?" David rests his forearms against the bar. "That is, providing she's not otherwise engaged."

"Not your business." Felix levels a death glare at our older brother, his good mood evaporating as though it'd never existed. "Matty, find me when you're ready, and I'll introduce you to the DiGregorios."

As Felix stalks away, I lean over the bar to punch David's arm, hard. "Dick."

"Perhaps not one of my smoother moves."

"You think?"

"I think his mopey ass needs a swift kick. Maybe that will motivate him to fix things with Lily."

"When has a kick motivated any of us to do anything but return fire?" I ask.

We stare at each other as I wait for him to work through his eternal tug-of-war between his desire to dictate an orderly world and acceptance he's not actually God.

"All right, all right. I'll apologize."

"Maybe give him a few minutes," Mateo says. "Like after he's performed introductions with the DiGregorios, so if he's arrested for murder, I won't miss my shot."

"You got it." David takes everyone's order then gets busy building the drinks. "Connor, you may want to delay asking Dad about the house until later. Right now, he's busy trying to stay one step ahead of the Chapman twins."

"Ah. Good to know. I'll be sure to steer clear."

"What's the deal with the Chapman twins?" Keira asks.

"Serial brides. At last count, they've had seven husbands between them," David says. "They're on the market again. Their term, not mine."

"They have a semipublic bet going to see which one can land Dad first," I add.

"Intriguing," Helena says.

"Don't get any ideas," Mateo says with a mock scowl. "You're getting one husband in this life. Me."

"Wouldn't have it any other way, sweetie." She anoints his cheek with a juicy smooch.

A spasm of grief, more muscle memory than active pain, shoots through me as I join in the laughter.

Dad should have had the chance to stay a husband to the woman he loved.

Though wherever she's hanging out in the hereafter, Mom's probably giggling herself silly at the Open Season sign taped to Dad's back these days. Poor guy, she'd say, before salting a giant bowl of popcorn and settling in to watch the show.

"I'll see about making peace with Felix after I do a round of cruise and schmooze with Celia." David comes out from behind the bar. Under cover of patting my shoulder, he slips a couple of condoms into my board shorts.

Same pocket as the two condoms I stuffed there after breakfast. And the pocket where Felix added one—stingy bastard—right before the first guest arrived.

Mack men. When we're not giving each other a hard time, we're there with a solid assist.

"Remember, Dad wants us to stick around after the barbeque wraps," David adds. "Says he has some news to share."

"All right. Catch up with you later." As my brother surfs into the crowd, I glide high on a wave of yes, doing a quick box step of anticipatory celebration.

"You think this is it finally? The thumbs-up on the Winstonian restoration?" Mateo lands a light punch on my arm.

"It's gotta be. Dad hinted at big news on the family group text earlier in the week. Drove David crazy by withholding the details." I chuckle at the memory of my oldest brother's increasingly annoyed poking and Dad's placid nonresponse. "Come on. Let's find Felix. While you initiate your charm offensive on the DiGregorios, I'll give Keira a tour of the grounds."

"A tour, huh?" Helena laughs with knowing eyes. "Far be it for us to delay that treat. You do you. We can navigate our way like big kids."

We agree to meet on the beach when it's time for Dad to speechify and make the ceremonial first cut into the roast pig.

"Fast hands, your brother has," Keira murmurs as I resecure the lock on the gate to a second, more private access to the waterfront. The curve of the staircase quickly leads us out of sight of the house.

"Caught that, did you?" Our shoulders brush. The fine hairs on my body stretch and sigh.

"You both practically radiated Don't Look, Secret Boy Shenanigans."

"Felix pulled a similar move earlier."

"Guess they want you to play it safe."

"No, I think they want us to get lucky." I smile. "They like you."

"First our friends, now your brothers." She pinches the bridge of her nose. "Please tell me your dad hasn't plied you with prophylactics too. I'm going to develop a complex."

"Nope." My grin widens. "But I wouldn't put it past him to have provisioned the boathouse with a decent supply."

"Definitely need to schedule time so I can develop that complex."

"Nah, I wouldn't bother. It's standard operating procedure in the Mack family. Our parents preached safe and consensual sex then made sure we had the tools to follow through."

We turn a corner on the wooden staircase, and the sprawling boathouse comes into view.

"Wow."

"Meet our Frankenstein's monster."

"You love it."

"One of my favorite places on earth. It started life as a shed, but every generation adds to its personality, hence the rambling mishmash you see today." I catch her free hand. "Come on. Let me show you."

"Romantic setting. Secluded from prying eyes. Indoor plumbing. Don't tell me, let me guess. This is the Mack family shag shack."

"Family lore says Great-Granddad Horatio was the first to outfit this puppy with all the mod-cons so he and his bride could shag in peace. Something about the main house not having enough privacy when all the kids were home."

"Is this the same relative whose brass bed you inherited?"

"Ah, now that was Granddad Floyd and Grannie Barb. Very keen on brass, they were. That partiality is well represented here." I guide us inside to the large main room. "Five bedrooms, five brass beds. Is it coincidence or fate that we happen to have five condoms? I say we strip down and test them all out."

"Not necessary," she says almost absently as she makes a leisurely tour of the wooden display cases and bookshelves lining the room. "The couch seems perfectly adequate for what I have planned."

"And what's that?"

"Tying you up, sitting on your cock, and taking a lazy spin." Glancing over her shoulder, she licks me from head to toe with her smoky brown gaze.

My board shorts shrink two sizes, crowding my suddenly rock-hard cock.

"Damn." I pat down my chest. "And me without a silk tie."

"Five condoms but no tie? And you call yourself a Scout." The quirk in her lips contradicts the stern frown she's attempting. She sets her half-finished drink on a coaster. "Guess we'll have to improvise."

"Or we could pass on the bondage this time. Skip the rules, strip down, hop on a bed. Lose ourselves in the moment and see if we wind up rocking the headboard hard enough to punch a few dents in the drywall."

"Now that's an image. It's your laundry, so we can muss all the clean sheets you want, but"—she shrugs a shoulder—"I don't fuck naked, I don't fuck without restraints, and I don't fuck without agreeing up front on what will happen."

"I— What? Never?"

"I'm sure you've clued in to the fact that I have control issues." She turns away, her body—loose and open a moment ago—now reminds me of a neon cactus blinking *stay back, I'm spiky.*

This isn't the body language of the proud, sassy, creative dominant who leads our playtime with her head held high and I double-dog dare you glinting in her eyes. This is a door cracked open to her inner self.

"Can you tell me why?" I ask, hoping to nudge the crack wider.

"Do you need to know?"

"I think I do. At the least so I'm not smacking into your boundaries like a dope. At most, maybe tell me because during our time benefiting each other we've become friends, and this is the kind of stuff friends share. Or, hell, tell me because you've never struck me as the kind of woman who'd allow a block to keep her chained."

She doesn't reply right away, and pressure builds in my chest to say it's okay. We can continue as is, instead of as if.

But if I speak first, offer an out, will we ever move from the shallows of this relationship to the deep end?

Hard as it is, I keep my lips zipped, letting the silence build, the discomfort grow.

"I need another drink."

"Hey, now. No booze crutches." I duck behind the bar and grab a couple of waters from the minifridge. "You're the one who taught me drink and kink don't mix."

"Yeah, yeah. All right." She folds onto the couch with a resigned sigh. "Let's do this."

Relief at her concession leaves me shaky. I hand her a bottle before dropping to the floor opposite her, leaning against Mom's beat-up recliner for support.

"You sure you want to hear this?"

"I wouldn't ask if I didn't."

Sucking her lips between her teeth, she peers at the green glass as though it's a crystal ball. Her pink-and-blue cotton candy pigtails are out of sync, too sunny and cheerful to match the frown etched between her brows. After a moment, she nods and sets her water on the side table.

"Growing up I had zero free will." She draws her knees up and wraps her arms around her shins. "My parents dictated everything, from what I wore to the sports I played, the friends I was allowed to have. What I ate, when I slept, how I studied. If there was a choice, they made it for me."

"That sucks."

"To put it mildly. When they agreed, everything was fine. When they didn't, I got caught in the middle, trying to please them both. A whole 'nother level of suck." She sighs from within her body fort. "Father was strict. Mother was indulgent. Their attention was addictive. The lack of it, devastating. Classic dysfunction, right? But what does a kid know? For a long time, I was happy, even eager, to let them mold me into whatever they wanted."

"What changed?"

"Middle school. I started hanging out with kids my parents didn't pre-screen. My early insurrections were pretty lame." A quick smile chases across her face. "Sneaking junk food and candy, watching R-rated movies, changing outfits once I got to school. Since I still played the perfect child on command, I don't think any of us could have guessed what was coming."

"That being?"

"Hormone blitzkrieg. I was a late bloomer, but I made up for it by going big. Zits, boobs, my period, and copious amounts of unhinged emotions. Kaboom, kaboom, kaboom. Each day arrived with a brand-new surprise."

"Good ole hormones." I toast with my water. "Drawing battle lines between parents and teens since the dawn of time. Sounds pretty typical."

"Yeah, maybe. But my parents were not the kind to tolerate a kid with a mind of her own." Her mouth pulls down at the corners. "The last straw for them was when I installed a lock on my bedroom door. I felt so smart, using a level, a drill. I might have celebrated that cleverness by inviting a boy over when I thought they wouldn't be home."

"Oh shit. What happened?"

"They grounded me and removed the door. Not the lock. The door. So I ran away from home."

"How—? What—? Were you—?" I stop, not sure what question to ask.

"I didn't get far. My father called in a favor from an old army buddy who runs a tough-love boarding school for teen-girl troublemakers. I was there for two years. No holidays, vacations, or trips home. No privacy, no autonomy, no downtime. The ideal setup for indoctrinating daughters of wealthy patrons on how to behave like proper little ladies."

"That's criminal." I set my water bottle down rather than give in to the desire to chuck it against the wall. The moment doesn't call for me to go caveman.

"Apparently not. The school keeps getting awards. I've checked." She snags a throw pillow and squeezes it against her belly like it's the only stable thing in her universe.

"I feel sick," I say, wishing I had a pillow too.

"Told you it was ugly. Want me to stop?"

"No. I definitely need to hear this. And maybe you need to share. Loads lightened and all that."

"If you say so. When my parents finally let me come home, I'd gone through a master class on how to bury my rebellions in plain sight, so there was nothing to find in my closets."

"Bet that wasn't on the curriculum."

"Not the official one, that's for damn sure," she says with a snort. "Father and Mother never did replace my door, but it hardly mattered. I became so good at playing their games, by the time I stumbled into the realm of kink the last year of high school, I didn't even have to sneak around. And finally, I caught a glimpse of the world as it could be. To have control or willingly cede it, to be up front and crystal clear about expectations and behaviors. No lies, no manipulation. No using without giving. Something just clicked into place. I looked at the future my parents had planned for me compared it to what it could be, what I might want it to be given the chance, and started planning my escape."

"I'm going to start crying in a minute."

"Don't blame me. You're the one who pushed for the origin story of what made me the control-freak goddess you worship and obey today."

"Goddess is right. Your strength amazes me."

"I don't feel strong. I feel wiped out and naked."

"Trust me, you're strong, and you aren't naked. I'd know if you were naked." I leer and toss in an eyebrow waggle for good measure.

"Dork." She rolls her eyes but relaxes her death grip on the throw pillow.

"I'm glad you told me. I understand better what you meant when you said there's no room for lies in a scene. I'm sorry about your parents."

"Thanks." She uncoils with a sigh, discarding the pillow. Her brown eyes gleam with unshed tears before she tucks in her chin, a shy gesture that finishes gutting me. "I could maybe use a hug."

CHAPTER 26

KEIRA

As soon as Connor scoops me into his lap, I shelter my face against his chest and breathe him in. He murmurs into my hair, half phrases of reassurance, his scent anchoring me as I fight the chaos swirling inside me like a tornado.

I only ever share like this with Helena, and even getting to that point usually takes copious amounts of wine. What makes this man so different? So easy to confide in?

Why, when I'm stripped bare of my trusty defenses, have I asked him for a hug instead of running for the hills?

And where do I go from here? How do I begin to regroup, rebuild my fortifications?

The pelt of questions defeats me, and I slump deeper into Connor's embrace, my last remaining piece of spine officially on strike. He shifts to accommodate me, not pressing me to speak, just taking care.

Silence stretches until it vibrates with all the little sounds that make up the nothing hum. The minifridge behind the bar. A couple of seabirds cawing over something on the beach. Connor's steady heart-beat in my ear.

He threads his fingers through my hair, dismantling my pigtails in soothing, generous pets that should continue for all eternity.

I snuggle closer.

"Ready to come out of hiding?"

"Nope." My voice is muffled by the muscled wall of his chest. I breathe in through my nose to get another soothing hit of suntan lotion, sweat, and Connor.

Only this time his rich, intoxicating cologne wakes the interest of General Hoo-ha.

I scrunch my already-closed eyes that last little bit shut against my sudden lurch into physical awareness. I've bared my soul, reliving the ugly underbelly of my life to the nice guy I'm supposed to only be boning, not falling for. I'm exhausted. I'm embarrassed.

Naturally my hormones pick this minute to make their demands.

Fast sex. Now sex. Sex to wash away the past. Sex to reestablish control.

Giving in to the surge of need, I lick his nipple.

It bunches up sweetly, so I follow up with a gentle bite and a wee tug of my teeth. He draws in a sharp breath, and my empty passage clenches with deepening want.

"Keira?"

"Shut up and kiss me." I slide up his body to sit astride his lap and attack his lush mouth.

I lick and tease and suck, pouring everything into my raid.

He doesn't fight.

Instead, he welcomes me, and the kiss turns from invasion to homecoming, from ground I try to steal to territory he offers for my delight.

The difference shifts the balance, but instead of gaining more control, I lose myself in the storm of sensation. The heat, the gooey, wanton need building within me. My hips rock, desperate for friction, for something to appease the craving making my body shake and my brain melt.

His cock, stiff and hot, pushes against me. It's not enough. Not enough.

He pulls back from the kiss. "Generalissima, order me to make you come. Please, I'm begging you. I'll sit on my left hand. Place it behind my back. Restrain myself however you want. Just let me touch you. Let me make you feel better."

"Yes. Do it. Either. Both. Now."

He tucks one hand behind his back. With the other, he finds the hem of my sundress and skims along the muscles of my inner thigh. I jump, the light pressure against my sensitive skin almost too much to bear.

"Shh, shh, we'll make it better. Promise."

Two thick fingers glide under the edge of my bikini bottoms right into my wet and ready pussy. I squeeze around their welcome intrusion, willing them deeper. They curl up, searching, searching. I gasp when they make contact with my G-spot.

"Easy now, we'll get you there." He begins a quick, steady rhythm.

The sounds of wet friction and our ragged panting fill the room. The scent of sex infuses the air around us, making me dizzy. I squeeze him again, urging him for more. More pressure, more speed. More flutters in my belly, rippling outward, building, reaching, yearning.

It's game over when he rubs his magic thumb over my clit.

I split apart on a shout, letting everything go. My confusion, my doubts, my fear. Consciousness. They all fade as my body shudders in orgasm.

Sometime later, my comfy mattress—ribbed for my pleasure—grabs my hips to heft me to a new position, dislodging my head from its cozy shoulder pillow.

"Quit it," I mumble.

"Too sorry, your generalship, but on the off chance you want to take Junior for a spin at any point in the hopefully extraordinarily near future, we need to return the blood flow to my lower extremities."

Another heft shakes my nap cobwebs loose, and I meet Connor's hungry, amused gaze. We're lying on our sides, belly to belly on the boathouse floor, half on the cushy rug, half on polished oak planking. The stuffed leather chair he leaned against during our talk is pushed back to make room for his long body. One arm is propped under his head, the other draped over my ass.

I try to pull back, but he massages my tailbone, and I wind up nestling closer. I swear, if I were a dog, my leg would start thumping.

"How are you feeling?"

"Honestly?"

"Boring." A devilish gleam lights his eyes. "In honor of our renewed truth-is-the-best-policy policy, how about a round of two lies and a truth?"

"Are you trying to gloss over any weirdness I may be feeling after my little episode of oversharing and overeager sexual demands by turning this into a game?"

"You know me by now. Of course I'm turning it into a game. Games provide fantastic cover for getting through socially awkward moments."

"You're a little too good to be true, you know." I settle my leg over his, and pull us closer together, shivering as the hair on his thigh tickles my skin. "Two lies and a truth about how I'm feeling is the challenge on the table, eh?"

"Correct."

"What do I get if I win?"

"Anything your heart desires." He rolls onto his back so I'm lying on top of him and flexes his hips, reintroducing me to his steel-hard cock.

The smug confidence in his grin has me squinting in sudden suspicion.

"If you were wearing sleeves, you'd be hiding something up one." His grin widens, two rows of straight, gleaming teeth. I hit him with the evil eye. "Come on, cough it up. What do you get if you win?"

"A date. Dinner. Dancing. Flowers. The whole works."

"I thought we agreed. No dates."

"Yeah. But then we had a conversation about you asking me out on a date."

"That's not how I remember it going." I poke his belly. "And anyway, I haven't asked."

"As I'm well aware." Grin widening, he snags my fingers and gives them a kiss. "But if we wait for you to ask, we'll be eighty. I decided to fudge the timeline a bit."

"I don't know—"

"There's one more term I'd like you to agree to before we go deeper into play." All teasing deserts his expression.

"What?"

"That our date includes a test run at naked sex. Think of the date as for me, the sex for you. Win-win."

"Win-win?" I stiffen, arching up. "Are you actually on crack now?"

"Come back down here. You're too far away." He cups my shoulders and applies a gentle pressure.

I cave, half-curious, half-wary, sinking until we're belly-a-belly again, our faces mere inches apart.

"You like control and open, honest communication when it comes to sex. Lucky for us, I like your control during sex, and I'm flat out addicted to our negotiations."

"If everything's so great, why push for naked?"

"Because naked sex can be a lot of fun. And I wonder if your rule is less a happy, well-explored fetish and more a flex you developed to take back control during a time when you lacked other options. I'm not arguing that we should strip down to bare skin every time we have sex." He shrugs, and I ride the ripple effect. "But I'd really like us to try it, see if we can figure out what will make it good for you, before we institute a permanent ban."

"Would this test run come under the umbrella of As If?"

"Absolutely." He flashes a dimple.

I try listening to my oddly quiet gut. Do I take a chance? Agree to another of his nutty-yet-effective As If challenges? Or do I stay stuck?

Put like that, I'd be a sucker not to try.

"Okay. If you win, we can attempt a date with a naked sex clause." His bear hug squeezes a yelp out of me. "On one condition."

"Name it."

"That we're on neutral territory. Neither one of us gets a home turf advantage."

"Sold." His hands skate down my back and over my hips to give my ass its own squeeze, making the nerves there dance and tingle.

"Easy, pardner. There's a very real chance you'll crash and burn on this little wager."

"Bring it on, Generalissima." He steals a quick kiss. "I double-dog dare you."

Two lies and a truth.

Truths pour into me, begging to be shared.

I'm so afraid of buyer's remorse, I rent a shithole apartment, and the fact embarrasses me, but I can't seem to get my act in gear to find a new place.

I'm this close to quitting my job and starting a new real estate group. And just like with the apartment, I can't quite make myself jump.

Some truths cross the line from begging to bullying, like they know me keeping my mouth shut is a doofus move, and they want no part of my silence.

My parents are in town. I wake up sick to my stomach each morning, wondering what they want from me. What they'll do to get it.

I'm falling for you, and it scares me to pieces.

No. Not ready to share any of that, the last two especially.

Connor waits for me, relaxed but for the long, poky, distractingly warm appendage making a home at the notch of my thighs. His hands have retreated from my butt to steady my hips. He'd say to protect me from falling, no doubt, but even money a good portion of his motivation is to maintain our current, cozy cock cuddle.

Fine by me. I like it too.

But enough with delaying. It's time to win.

"I soaked through my underwear fifteen minutes after meeting you for the first time at Mateo's happy hour. The next month, I snuck into the bathroom at Sully's and gave General Hoo-ha the business before hitting the crowd in an attempt to preempt my inconvenient lusting. But it was getting a view of your seriously fine backside as you squatted to pick up a drunk chick's purse that finally convinced me to make a move."

In reality, my thong was toast within five minutes that first night. I didn't even have to meet him. From my seat at the bar, I watched as he worked the room, laughing, smiling, radiating good-guy vibes all over the joint. Add in his stone-cold hottie good looks?

Bam, soggy lace placket.

The second month, after weeks of fantasies starring him, I couldn't even hold off until the bathroom at Sully's. No, instead I locked the

THE ONE THAT I WANT   163

door to my office, dug out my emergency bullet vibe, and spent the most satisfying ten minutes of my life working him out of my system.

Until later that night when he just had to go and be *nice.*

The jerk.

A gal with one too many cocktails under her belt spun away from the bar and knocked into him, spilling her drink down his front before dropping the glass, her purse, and, somehow, her glasses.

When she burst into tears, without missing a beat he made sure she wasn't hurt then rescued her personal items, arranged for cleanup, corralled her friends, and ensured their safe passage home. No shaming the women. No strutting to show off his good deed. No fuss. He simply took care to do the right thing.

A fine ass and a finer sense of honor?

Even my grumpy self couldn't hold out against such an irresistible lure.

"I think we can safely cross off your first sentence as a lie."

"What? So easily?"

"I clocked you clocking me that first happy hour. We made eye contact, and the rest of the room ceased to exist. All I could see was you, looking at me, crossing and uncrossing your legs, shifting on your stool, sucking on cube after cube of ice. No way your panties lasted until fifteen minutes after we met. My dick sure didn't. Poor Junior turned full I-beam in two heartbeats. I stand by my decision. Strike the first sentence."

"Hmph. Let's hear the rest of your logic."

In response to my sulk, he runs a hand up my spine to tug at my hair. A bright arc of goose bumps chases over my skin. My nipples harden into achy points. In retaliation, I wriggle against his pride and joy.

"All right, all right, settle down. I'm trying to win a date here. Quit trying to distract me."

"Got you stumped on the last two, don't I?" I lick his neck. It tastes like victory.

"I'll give you thirty minutes to stop that immediately." He angles his neck to grant me greater access. "While I wouldn't put it past you to crank one out at Sully's, what you don't know is I was behind you, enjoying the view, when you arrived the next month. You're not the one who stopped into the restroom for a quick spank. That would be me. Which means our third option must be the truth."

"That's not fair." I pull back to glare. "You cheated. Insider information. I'm calling the SEC. What's their number?"

"We can do a search for it later. After you explain the connection between me picking up a drunk woman's purse and how you're feeling."

"The thread between then and now?" My stomach flips, but I push and give him more. "Your gallantry."

"Me, gallant?" He chokes out a disbelieving laugh.

"What else would you call it? You flew to the rescue without pausing to undertake a cost-benefit analysis. I grew up with parents who never once acted without weighing the payoff. Do you realize how rare someone like you is? Of course, I had to jump your bones. For all I knew, you'd turn into a pumpkin or a mouse or something equally useless if I didn't do something quick."

"Fuck me to save me?"

"Brilliant, right?"

"Think I'd call that convenient and highly suspect reasoning, but I'm not complaining."

"You better not. You're getting a date and naked sex out of me. Be happy."

"What's that I heard?" He cups his ear. "You, conceding defeat?"

"Don't be a sore winner." As he snickers, I lever up to sitting, done with slippery emotions and pesky insights and truths and lies. "Wanna play?"

"With you? Always."

"With no tie, I'm going to need you on your best behavior. Think you're up for it?"

"Very, very up for it." He arches, pressing his erection into the vee of my thighs. I hum with pleasure. Possessiveness. The heat, his hardness. All mine.

"I'm convinced. Okay, now lace your hands together behind your head. That's your binding."

As he complies, I glide my fingers over his chest with a barely there touch. His stomach hollows out as I count his ribs, outline his muscles, mapping his most responsive spots. Beckoned by his nipples, pinched tight and browny-pink, I lean in, sucking and biting, soothing with my tongue only to nibble again. Each groan I pull from him plucks a string deep within me, and I grow wetter and wetter, needy and needier.

Hinging back up, I grind my hips against his. Connor's breath catches. So I do it again and again, throwing my head back as thought-stealing sparks charge up my body from my clit to my belly to my brain.

Gathering my sundress out of the way, I grab the string at one hip and undo the bow on my bikini bottoms. I repeat the move on my other side then drag the bottoms free, pressing them sticky side down on his belly. He makes an animal noise.

"You're killing me."

"Pthpt. I think you can handle a little more."

"Would that more include a peek at your tits? Fair's fair. You played with my nipples. I've been dreaming about yours for months. How will they feel under my tongue? Simply amazing or outright awesome? Are they pierced? So. Many. Questions. So much to discover."

His words coax a new flood of desire in my empty pussy. I tighten around nothingness, achy and wanting. Tempting. So tempting to let go, strip away the last of my protective shielding, and let him explore me, body and soul, no holding back. But it's too much, too fast. Today, in this moment, I can't.

Maybe on the date I'll be ready for the *more* he seeks.

"You'll have to keep dreaming for now." I rock back and forth, reveling in the more intense sensations that going bottomless allows. "I didn't set the terms of the deal. One date, with flowers, et cetera, with an attempt at naked sex. Nothing in there says you get a naked preview."

"Yes, ma'am. Understood, ma'am. Can't blame a guy for trying, ma'am."

"I could, but how about we try this instead? Connor Mack, I'm about to fuck you hard. Are you okay with this course of action?"

"Couldn't be okay-er." His wink does something hinky to my heart, making it double kick.

Ignoring the aberration, I scooch down his thighs and loop my fingers into the waistband of his swim trunks. He lifts up helpfully, allowing me to navigate the material over his massive bulge. His cock springs up rooster proud, straining toward me, satin over steel and looking like the missing piece to my puzzle.

I give it a kiss, sneak a little taste, the scent of his salty musk giving me a contact high.

"Yep," he pants, "definitely killing me. At least I'll die happy."

"Oh, I have plans for you. No dying today. Not until we've put this big boy to good use."

Wrapping both hands around his base, I squeeze. His panting turns to a gasp, and he thrusts into my hold, invoking my name like a prayer, and poof, my plans for any further torment disappear.

"Which pocket?"

He blinks at me as though his brain has left the building. Too impatient to ask again, I poke around in one pocket, letting out a huff of disgust when I come up empty. Frantic, I dive for the other, letting out a woot of triumph when I hit pay dirt.

Fingers trembling, I roll the condom down his length and shift up his thighs, lining his tip to my entrance. Slowly, slowly I take him inside, inch by inch adjusting to his fullness, the pressure, both of us shuddering as we lock into place all that lovely potential for pleasure.

Then slow is a memory.

Setting a demanding pace, we sprint toward orgasm, as if there's a shortage and we'll die if we don't get our fix. I grind, and he twists. He growls, and I moan.

"Touch… yourself," he chokes out, face red. "Please. I'm there, I'm there. Come with me."

Zeroing in on my clit, I time each touch with the thrust of his cock. The slick knot of nerves is swollen, hypersensitive to my lightest touch.

Imagining it's him—touching me, teasing me—sets me loose. I shatter apart on wave after wave of electric bliss. Connor shouts as my climax triggers his, hips pumping, chasing down every last zap of sensation. The movement shocks me into a second orgasm, and I squeeze tight, trying to make it last.

Lungs heaving, sweat pouring down my face, my back, between my breasts, muscles like noodles, I collapse into the cradle of Connor's arms.

"One hundred percent, definitely dead," he croaks. "You killed me."

"What a way to go."

"No arguments here." He pats my butt. "I need to deal with the condom."

"Right." I don't move.

"Upsy-daisy, now. We don't want a leak."

Reluctantly, I push off until I'm kneeling beside the display that is Connor in the Aftermath. Eyes at half-mast, skin burnished to a bronzy pink. His spent, condom-covered cock still one proud dick.

He makes no move to cover up, to hide from me. Neither embarrassed nor ashamed, he's simply present, living in the moment. Maybe that could be me one day. Maybe, if I hang around him long enough, his self-acceptance will rub off and I can learn to relax some of the rigidity that rules my life.

He stretches and yawns, a satiated, sleepy nice guy in his prime. His stomach rumbles, making me chuckle.

"Guess I could use a little refueling." He rubs his belly, and just like that, I'm hungry for him again.

Forget food, forget parents and uncertainty and bad bosses and the sex-only boundaries he's making me question with his relentless optimism. Just dive headfirst back into the fizzy, spicy fun that bubbles me aloft every time we're together. The fun, and the safety I'm beginning to think I'll miss should he ever decide I'm too much to handle.

Scrambling to my feet, I pluck my bikini bottoms from the floor and turn away. I've already leapt off one cliff today. No need to push my luck.

"Got a bathroom in this five-bedroom shack?"

"Several. There's one down that hall on your left I think you'll like. Lots of adjustable jets. Use whatever you need."

Hesitating at the entrance of the shadowed hall, I say over my shoulder, "I didn't confess the whole truth earlier."

"No?"

"No. It was your kindness. That night at Sully's. What you did for the woman was gallant, but it was also kind. Listening to my tale of woe now, holding me after? Kind and kinder. You're a nice guy, Connor Mack." I take a quick breath. "I like you."

I disappear before he can reply.

CHAPTER 27

CONNOR

Keira's wet pink-and-blue hair is slicked back, leaving her face naked but not open. Her eyes are puffy, hinting at a crying jag in the shower. I crack my knuckles, rerouting the ugly urge to punch dents in some drywall. No wonder she feels the need for privacy before allowing her guard to drop. Her parents leave a lot to be desired in the nurturing healthy boundaries department.

Daring greatly, I take her hand as, wordless, we mount the stairs back to the pool terrace. Her shoulders relax as she permits this small comfort. Her body knows I'm no threat, even if her brain is slow to accept.

Kindness is her trigger.

My body strains, that primitive desire to smash rearing anew. What a fucking horrible legacy to give a kid, to make her react to compassion as though it were an enemy capable of breaking her apart.

Her restraints and contracts and negotiations. The restrictions on dates and adult sleepovers and plain freaking friendship.

They're all attempts to keep her hard-won peace.

Part of me wants to cover her in Bubble Wrap, or better yet, sneak us into my childhood bedroom. We could purloin some snacks, build that blanket fort, and the world could go hang for the rest of eternity.

Instead, I remain close as she recovers her balance. We wander through the afternoon, not always working the same conversations but always in the same orbit. When she laughs, my chest squeezes. When she takes my hand, my heart trips.

After a late lunch, the flow of the crowd finds us face-to-face with my family. As though she's always been part of our inner circle, Keira quickly allies with Celia in the never-ending zinger exchange among my brothers and me, the two of them working together like a well-oiled volleyball team. Set, spike, and repeat. Dad lands the occasional dry burn, though mostly he hangs back and lets us run wild until hosting duties call him away.

A covetous pirate, I stockpile each small moment with Keira in my treasure chest. Every shared glance, every impish grin, adds to my trove of riches.

The barbeque ends too soon.

"Damn it. Eager as I am to hear Dad's verdict on the restoration project, I resent like hell not being able to drive you back to the city myself," I say as I slow-walk Keira around the beach house toward the driveway.

"Feeling a yen for a little car sex? That has possibilities." She purrs her approval of the idea.

"And that's a boner I wasn't expecting, thankyouverymuch." I pull us to a stop beside a cove of tall shrubs and adjust the fit of my board shorts. "I had in mind more touching base, not rounding the bases."

"Touch base on what?"

"Today was a turning point for us. And pop-up erection aside, fear has my balls locked in its fist. Are you going to retreat once I'm out of your sight? Are we headed back to square one?"

"You." Hands on hips, she leans into my space. "Always with the pushing."

"You want me to stop?" My heart stutters.

She contemplates me in the evening shadows, letting the silence build. There's enough light left in the sky to make out the frown line between her brows and the pursed bow of her lips.

"No." She lets her arms drop and falls into me. My arms wrap around her before my brain relays the order. "I figure today falls under our As If clause, where I act as if this kind of intimacy doesn't scare the ever-loving toast out of me."

"Toast, huh?"

"Ever-loving."

"So, what's our next step?" I ask.

"You're asking me? I'm the poster child for relationship dunces. How should I know?"

I laugh into her hair. She gives me more of her weight.

"All right. We'll keep making shit up as we go along. How about a new clause to our contract?"

"You know I love when you whisper dirty business in my ear." She nips my chest, right above my nipple, and my cock sproings in renewed approval against her belly.

I tangle my fingers in the hair of her ponytail and gently tug until her face tilts up to mine.

"Stop distracting me, woman." Her evil grin promises nothing. "All right, as a subsection under the As If clause, let's agree to continue with the nightly texting."

"I'm a go for that."

"And let's agree that you need to ask me for our date no later than Wednesday of this week."

"Wait a minute. What's this about me asking you on the date? Aren't you the winner of that little trophy?"

"I may have won the date, but a man still likes to be wooed. Besides, I figure you'll get off on having control over the details." I raise my eyebrows in question. "Tell me I'm wrong."

"You are super wily," she huffs. "And right, damn it. I want my fingerprints all over this date."

"That's handy since I want your fingerprints all over me."

I nibble my way down from her temple along her jaw to her mouth. She meets my kiss, our tongues gliding in a languorous "hello again" exploration.

A cool night breeze wafts in off the ocean, chasing away the heat and humidity of the day. Insects chatter as they begin their evening rounds. The layered scent of this woman in my arms, shampoo and lotion and *her*, calls me close and closer still.

The sweetness builds until it breaks, our kiss pivoting from *nice way to end the day* to *let's have sex right now*. Her hand heads below my waistband to take firm possession of my cock. I thrust against her palm and scramble to raise the hem of her dress.

With four condoms left, a quick bang in the shadows is totally doable.

"Yo, lovebirds. You're scaring the wildlife," Mateo calls from the circular drive. "Unless, Keira, you don't need a ride anymore? I mean, a ride back to the city?"

We jolt apart. Her lips are plump, swollen, her cotton-candy-colored hair no longer neatly restrained. Every shallow breath she takes presses her breasts into my chest.

The caveman in me revels in how mussed she looks from my touch.

The twenty-first century dude notices the estate lights have turned on for the evening, and our shadows are blown up, large and in charge, against the side of the house.

Whoops.

"You okay?" I chafe her shoulder.

"Fine, fine. Mateo may need a smackdown, though." She sends a glare toward the driveway.

"The nerve of him, to interrupt our exhibitionism like that."

"Exactly."

We exchange grins, just two regular folks lighting up at the possibility of getting caught in the act. As we trek toward the driveway, our fingers tangle together accidentally on purpose. Her touch is the only thing keeping me tethered to the ground.

A date with Keira. The prospect of practicing naked sex. And, in a few more minutes, the official nod on leading the Winstonian project.

No wonder I'm soaring.

We arrive at Mateo's SUV rental to find Helena and him deep in a lip lock.

"Thought you were in a hurry to leave?" They spring apart, and I wouldn't be human if revenge glee didn't make my grin a little on the villainous side.

"When in Rome." Mateo shrugs with a "whatcha gonna do" lack of repentance. "Though it's about time your slow as molasses asses got here. Some of us have work in the morning."

"Ugh, don't remind me," Keira says. "I'm looking at a crazy-busy week, and it starts at seven thirty tomorrow morning."

"Right then, you better head out." I squeeze her hand. "I'll talk with my dad about hosting the party here and let you guys know. I'm sure he'll say yes."

"With the location sewn up, the rest of the party details should be a snap," Keira says.

"Your lips to the engagement party goddess's ears." Helena flattens her palms together in a prayer pose. "May The Moms take a surprise vacation and leave the rest of the planning to you."

"Meddling again?" Keira asks.

"Like they ever stopped," Mateo replies. "Gives me cold sweats just thinking about how they'll act with grandchildren."

"Family. Can't live with 'em, can't tie 'em up in the attic for six months while you get on with business," Helena says with a "gosh darn it" snap of her fingers.

"No worries," I say. "We won't let this turn into anything less than the party of your dreams."

"Thanks." Helena smacks twin kisses on my cheeks before letting Mateo guide her into the front passenger seat.

As he rounds the hood, I open the back passenger door. Keira lets me crowd her. I fall into her dark-brown eyes, liquid and lovely.

"I had a good time today," she says quietly.

"Me too." I brush my lips over hers. "Text me later. Let me know you got home all right."

"Sure thing, Mr. Worrywart."

"If I suggest you sext me instead, would that feel less warty?"

"You are a goof." The curl of a barely-there smile contradicts the shake of her head.

Instead of debating, I help her into the SUV, managing maximum body contact the entire time. She matches me with a host of her own handsy touches.

"If being a goofus maximus nets me your sneaky fingers fluffing my junk, sign me right up," I whisper before I give her ear a little nip and pull back. I raise my voice so Mateo and Helena can hear my singsong, "Buckle up, children."

"Yeah, yeah, old man. Clickety-click it, we don't want a ticket." Mateo gifts me with a dry look over his shoulder. "Now kiss your girl and shut the door so we can hit the road."

"Since you insist," I say, bending toward Keira to comply with my pal's most excellent order.

She grabs a hunk of my hair and steers my mouth to hers. The kiss is short and brutal and hot enough to leave me needing a cold, cold shower.

"Good thing you're so cute," she whispers against my lips before pushing me away. "Bye, boy."

"Later, Generalissima."

After shutting the SUV's door, I give the roof two good luck knocks. Mateo gives a light tap of the horn and heads left out of the drive.

I follow the taillights, savoring the taste of Keira on my lips. Savoring each moment of the day. My gut informs me that a lifetime of days like this will never be enough.

I'll always be hungry for more.

More passion. More sharing. More quiet belonging.

More Keira.

"Sorry to interrupt your mooning, lover boy." Felix strolls up beside me. "David's back downstairs after coaxing our cranky, sleepy sister-in-law into bed. and Dad's kitchen pace is getting out of hand."

"The kitchen pace? That's for suck news. I was expecting his bar-prep two-step." I catch Felix's arm as he moves toward the house. "You think he's having second thoughts about the Winstonian?"

"Do I think the world revolves around your pet project? Not particularly."

"Asshole," I swing a punch at him, more from reflex than heat, and he dances away with the ease of long practice. "Seriously, you don't think anything is wrong, do you?"

"Seriously, I think we'll find out once we hit the kitchen." We climb the wide steps to the front entry. He opens the door but stops short with his hand on the doorknob, brows arched in challenge. "Twenty bucks says the big news is a brand-new stepmama."

"Har har, very funny. Easiest twenty I'll ever make." I shove him against the door jam. "Race ya."

We tumble down the hall toward the family room off the open kitchen, cursing and laughing. It's the most positive energy I've seen from him in weeks, and it adds to my buoyancy. Wrestling for top dog position, we knock into a floor lamp, and David catches it before it crashes.

"Do I need to pinch your ears?"

"Suck it, Davey," Felix huffs, chest pumping.

He and I share a look, mind meld, and turn on our big bro, taking him to the ground. He has this one ticklish spot…

"Not inside the house, boys." Dad's voice is filled with either amused tolerance or tolerable amusement. Possibly because he's given us a similar warning before a time or three thousand. "You'll wake Celia."

We grin, unrepentant, from our puddle of arms and legs. Well, David doesn't grin. He takes the opportunity to lay a noogie on Felix. I find the tickle spot, and we start up again. Dad dives in, giving as good as he gets.

Finally, we tap out to lie on our backs, sucking wind like washed-up racehorses, not as young as we once were.

With a groan, Dad pushes to his feet, and we scramble up with him, still panting.

"You three. You burst my heart, I love you so much."

He pads into the kitchen, dim but for the under-cabinet lights. We belly up to the breakfast bar, almost choreographed in our synchronicity as we sit on the stools like we used to do as kids when Mom would serve up lunch. Her baby birds, she'd say, waiting to be fed.

As he pours four scotches from the emergency bottle stashed in the cabinet beside the fridge, my brothers and I share a round of "what the hell" frowns.

Disappointment streaks through me, knife sharp. He's decided not to tap me to head the restoration. All right. Okay. I'll learn. I'll get better, be ready for the next one. But surely telling me doesn't need to be this drawn-out production?

"What is it?" David asks, short and direct. Another move from our youth when he took the lead in parental negotiations, especially when we were facing a lecture.

Face in shadows with the lights now behind him, Dad passes around the tumblers. He lets the silence stretch, fixated on the amber liquid in his glass as though it holds the key to the universe.

My hands turn clammy, and I curl them into fists in my lap. I'd drop anything I pick up.

Time to stop pushing away the obvious.

This isn't about the Winstonian or my laddering up at the firm.

I race through disaster scenarios. Uncle Aloyisus had another stroke. Cousin Demeter's baby is back in the hospital. One of our linchpin clients has gone bankrupt and can't pay their bills.

"Boys, I—" He laughs and sets his glass down. "I didn't know how hard this was going to be."

"Spit it out, Dad." The brief lightness in Felix is gone. "If it's bad news, just tell us."

"Right, right." He runs a hand through his salt and pepper hair—when did it get so gray? "Now, let me preface this by saying it's not great news, but I don't want you to freak out. It's not the end of the world."

"Not really helping, Dad," I say.

"Fuck. If your mother were here, this would be easier. Damn it, why isn't she here?" He snatches the tumble, and slams it into the sink. It shatters, spraying glass shards and scotch all over.

Felix and I freeze, but in the space of a heartbeat David rounds the island to wrap Dad in his arms.

The reversal of comfort roles chimes a pain-filled chord.

The last time I witnessed this flip was right after Mom died, when Dad fell apart and David aged a decade overnight.

"Are you dying?" My voice comes out high, squeaky, like I've entered reverse puberty.

Felix's hand clamps my shoulder. I lean into the pressure.

"No, I'm not dying." Dad pulls free from David with a quick

squeeze at the base of my brother's neck. "The doc tells me my prostate's decided to get a little funky, is all."

Felix stalks into the family room, fingers stabbing into his hair. David rocks back against the sink counter, uncaring of the glass and booze carnage. He looks like how I feel.

As though someone's sucker punched me and I can't breathe right.

"Shit, I'm making a hash of this. I'm sorry." Dad closes his eyes as he takes a deep breath. "It comes at me in waves, missing your mom. Some days I don't think of her at all, which feels like betrayal and relief all in one go. Other days I'm so damned angry she isn't here to help me with this. With you."

"It's okay, Dad. We know. We've all bitched her out for leaving us a few hundred times," David says. "Tell us what's going on. How can we help?"

Dad and David hold an actual conversation with nouns and verbs, questions and replies.

The words wash through the room, maybe one in ten sticking in my ear canal for longer than a half second.

Monitor the situation. Risk. Cautious optimism. Treatment options. Recovery.

Felix wanders back, knocks down his first shot of scotch. He leans over the bar to grab the bottle and pours himself a hefty second serving.

I sit in a haze, mind and body inhabiting two separate planes.

Cancer.

Dad is bigger than life. True blue, steady, honest, and decent. The one I can count on no matter what.

Funny, I thought Mom's death was the worst thing that could ever happen.

Keep your wars and famines. Life without my spirited, sweet, smart mother drained the world of its color.

Lately, that color has been seeping back. Hair, first blue then green then pink, a kaleidoscope of shades. Red power suit, tailored to cut a man off at the knees. Green thong wrapped around my wrist, reassuring and snug.

Brown eyes laughing at me, teasing and luminous.

All the Keiras of the rainbow, each hue another jab waking me up from too many years of going through the motions, sleepwalking on empty while pretending I had it all together.

Now this.

Dad's news threatens to plunge me back into the deep end of the gray scale.

Felix-style, I down the contents of my tumbler in one long, open-throated gulp and resolutely pour another dose of numbing agent.

I'm not ready. I'll never be ready. Not for this. So tonight, I'll let the booze handle my emotion.

Felix knocks the base of his glass into mine in wordless solidarity.

Sheepdog caretaker that he is, David collects a replacement tumbler for Dad, the Johnnie Walker bottle, and us, shuffling our shell-shocked selves into the pillowy embrace of the family room's oversized couches. Next, he fetches water and the after-party tray the caterers make for us each year for midnight fridge-raiding, a holdover of Mom's foresight from when we were teens with tapeworms for bellies.

"Fuck cancer," David raises his glass.

It takes us a minute, but my brother keeps his arm stretched out, patient and determined. He's not going to let us retreat to our corners.

We fall like dominoes to his persuasion, lifting our glasses to his, first me then Dad then, finally, Felix.

"Fuck cancer," we say as one, Mom's old battle cry I thought we'd buried with her.

The scotch disappears in a blink, and we thunk the tumblers on the coffee table like we're in some kind of Russian mafia drink off. David pours the next round.

Yeah, this liver-pickling fest is going down.

CHAPTER 28

KEIRA

"Cough it up, sister," Helena says, twisting in the confines of her seat belt toward the back seat to give me a thorough examination. "Are you and Connor official now?"

"Define official."

"Oh, for crying out loud, are you two dating or what?"

"The clever SOB tricked me into a test date. You tell me whether that's official."

"A test date? What the hell is that?" Mateo asks. "I don't understand all these newfangled mating rituals. An old-fashioned bar hookup was good enough back in my day."

"Your day. That was all of a year ago." I can hear Helena's eye roll. "Who says the hookup was the determining factor, huh? Maybe the hookup was beside the point. Maybe it was that I realized I couldn't live another moment without a man who can talk dirty to me about quarterly financial projections."

As my bestie and her fiancé seduce each other all over again with ROIs and mortgage rates, I picture the Mack family by the pool,

Connor letting out a huge whoop as his dad announces his new role as lead on the Winstonian restoration.

Felix pops the cork on a celebratory beverage. David slaps Connor on the back with congratulations before shoving him into the deep end with an evil, doting, big-brother grin. Celia tosses in a floatation device, half-helpful, half-teasing. Connor rises from his dunking, shaggy-dog shakes to get everyone wet, and claims the first glass for the toast.

The details might be off but probably not by much.

Their family bonds run counter to everything I learned about family growing up. Passing out support and pride in achievement without expecting a return? A human interaction that is not a transaction? Unthinkable.

My parents always look for leverage. Over me, over their competitors. Even their business partners. They use whatever and whoever they can to achieve their goals. No doubt, they'd see my growing relationship with Connor as something to exploit.

Which is why I'll never relax the distance I keep between us. Bad enough I polluted Connor's air with talk about them today. Maybe letting down my guard to do a trust fall into the embrace of a nice guy didn't flip the world on its axis or conger my parents into existence in a puff of acrid smoke, but some boundaries are meant to stay in place.

Tomorrow, the tides will go in. Or out. Or whatever tides do. The sun will continue to blaze through its perpetual summer hot flash.

And I will not let my parents steamroll over my life. Never again.

I begin sketching the outline of our date. Glossy, over-the-top, vintage Hollywood rom-com material. He wants romance? Flowers? Wooing? I'm bringing it. Tenfold.

At least for the night. No need to get ahead of ourselves. It's just a test date, after all. Just an As If practice drill.

Are heart palpitations dancing around like jumping beans a common occurrence in the dating world? I wipe my hands down my thighs. Dinner. Dates usually include dinner. I flip through all the high-end restaurants I know, axing one after the other. No, we don't need luxury.

We need Sully's.

A trip to our usual stomping grounds, but this time with no sneaking into the restroom like we have something to hide. Or more, like I have something to. Pretty sure he'd engrave a sign and attach it to the wall behind the bar to let the world know we're on a date.

With each other.

Damn it, how can that sound both appealing and scary at the same time?

I thump Helena's seat.

"What?" She breaks from cooing about spreadsheets. Mateo fidgets with the neck of his T-shirt. Huh. Who knew pivot tables could be so stimulating?

"I'm not ready to use the O word, but I've decided I'm taking him to Sully's for the dinner part of our date, so give me some points for being willing to go public."

She squeals, undoing her seat belt and launching into the back seat for a tackle hug. I return the embrace as much as I'm able with her arms and legs wrapped around me like a boa constrictor.

"I'm so happy for you." She mashes a noisy buss on my cheek.

"It's just a test date. Could be a disaster." I can't help adding the warning.

"Whatever, Eeyore." She loosens the hug to settle into my side.

Helena has always been comfortable with casual touch. From the very start of our friendship, she ignored my fifty-yard personal space boundaries as though they were nonexistent. Until Connor, she was the only one in my life who ever touched me with simple affection. I lean into her, more grateful than words could convey. She pats my hand. She knows.

"Regardless of how the test dates goes or how many test dates you have to run through before you decide to give the relationship an official label, I'm glad you and King Con found each other," Mateo says.

"Why's that?" I ask. "I mean, surely Helena has shared I don't exactly have a stellar track record when it comes to the girl-boy dance. I'd think you'd be laying down the law about not fucking up your best friend."

"I guess because you're nothing like the woe-is-me princesses he's always gone for, starting with little Libby Leidecker in kindergarten right through to Sherry. You won't let him carry the whole load of the relationship like you're too precious to wreck your manicure. I think you'd pop him a good one, metaphorically speaking, if he even tried."

"I hope you're right."

"Don't worry." Helena pats my thigh. "As in incentive for not fucking up, keep in mind I'll stick you with forty jillion more wedding-related tasks if you do. You'll have plenty of time to regret the error of your ways while you're running around town, trying to appease The Moms."

"I'm shaking in my flip-flops."

We hit Manhattan, and Mateo navigates to my neighborhood, pulling up to my skanky apartment building.

"This dump is an affront to real estate." Helena wrinkles her nose.

"It's close to a subway, and my favorite coffee shop is down the street. Location, location, location, right?" I deflect. "Besides, the rent's cheap. Depending on how things go with Rat Bastard and my parents this week, I may need to live lean for a while."

"You know we won't let you starve. Or get evicted," Helena says, only half teasing. "You're talking with Brad tomorrow?"

"That's the plan. If he gets his head out of his ass, we may be able to salvage our working relationship. If not, then the Magic 8 Ball says I'm striking out on my own sooner than anticipated."

"Proud of you, lady." Helena bumps her shoulder into mine. "Whatever happens, you can walk tall knowing you dealt with this situation exactly the opposite of how your parents would."

"Professional ethics for the win." I play air guitar with mad chops. Helena and Mateo laugh.

"Let us know how it goes," he says, ducking out of the way as Helena climbs from the back seat to the front. "In fact, come over for dinner tomorrow. I'll chill some champagne. Consolation or celebration, we gotcha covered."

"You guys." I wipe away a faux tear with my knuckle and sniff. "You like me. You really like me."

"No, honey. We're family, and we love you," Helena corrects me gently. "Now go tuck yourself in and dream sexy dreams about Connor."

My phone buzzes from the depths of my beach bag as I unlock my apartment door's fourth dead bolt. Connor. A warm fuzzy swirls in my bloodstream, leaving me tingly. The man couldn't wait a full two hours.

I could get used to being the one Connor reaches for first regardless of how long we've been apart.

I slow-walk my homecoming routine, stretching out my anticipation. Lock the door, triple check the bolts, shuck my shoes. I trail keys, sunglasses, a lightweight sweater in my wake as I set course for the couch.

"Camuel, looks like Helena was right." I flip on my lava lamp and set the beach bag on the floor. "Approaching sex with my no-strings battle plan was doomed to fail."

From his nest among my jewel-toned throw pillows, my stuffed camel stares at me, his permanent half-mast gaze taking me in with sleepy nonjudgement. I wiggle into my cozy spot on the couch, curling an arm around his skinny neck and landing a kiss on his cute bulbous nose.

"Sext first, ask on date second, or vice versa?" My strong, silent dromedary allows me to work out the answer for myself, though he does give me a little side-eye. "Yeah, okay. I'm not sure what I was thinking either. Of course, sext first. Sheesh."

Connor's staying in his childhood bedroom.

Digging for my phone, I speed through possible scenarios, landing on stern lady of the manor and naughty cabana boy.

"Cammie, I think I have our theme for the night."

Camuel keeps his dignified peace. I turn his face to the wall to spare him his blushes.

General Hoo-ha begins to tingle in preparation for the fun to come, sensations zip-zapping through my insides and tripping my breath. I'm light, floating and giddy.

I'm planning a date with a nice guy, and we're about to embark on sexy times via text.

How normal. How astounding.

I polish the screen on the hem of my sundress, dragging the

moment out, teasing myself with a little short-term denial the way I would Connor during a scene.

"All right. Let's do this thing." Big breath. In. Out. Unlock.

Sunday, 10:42 p.m.

> Bastard, Rat: Canceling tomorrow. Resched to Tuesday @ 8 a.m.

> Keira: Brad, we need to talk.

> Bastard, Rat: And we will. Tuesday.

"Aaand, end scene."

I'm tempted to reply with a poop emoji followed by I QUIT.

Instead, I send him confirmation of receipt. There was a time not so long ago, I'd have shot him a middle-finger emoji, cracked a joke, and reassured him I could, indeed, wait—or argued why waiting was impossible. Whatever I thought was the right course of action to stay on track with our business goals. Tonight, his brush-off settles on my back like that final piece of straw.

I'm done.

Scrunching deeper into the couch, I reposition Camuel beside me before pinging Jessica to arrange a breakfast meeting for the two of us tomorrow.

With her salute-emoji reply, Operation New Real Estate Group with New and Improved Terms is officially a go.

"I should probably think deep thoughts about how my life is changing, Cammie, but I'm gonna ask my guy on a date instead." I nod Camuel's head up and down for him. "Glad you approve."

I text Connor, asking him to meet me at seven on Wednesday evening at the Central Park entrance at Columbus and 59th. Well, tell him, really, having left off a *will you* and a question mark.

Close enough.

While waiting for him to reply, I build the first-date flower offering in an app they've got for that, aiming for quantity, quality, and maximum scent. Flower-level achievement unlocked, I pull up the business plan I've been piecing together on and off for years, a vision for my future that's deliberately the opposite of anything my parents and Brad would recognize as a road map to success.

I nibble my thumbnail in between making minor edits. I'm good at selling real estate and throwing attitude. Persuading people to follow me into the unknown? That's a stretch. But damn if I'm not ready to As If this dream into reality and do my best to lead a kick-ass team there with me. Bringing Jessica onboard will be my first test.

An hour and a half later, my eyes are bleary, and I haven't heard back from Connor.

"That must be some celebration the Mack clan is tying on, Cammie. Think this calls for a razzing in the morning?"

Keeping his own counsel, my support camel hitches a ride to the bedroom on my shoulder and waits patiently as I prep for sleep.

"Brilliant, Cam, as usual," I say as I slip into my sheets. "This is indeed a perfect setup for stern principal and naughty student. I wonder if Connor still has his high school uniform tie?"

CHAPTER 29

CONNOR

Monday morning, Dad and I lie on a pair of loungers under the trellis by the pool, nursing morning-after recovery sludge, an old family recipe that tastes like dog but works miracles. I welcome the suck of our hangovers, the perfect excuse to drift in a "why did we think that was a good idea" haze. No need to get chatty or bare our feelings.

Hey, Dad, I hope you don't die?

Hey, old man, what the hell do you mean, bringing cancer back to our family?

Hey, dude, I'm kinda scared. Are you scared too?

With a glance through the open folding glass doors, I check if David or Felix are stirring yet, maybe grubbing up some eats. Between David's caretaker gene and Felix's cooking class hobby, one of them usually pulls the hangover breakfast-prep short straw.

Better them than me. My egg game is pretty pathetic.

"Celia and David headed out a while ago," Dad rumbles in a voice not ready to be awake. "Felix was passed out in his room last I checked. You're stuck with me, kiddo."

"You want I should attempt eggs?" I ask.

His crack of laughter makes us both wince.

I turn my reflexive probe to see whether my head's still attached into a suave hair pat. Dad and I share a grin when I catch him pulling the same move. What did Keira say about chips and blocks?

"It's not that bad, Connor." He resettles on his lounger. "We caught the cancer in good time, and I have a stellar medical team in place."

"No cancer is good."

"No. No one's saying cancer is good. I'm saying this isn't equivalent to your mother's situation, so don't go down that rabbit hole. We're going to have enough trouble with Felix."

"Nice deflection, Pops." I raise my mug in salute. "Leaving my completely justifiable anxiety aside for the moment, any idea what's going on with him and Lily?"

"Maybe." He massages the bridge of his nose. "His story to tell, not mine. I just wish he…"

"He what?"

"I wish he had half your resilience."

"What do you mean? Felix is Mr. Stoic. I think he uses stone grit as a mixer. I'm here one step away from bawling my eyes out."

"You're proving my point. Felix stuffs things down and muscles through with his face stuck in front of a screen. That's not coping, that's avoidance."

"Whereas crying like a baby is the height of emotional maturity."

"I'm saying that at some point this week, you're going to tag Mateo, and the two of you are going to whack the crap out of a bouncing squash ball. You're going to charm your girl. You're going to hang out with your brothers and keep scheming ways to treat your old man like a geezer without letting on that you're handling me. Good luck with that, by the way. You're going to dive into the Winstonian project headfirst, and the thrill of a new challenge is going to balance your anxiety about my health." He reaches over to give my shoulder a squeeze-shake. "It's taken a while, sure, but in the years since Mom's death, you went and built yourself a full, balanced life. I'm proud of you."

A stinging sensation hits my nose and the backs of my eyes. Swallowing over the knot lodged halfway down my throat hurts like a mofo, but I do it anyway, a series of reflexive twitches geared toward keeping the saltwater sloshing around my sinuses from leaking down my face.

My brain catches up with my ears after a moment. I twist up and around until I sit facing Dad. My mouth flaps open and closed a couple times before the jumble of words in my head line up to something intelligible.

"Did you just sneakily tell me I got the project?"

"Didn't think that would get past you for long." Dad salutes me with his mug. "I should have told you before, but the prostate thing knocked my plans for a loop."

"You're really going to be okay?" I ask for the third or sixth or twenty-eighth time.

"Yes, I'm really going to be okay," he says, using the same patient tone he had when I was a kid badgering him at bedtime for one more story from the Mack family vault of colorful characters. "I've cleared Project Room Three. Your assistant's been working with me to get it set up with the basics of what you'll need to get started."

"Thanks." The single word seems an inadequate acknowledgement of his faith in me. I look off to the side and cough to clear the sudden block in my throat. "When this puppy's done, Mack Family Architects is gonna clean up on the awards circuit and win us a ton of new business. I promise."

"Never change, Connor, never change. You, conquering the world, is one of my favorite things."

We exchange manly "I'm not emotional, you're emotional" mug clinks, sip, and grimace. Dog is an unfortunate flavor of beverage.

I settle back into my lounger, brain teeming with lists and first steps.

"I like Keira," Dad says after a few minutes. "Things between you getting serious?"

"Think so. Hope so. She's gun-shy about relationships. Hell, so am I after the mess I made of things with Sherry."

"I don't recall you being the one who made the mess."

I shrug a noncommittal shoulder.

"You crashed and burned with a woman who wasn't interested in being an adult." Dad plants his feet on the ground, leaning into the space between us. "Your pain but ultimately her loss. Chalk it up as a lucky miss, and let her memory go."

"Easy to say, Pops."

"You're right. But letting go would be easier if you take your blinders off and allow yourself to see the truth. Sherry couldn't hack you paying attention to anyone but her. Not even your dying mom. That's not on you. You deserve someone who has the chops to walk by your side through thick and thin."

"Like you and Mom."

He smiles, his body losing some of its tautness. "Like your mom and me, yeah."

"Keira has some booby traps we're working on diffusing, but I'm pretty sure she has titanium chops underneath."

"She strikes me as a woman with a good head on her shoulders. Plus, she laughs at your jokes. Don't underestimate the intimacy of humor. Gets you through a lot of hard times. With the added bonus that if you get good enough at it now, by the time kids come along, you'll be able to embarrass the hell out of them with practically no effort."

I groan. He chuckles.

My headache is fading, and my inner terrain starts to match the day, bright and filled with endless possibility. I yawn and stretch, finally able to enjoy the sun on my face.

"David told me this morning you want to use the beach house for Mateo and Helena's engagement party."

"David has a big mouth." I shift until I sit facing him. "I wasn't going to ask, given the circumstances."

"You know better than that. A little cancer treatment can't stop a Mack family party. Especially since you'll be doing the work. All I'll need is to show up and look pretty."

"Thanks." I catch his gaze. "You swear you're going to be all right?"

"I promise." His blue-gray eyes pierce me with fierce-dad sincerity. "No way am I letting my boys escape routine mortification from their father a minute sooner than absolutely necessary."

"Okay then." The threat of decades more teasing brings a comfort that none of his doc talk has managed.

"Let's go wake Felix. I'll play the invalid card and guilt him into making us some brekkie. I could eat a horse with a side of bacon." He scruffs the top of my head, chuckling when I curse and duck away. "We'll get through this, Con. Concentrate on Keira, the party, and the Winstonian. Don't worry about me."

By the time we rouse Felix, David and Celia have returned with all the fixings for a full brunch. Felix launches into short-order cook mode, and we end up gathered around the kitchen table, comfort eating through the afternoon, sharing family stories and memories of Mom. Felix suggests names for Celia and David's baby. Everything from Junior, which I argue vociferously against, to Leonidas to Myrtle to Flossie. The post-party party breaks up when Celia bounces her balled-up napkin off Felix's nose and announces it's time for a nap.

We're all secretly happy she made it through a meal without barf-ing, so we don't voice a peep when David cuts out on his share of the cleanup to fuss over her.

After a shower, I'm ready-ish for the real world and power up my cell. Emails and texts download in a cascade of pings and buzzes.

Mateo wants to hit the court on Thursday. Damn, Dad called it. I shoot Matty a yes and zip through the rest of the easy stuff. Yes, no, later, never, I'll get back to you. My thumbs race over the screen to clear my path. Last, I set up time with my assistant early tomorrow morning to settle into our new project room.

After dealing with the have tos, I turn to the one true want to in my queue—a slew of texts from Keira.

My thumbs hang in the air over her name.

She's not Sherry. Not a drama queen, not an attention hog, not someone who'll rake me over the coals for fucking up my commitment to our nightly texts. Especially once she knows my why.

Still.

What happens when I tell her about Dad?

Sherry and I might only have been engaged for a few months before Mom's cancer diagnosis, but we'd made promises to each other. Dreamed about the future together. And she quit. Flounced away with my ring and my heart.

The prospect of Keira disappearing from my life sours the minty freshness of my toothpaste-flavored mouth. Our relationship is new and, despite all our verbal contract mumbo jumbo, basically undefined. Can it survive the same pressures that imploded my engagement?

A voiceless whisper in my ear says don't tell her.

I knock that piss-poor advice away with an abrupt shift of my shoulders. Hiding shit out of fear isn't the right path forward. I ended up tiptoeing around the hard stuff with Sherry, and my instinct to smooth things over, to avoid conflict, was part of our problem. I'm not on board for a replay of that move. Besides, falling back into that habit would break my promise to tell Keira the truth.

The word brings clarity. Eyes closed, I let the sense of rightness flow through my veins.

Truth is always the answer with Keira.

Sunday, 10:59 p.m.

> Keira: 7 p.m. Wed Centrl Prk Columbus & 59 St. entrance. Be there or else.

Monday, 6:02 a.m.

> Keira: Hey, slugabed. Wake up. You have a date proposal to reply to.

Monday, 6:37 a.m.

> Keira: I think my barista is asking me to top
> him. [picture of cuffed hands made of latte
> foam, accented with small foam heart]

Monday, 10:00 a.m.

> Keira: Must have been some after-party
> celebration for you to stay off your phone this
> long. Congratulations! [party-hat-wearing emoji
> face, confetti emoji, high-five emoji]
>
> Keira: Now text me back, damn it.

Monday, 1:13 p.m.

> Keira: Okay, I get it now. One-way texting
> sucks. [GIF of toddler having a tantrum]
>
> Keira: But once you come back to the land of
> virtual living, here's a hint of what's in store for
> you Wed. nite. [GIF of basketball fans doing
> the wave as a player makes a three-pointer
> and the words he shoots, he scores blinking
> across the bottom in rainbow colors]

Half laughing, half-hard, I punch the call icon instead of texting a reply.

No, this woman is nothing like Sherry. For that, I'll gladly hit my knees to worship at her altar.

Maybe we can play repentant sinner and authoritarian abbess on our date.

"Took you long enough." Her non-hello grumping makes me chuckle.

"Miss me?"

After a brief pause, she says, "Yeah. I did."

"Uh-oh, you copped to a squishy emotion. When did you last eat?"

"Haha. Fuh-ny. I'm not hangry. I want an answer to my invitation."

"You want a 'yes ma'am, sir, ma'am' to your dictatorial order."

"What, that's not the same thing?"

"I missed you too." I sit on the edge of my mattress, wiggling my toes in the carpet pile. Would that I could stay in banter mode and put off my confession for a few decades. "Sorry I didn't respond sooner."

"Don't sweat it. I figured you were caught up in the moment. Tell me everything. Your dad give you the thumbs-up?"

"Yeah, but, ah, that's not why I didn't text. Dad kinda pitched a curveball. We're... we're all, uh, scrambling in the aftermath." I push past the unwelcome tightness in my throat. "So, listen, I'll understand if you want to table the date for another time or, you know, postpone indefinitely."

"How about you explain what's going on before offering me an out?"

"Right, right." I massage my throat, trying to keep it from shutting down completely. Saying the word will make it real all over again. "He's, uh... he's—"

"What is it? What's wrong?" she asks, voice a whipcrack of alarm.

"Dad's got cancer."

"Oh fuck. I'm sorry."

"The doctors caught it early. Prostate." I make a shrug she can't see. "He'll recover fully, they say, but it's..."

"Reminding you of your mom. How could it not?"

"Yeah." I fall backward across my bed. The white ceiling above me is as blank as I'd like to feel. I close my eyes, but scenes from my mom's illness stream behind my eyelids, a too-familiar highlights reel from my nightmares.

"Are you first up on the dad-sitting duty roster?" she asks. "I can imagine the wicked game of rock paper scissors between you and your brothers vying for the privilege."

"It's like you know us."

"I've been paying attention."

"Dad nixed the idea before David could finish suggesting it." I bounce up to pace the confines of my bedroom, crazy ready to do something, anything, to burn this helplessness away.

"Like that's going to stop you." Her dismissive snort echoes the three-way look David, Felix, and I shared when Dad tried laying down the law. "Luckily, until your stealth sentry duty has a chance to kick into full gear, the perfect anti-fret remedy is within your reach."

"And what's that?"

"Duh. A date. With me. And naked smashing." She clears her throat. "Probably naked. We'll see. But definitely smashing. Now, could there be a more effective pitch for a stress-management solution? I don't think so."

"Sold." I'm still fidgety, but now it's anticipation, not helplessness. "I accept your invitation."

"Took you long enough."

CHAPTER 30

KEIRA

atcliffe and Associates is deserted Tuesday morning, with rounded chair backs poking up behind each empty desk like ergonomic gravestones in an urban cemetery.

Jessica's legwork. Our breakfast meeting yesterday lasted until it was time for me to head off to Helena's for dinner. I started off unsure whether I could persuade her to join forces with me. Leaving a bad work environment is one thing. Logical. Maybe even necessary. Leaping into a start-up led by a woman with no track record of running her own shop? Risky. Maybe even foolish.

But she not only stopped my fumbling, convoluted invitation mid-ask with a no-nonsense yes, by the end of our marathon session, we'd hashed out a road map of next steps that included her holding a breakfast meeting today with the rest of the squad to see who wants to take a chance with us.

The lack of people in the office this morning speaks volumes about the current state of affairs.

Not my problem. Not any longer.

Giving myself a shake to ward against any ghosts that might want to haunt me in this spooky, abandoned space, I head to my tiny office to pack up. It doesn't take long. Eight years of work flotsam fills about half of my leather tote. A tin of forgotten breath mints. Some emergency makeup, a box of tampons. The stash of superior fountain pens I hand out to clients as a gift when we go to closing.

No photos, no tchotchkes. Not even an office philodendron.

So little to show after so many years.

I tilt my head back and blink back the prickling behind my eyes.

Leaving Rat Bastard's employ is a Good Thing. See points logical and necessary above.

So why am I getting all sad-sack philosophical?

Connor's fault.

Connor's and Helena's and Mateo's and Jessica's. Instead of leaving my moody ass alone to lead a life heavy on nonfraternization, light on human connection, they started butting into my beeswax, making me laugh and care and come. Okay. Only Connor makes me come.

Still.

Their friendship means I'm no longer doomed to live in the dark. After being lost in my cave for so long, I'm finally touching daylight, and the sun on my face is a kiss of freedom.

I can't hit reverse. Won't face returning to letting the only brightness in my world stem from dyeing my hair and too-rare outings as the third-wheel to my bestie and her beau.

Checking my reflection in the door-mounted mirror—a leftover from the previous holder of this office—I straighten my spine. The whites of my eyes are clear. No telltale red veins or mascara streaks. No puffy lids. My mini freak-out remains my secret, too short to leave a trail. I sleek my hair back. Maybe gray ombré for my date with Connor. Make it fifty shades to honor my transition from the shadows to the light.

I perform one final idiot check of my office. Antiseptic. Drained of even the smallest spark of personality.

Strange how musty the room smells, as if it's already part of the distant past.

In the conference room, I shrug my tote onto a chair and carefully place the manila folder containing my letter of resignation on the table. The modernist wall clock shows it's almost go-time.

Rat Bastard strolls in forty-five minutes late.

"Our meeting was for eight o'clock." I replace the "what the fuck" begging to break loose with a more diplomatic, "What gives?"

"Knew you'd wait." Brad shrugs before taking a seat at the head of the table. "You're predictable that way."

"You mean dependable."

"Do I? Okay. You're dependably predictable." His gaze flicks between the folder and my face. "I admit, I didn't see that potential when you first came sniffing for a job. Couldn't see past the runaway princess with mummy and daddy issues. But your parents assured me your upbringing would kick in once you settled down, and they were right. You became an effective little hustler and made us all a lot of money."

"I don't understand. What did my parents have to do with you hiring me? I never mentioned our connection."

"You really think Julius and Ava Tanner would let their only child travel across the country and not pull strings to see she ended up exactly where they wanted her?"

I blink, stunned mute.

"Think of your time with me as a modern-day form of medieval fostering. You had a place to test your wings, cross-train your skills. In return, I received a healthy stipend and a good little doobie who was willing to sweat but not entitled to equity. The ultimate in business success."

"That's deceit, not success."

"And not worth my time arguing over." He points at the folder. "That your letter of resignation? Or yet another plan to restructure the agency?"

I slide the beige rectangle closer to me, protective of its contents and all at once unsure of… everything.

"Let me save us both some agita," he says. "As of last night, your parents own Ratcliffe and Associates. Talk with them about any new schemes you want to hatch. I'm headed to Antigua."

"You sold out. You sold me out."

"Years ago." He stands, adjusts his tie. "I wouldn't worry, whatever happens. Your parents have big plans for you. My advice? Get rid of the stick up your backside and cultivate a little gratitude for the gilded lily you were born into."

"Gilded cage," I correct in a monotone. "The term is gilded cage."

"See a doctor about that stick, Tanner. No one likes a humorless, moralizing woman."

After his mic drop, Brad leaves. I stare at the far wall, alone in the silence, a statue with clammy palms and a heartbeat fluttering way too fast.

They've done it again, my parents. Decided that their goals, their plans, supersede any of my own. I'm still a pawn to them, a puppet they have free license to manipulate. If what Brad said is true, they never stopped thinking that way. Never stopped meddling in my life.

I close my eyes, but that only magnifies the rush of my racing pulse.

The cheery two-tone chime of an incoming text from Connor spikes my budding freak-out. I take a deep breath and try to release my tension on the exhale.

I'm not a teenager any more, subject to their whims. Starting the new real estate group means I won't be beholden to them for a paycheck. But I need to deal with them. Deal with them before they ooze into other parts of my world, with their judgements and string pulling. I can't let them get anywhere near Connor.

I wouldn't be able to stand it if he were hurt by their manipulations.

My cell rings with a call from Helena.

"How'd it go with Rat Bastard?"

"Somehow worse than even I could imagine." I fill her in on the details.

"I'm sorry, honey. That level of bullshit is hard to fathom. You finally going to let Connor know what's going on?"

"No. Nope. Negativo."

"He's going to find out sooner or later. You're starting a new business! That's not something you hide from your boyfriend!"

"Stop shouting. I'll tell him. Everything. Eventually. You convinced

me of the wisdom of that relationship maintenance nugget last night."
And if her words hadn't, the blob of guilt in the pit of my stomach that
fattens each time I let the opportunity to say something pass by would
have soon enough. "But please, please understand me when I say I
need to fix the situation with my parents before I come clean."

"You know I have your back through thick and thin and stupid
decisions. Connor's going to be hurt you didn't confide in him, but
he'll survive, and you'll make it up to him with chocolate chip cookies
and sex, as nature intended. Now, what's the plan with your parents?
What are you going to do?"

"Grant them their wish. Part of it, at least." I breathe out again,
slow and steady. "I'm going to meet with them. One final time."

CHAPTER 31

CONNOR

"That's it." David makes a gimme demand with his hand across the table at Sully's on Tuesday night. "You've lost your phone privileges for the rest of the night."

"Like hell." I hide my cell on the padded bench beside me after another quick peek shows Keira hasn't texted in the last zero point zero one seconds. "You're not the boss of me."

My brothers and I have taken custody of our usual booth, waiting for Dad and Celia, who are caught in traffic on their way back from a meeting with clients, to show. Beside me, Felix is nose deep in his laptop. Which leaves David—testy because two and a half of his pack are missing—and me—obsessed with checking my texts to see if Keira's responded yet to my latest Dick photo series—to crab at each other.

"Of course, I'm the boss of you." He sends me a pitying look. "Sad how you turn thirty in a week and a half, yet you're still so naïve about the natural world order."

"Gentlemen." Felix flips the laptop closed. "Much as it pains me to trot out the voice of reason—David that's your job, you slacker—remember what happened the last time you fought here."

"Not our fault," David and I say in tandem as Dad and Celia arrive at the table.

"What's probably all your fault?" Celia nudges David deeper into the u of the booth and slips in beside him, her baby bump making it more of a scoot waddle. Dad takes the end of the bench.

"David is having delusions of dictatorhood," I say. "Tell him that he can pry my phone away from my cold, dead hands."

"Were you texting at the dinner table? Tsk, tsk, you know better." Celia steals the pretzel bite from David's hand. He moves the pretzel basket closer to her. Felix nudges the tub of melty cheese within reach.

"How is a phone worse than Felix's laptop?" I inch the mustard forward. "No one ever gets on his case."

"You stopped midsentence to look at your phone." Felix slides his computer into a neoprene sleeve. "Three times."

"Mm, rude," Celia says around a mouthful of pretzel. Looking smug, David swings an arm around her shoulders.

"Now wait a minute—" My phone vibrates, and I check the lock screen. "Okay, uncle. I'll ditch the phone for the rest of the evening, but for the record, it's because I choose to, not because you all ganged up on me."

"It's your brothers' solemn duty to rib you at every opportunity." Dad waves one of the waitstaff over. "But you know the deal, no—"

"Electronic devices at family dinner," my brothers and I singsong.

I stash my phone. Obsessive checking might feel like action, but it's not going to prompt Keira to respond any sooner. I give it a rest so I can join forces with my brothers to convince Dad to agree on some ground rules.

Like letting us come to his treatment on Friday.

"I refuse to be treated like I'm a feeble old man." Dad pushes his plate back. Lasagna, mostly demolished. A forlorn line of cooked carrots decorate the plate's rim. Phew. Normal appetite. But for how long? "Damn it, stop looking at what I ate. I'm not sick."

"You have cancer," David states the obvious.

"It's not the same as your mom's. I'm not losing half my body

weight. My hair's not falling out. I'm just getting a radioactive dick—"
Blushing, Dad cuts a glance at Celia.

"I sense a superhero origin story in the making," she says with a
wink. "But seriously, I think you're going to have to give in on the
honor guard. I'm surprised this crew has let you out of their sight long
enough to use the bathroom."

"Fine." Dad tosses his napkin on the table with a sigh.

"You sound like Felix when he's grumpy," I say.

"Is Felix ever not grumpy?" David asks.

"When am I not grumpy?" Felix demands at the same time.

"Smartasses. Every last one of you." Dad shakes his head. "I'm
going to visit that ridiculous restroom of David's. Alone."

"Don't forget to wash your hands." Felix dodges Dad's mock ear
cuffing, a small grin proving my brother's needle only mostly points to
grumpville.

"That went well," David says.

"Five will get you ten he tries to ditch us Friday morning," Felix
replies.

"No bet," I say. "I'm not losing money on a sure thing."

"We just need to think squirrelly, like he does," David says. "With
three of us, we should manage it."

"Glad you boys have a plan," Celia says. "Now on to more urgent
business. Who wants to share a brownie a la mode?"

"Not me," I snort. "You're a brownie hog. I'm ordering my own."

Back at my condo, I toss the package I've been expecting on the
coffee table and sprawl face forward on the couch, groaning like a
beached whale. My gurgling digestion is interrupted by a buzzing
against my chest. Rolling to my side with another full-belly groan—it's
possible I should have passed on the brownie—I pluck my phone from
my jacket.

And there she is.

Tuesday, 9:03 p.m.

Keira: I had to look these Dicks up, but your secret message was easy to decode. Sargent and York starred on Bewitched. Ergo, you find me bewitching. [witch emoji, magic wand emoji, wink emoji]

Keira: Don't bother trying to tell me any different.

Keira: This is now canon and not up for debate.

Keira: It's been...

Dots bubble like a heartbeat on my screen as she types and types without a message coming through. I flip over to the phone app— maybe a good-night call will save her thumbs from writing a book?— when her next text pops up.

Keira: It's been a day. A long day. I'm headed for bed.

Keira: See you tomorrow night.

Keira: Don't be late. I have plans for you. [GIF of Jessica Rabbit displaying ample side boob as she slinks across a room, come-hither finger curling in demand]

The va-va-voom cartoon is sexy but nearly as captivating as the sender behind the GIF in all her intriguing complexity. Playful, curious, sharp. Unexpectedly tender. I could spend forever exploring her facets and never learn enough.

Connor: Dad and Mom used to watch the reruns. Samantha was cute and all, but Endora was my favorite. Bold, ballsy, and brilliant. Liked to change up her appearance. Kinda reminds of someone…

Connor: Sleep tight. See you in twenty-ish hours.

I break open the package lying patiently on my coffee table and inspect the special tie I hunted down in a fit of inspiration. Running my finger down the cool, smooth fabric, I pause over the sepia-tone quotes silkscreened onto its cream base. Oh yeah. This is subtle, yet mighty, big Dick energy.

Perfect for our first date.

CHAPTER 32

KEIRA

Wednesday evening, I stand near the carriage ride kiosk, passing a florist box from hand to hand. Palms sweaty, back sweaty, nape sweaty.

Annoying that I can't blame my physical state solely on the summer heat.

Why did I give in to Connor's charm and ask him on a date?

A light breeze chases through the air, brushing the hem of my take-no-prisoners dress against my thighs. The silver chiffon kisses my skin, and a pop-up army of goose bumps marauds the length of my body, tickling me into a laugh.

Ah. There's my answer. This dress is going to melt his brains into goo. Goo is good. Goo means he won't have the ability to worry about his dad. Maybe some will rub off on me, and my own doom looping about my parents will stay quiet the rest of the evening so I can sink deeper into enjoying the night I have all mapped out.

Flowers, carriage ride through Central Park, dinner at Sully's, a short stroll to dessert at Buon Gelato, and a room at a hotel in midtown.

Followed by naked banging, smashing, bumping, and grinding.

Naked. I press my stomach, hand spread wide. A squadron of butterflies quiver in reply. Naked can't be that hard. People do it every day.

Hahaha. *Do it.*

I blow a few multishades of gray strands of hair off my face. Connor better arrive before I revert any further into tweenage-virgin humor. Otherwise I might point and laugh when we get to shedding clothes. Poor, trusty Junior does not need to be ribbed like that.

Ribbed. Hehehe.

I shake my head. Two more minutes. Then I'm hunting down a drink and forgetting this whole nudie As If experiment.

"Are you an angel? Because you look like the answer to a prayer," he whispers in my ear, his body close and solid behind me.

"Did you buy that line off a guy selling genuine solid gold wrist-watches? He throw in the Brooklyn Bridge too?"

Ignoring my heckle, Connor traces the crisscross of straps keeping my dress legal, a slow glide that leaves fire in its wake. He ends at my neck, toying with the string bow.

One pull. A quick tug.

That's all it would take.

Air stops up in my lungs. My goose bump army returns with rein-forcements.

"I'm sorry, could you repeat that?" He closes the remaining minis-cule distance between us. "I'm a little distracted."

"Never mind," I say in a rush as I turn. "Kiss me right now, or risk my spontaneous combustion."

"We wouldn't want that."

"We sure as hell—" The rest of my reply is swallowed by his lips settling on mine.

More heat, this time slick and silky and soft. It only takes an instant before we're pressed hard against each other, as close as two fully clothed humans can be.

Immolation is imminent.

I make a hungry, impatient noise. He feathers my bottom lip with tiny licks of his tongue. I curl my ankle around his calf.

Someone clears their throat, the dry, wry cough of a woman who's seen it all yet still finds the world amusing. "You dropped this."

We keep kissing.

"Also, there's a cop giving you the stink eye heading this way. Personally, I think you're adorable, but you might want to cool your jets if you don't want a ticket for public indecency."

Connor retreats. I grab hold of his tie so he can't go far. He smiles, a lopsided quirk of wet, swollen lips.

He likes being claimed. I like claiming him.

"Here." The woman thrusts the dented florist box into my free hand. "Nice taste, honey, I'd climb him like ivy on a pole, too, given half a chance."

One of those New York City elders who wear layers of black to set off their statement jewelry, the woman winks, and strides away in a flutter of scarves. The cop halts his progress but not his stinky eyes. Connor gives the guy a chin nod before shuffling us behind the carriage ride kiosk.

He backs me against the clapboard wall. "Hey."

"Hey." My heart pumps in a souped-up cha-cha-cha. "That went a little sideways."

"Not quite sideways enough." He adjusts the fit of his slacks.

"Perv."

"Horny perv," he agrees with a wink.

Happy sighing, I fiddle with the tie I've yet to relinquish, skimming over the design without taking it in. I smooth and tuck until he's presentable and I'm simmering with need but no longer in danger of boiling over.

"Right. Time to go over our agenda."

"Our date has an agenda?" Laughter dances in his blue eyes.

"Did you expect any different?"

"Now that you ask, not especially. Wouldn't want it any different, either."

We share smug smiles, pleased with each other.

"If at any point you wish to amend, delete or otherwise alter the agenda, speak up and we'll negotiate an alternative."

"Acknowledged." He inches forward, shaving the scant space between us by half. "Lay it on me."

"First, romantic carriage ride through Central Park with flowers, hand-holding, coy flirtation, and innuendo-laden banter."

"Sounds promising."

"Second, dinner and dessert." I double tap his chest. "If you play your cards right, there might be foot canoodling."

"What're the odds of foot canoodles segueing into knee squeezes and thigh pets?"

I purse my lips. "Pretty good. Frankly, I anticipate a near one-hundred-percent probability of some initial forays into thigh territory while we're crossing item one off the list."

"I'm in agreement so far. Continue."

"Third, we'll repair to a hotel and practice getting our naked monkey sex swerve on."

"One question." His dancing eyes turn crafty.

"What?"

"Any chance we can reverse the order of the agenda? Start at the hotel and work our way back?"

"This date was your idea, buster." I thump his arm. "But by all means, let's junk my sweat equity."

His gaze gentles, and he kisses my nose. Rather than be charmed by the tacit apology, I cross my arms and grump at a nearby shrub.

"*Vices are sometimes only virtues carried to excess,*" he whispers against my neck before suckling the delicate skin below my ear. "Blame my overeager enthusiasm on a predilection for eating dessert first. I fucking can't wait to eat you."

"Hmmph."

"I approve your agenda as submitted, Generalissima, ma'am." He nibbles his way to my mouth and lands a quick kiss before stepping back. "Might the contents of that box be for me?"

CHAPTER 33

CONNOR

Keira tilts the florist box, brows furrowed as though wondering where it came from. So fierce, so uncertain. So game for making this whole As If thing her bitch despite her misgivings.

My insides flop over in happy surrender.

"Here." She shoves the box at me.

I open the lid and start laughing.

"You wanted flowers. Boom. Flowers." She points at the floral behemoth in the box. "Crazy-romantic, first-date flowers."

"Roses and orchids and lilies, oh my," I say, batting my eyes. Charcoal and silver ribbons wind through the pale white blossoms, echoing the grayscale rainbow of Keira's hair and the shimmer of her I-almost-swallowed-my-tongue-at-first-sight dress. "It's a stunner of a boutonnière."

"Boutonnière? You think I'd go through the hassle of outfitting you with flowers, and end up with a mere boutonnière? Yeah, no. This puppy is a full-on man corsage. You'll wear it and like it, you got that?"

"Yes, ma'am."

Head bowed to hide the fierce *fuck yeah* searing through me, I wait as patiently as I can for her to pin me with blooms worthy of a Kentucky Derby winner.

There's no question she's turned us into a matchy-matchy couple for the evening. Or that she's trying to brush the flowers off as an elaborate gag.

But this painstaking attention to detail is no joke.

It's proof she cares. That our date is important to her too. I refrain from stealing another bone-dissolving kiss—we have an agenda to follow, after all—but it's tough.

"There. All set." She cocks her head to admire her handiwork.

"Thank you. *I will honor this in my heart and try to keep it all the year.*" Hand to heart, I make a half bow.

"You're being weird. How is it you make that so appealing?" Muttering under her breath, she stalks toward the carriages.

I straighten the knot of my literary tie and follow in her wake, filled with great expectations for the night.

Despite early rumors of leg petting, ten minutes into the ride, we're struggling. She makes a comment about the weather. I agree it's very weathery. I say something about the Yankees. She nods like she gives two hoots about the Yankees. I fight the urge to tap my foot. She picks at the plaid blanket wedged between us that no lovebirds in their right minds would cuddle under during a summer heat wave.

Civil. Mature. We're adulting the shit out of this first date.

It's tedious as hell.

Thankfully, the horse farts.

"What died?" Keira croaks, pinching her nose, waving her free hand in a futile effort to fend off the attack. My eyes water against the sting.

"Me poor Mauvereen's been a wee gassy this week, alas," our driver says over his shoulder. "Usually, 'tis a short-lived t'ing."

We're pummeled with another swell of pony pong. I sneeze and sneeze some more. I swear the orchids in my corsage shrivel.

"That's it. Pull over. We're done," Keira says, wheezing.

"You sure, lass? I'm after reminding you there'll be no refunds for incomplete rides."

"Don't care. I'm not willing to go blind from the stench. Pull up, buddy, and let us off this unholy toot wagon."

We're gifted with another ass belch. This time even the driver shudders.

The carriage comes to a stop, and Keira races for the other side of the path as though the whole contraption is moments away from exploding. I clamber down and join the driver at the unsmelly end of poor Mauvereen, where he's whispering encouragement to her in a Bronx accent.

"She going to be okay?" I ask.

"Yeah, yeah. She's fine. Like I said, a little gassy. It'll pass eventually, if you know what I mean." He elbows me in the side in case I'm slow on the uptake. "She's just tired of the heat. Aren't you, pretty baby num-num face?"

"Glad she'll be all right." I pass him a twenty. "Maybe you can get her a ginger ale or the equine equivalent. Something to settle her tummy."

"Thanks, man. Poor Mo's sorry she ruined your night."

"Ruined? You underestimate us, my friend." I take in Keira, who's shaking her head at me, the hint of a smile gracing her lips. "Our night can only go up from here."

She bursts out with laughter as I approach. I catch her in my arms, swirling us in a circle as her joy breaks free to tickle the treetops. I may not know why she's frothy with giggles, but I could spend the rest of the night, maybe the rest of time, spinning loops with her face shining up at me. Her stomach growls, though, and I follow the cue to bring us in for a landing.

"You can't help it, can you?" she asks as her feet hit the ground.

"Help what?"

"Being nice." She hooks her thumb toward the carriage. "That guy played us, and you tipped him."

"Not his fault Mo's having an off night."

"Not your responsibility to help pay his vet bill."

"'Tis love that makes the world go round, my baby." I etch a circle in the air with my finger. "I merely did my bit to keep it going."

Frowning, she studies me like she can't quite figure out what I'm up to but knows it's something. I smooth my tie.

"You're a nut." She shakes her head. "An odd, thoroughly nice nut."

"Oh no." I catch her shoulders. "No, no. Please, do not label me Connor Nice Nuts. Not with my brothers. Family dinners would be agony for the rest of time. I'd have to emigrate."

"It has a certain ring, though, you gotta admit." Devious. Her smile is positively devious.

"Nope. Uh-uh. We're not making this a thing. We're moving on to item two on our date agenda. Dinner, dessert, and thigh pets. What fine-dining establishment have you chosen for us? Something French, exclusive, and *je ne sais quois*-y? Or Italian, dramatic, with wax-covered Chianti bottles and a wandering troubadour?"

"Not even in the ballpark of close." She rocks toes to heels, chockful of delicious secrets and ready to burst. "But I guarantee you'll like it."

"I pretty much like everything you dish up. Carry on." We stroll toward one of the park exits, heading toward Fifth Avenue, and I thread our fingers together. My pulse jumps when she gives a squeeze of welcome. "How's your week going? From your text last night, I get the impression your boss's mystery clients are still running you ragged. Any sign of a light at the end of that tunnel?"

A dog barks. Some kids shout. Nearby, someone starts tuning a guitar. The park showing up for its early evening shift as we walk, and I wait for Keira's reply.

"You could say that, though the end won't come soon enough for me." She kicks a pebble off the path with enough force to make me wonder if it's a stand-in for her boss. "How about you? How's your dad? And the new project. Are you sinking or swimming?"

"We ganged up on the old man last night. Convinced him to let us come to his first treatment. In retaliation, he gleefully overmanaged me today. A fair trade."

After we flag down a cab, she asks a follow-up, and—responding to her obvious desire for a conversational pivot—I geek out over historical blueprints, archival photos of the Winstonian's construction, and the push-pull between preservation, restoration, new technology, and ensuring the usability of space for the next generation. That leads us into a philosophical debate about the future of the Manhattan real estate market.

One topic blends into the next and the next and the next.

It's the kind of exchange Sherry and I never practiced, this wide-ranging exploration of passions, the mundane, dreams, and daily grind. Things that leave us breathless with awe, speechless with anger, or shaking our heads over evidence of the world's more-than-occasional whatthefuckery.

"I closed four sales over a weekend within my first two months at the agency," she says on the way to our ultrasecret dinner location.

"Overachiever."

"Says the pot. That weekend changed my life. I'd been mired in a tub of self-pity since relocating here after college. Helena ordered me to get my head out of my ass before I was evicted and forced to shame sleep on her couch."

"With friends like that—"

"Who needs therapy?" Grinning, she knocks shoulders with me. "She made me mad. I'm grateful. Those two days gave me a taste of my potential, of who and how I wanted to be outside of the world I was raised in. I got good at it. Then I got better. And I'll get better yet, you watch."

"Have I ever mentioned how much I like to watch?"

"Again with the pervitude."

"Just keeping it real."

Our cab stops, and she slips a credit card from the neckline of her dress with a "don't even think about it" slant of her brows when I reach for my wallet. Distracted by the sneak peek of her shimmery platinum bra, I miss a prime opportunity to pretend complain about being a kept man, too busy proving my point about my viewing pleasures.

I tumble out of the vehicle behind her, not paying attention to where we are, meditating on the uncanny architecture of women's intimate apparel.

"Damn it." She stops short. "Of all the nights."

"What's wrong?" I rip my gaze from her near-naked back.

A sign on the door of Sully's reads "Closed for Staff Outing. Play Ball!"

"Sully's? Our grand romantic date night dinner was going to take place at Sully's?"

"I thought you'd appreciate the symbolism." She jerks her shoulder. "A different kind of naked."

CHAPTER 34

KEIRA

"But you know what? Forget it. This date is cursed." First, the poison gas attack in the park. Next, the staff at Sully's goes AWOL. And now Connor thinks it's a lame date location to boot. "We should just cancel."

"Trifles make the sum of life," he intones, adding to his growing collection of weirdisms for the evening. Before I can comment, he tilts my chin up with his forefinger. "I was no English major, but I'm down for naked in any form it takes. Allegorical, skin, whatever."

He kisses me, gentle fusion, affectionate pressure. The urgency from earlier is missing. Instead there's comfort and familiarity.

A learned knowledge of each other's ins and outs.

If I lick here, his lips quirk in a half smile. When I steal into his mouth, his tongue welcomes mine, a raspy glide with playful tickles. If he pulls me close, I give him my weight. When I encircle his wrists, his shoulders relax.

It's new, this ability to anticipate, to coax pleasure based on knowledge, not theory.

The kiss spins long and lazy and thoroughly luscious.

I could bliss out standing here until Sully's reopens. But my stomach renews its ruckus, and this time Connor's belly grumbles in peckish sympathy.

"Trifles make the sum of life, eh?" I ask, releasing his wrists with reluctance. "Would that be the dessert kind of trifle?"

"Naturally. Imagine the whipped cream."

"Mm. Whipped cream. Okay, I'm sold. What would you say about dessert for dinner?"

"I'd say I like that suggestion about as much as I like naked. Which would be a lot."

"Fantastic. There's this yummy little hole-in-the-wall place around the corner—"

"Buon Gelato? It went out of business last week."

"Of all the— You've got to be kidding me. This is ridiculous. It's like fate doesn't want tonight to succeed."

"*Injustice breeds injustice.*" He adjusts his already perfectly straight tie. "Maybe fate wants us to fast-forward to hotel hijinks."

"I'm halfway tempted to accuse you of date espionage."

"Innocent party, I swear." He curls a strand of hair behind my ear, his intent blue eyes taking my measure. "I understand your goal here. No hiding behind louvered toilet stall doors. No pretending to be cool when we're running hot. The man corsage was a fun, funny way to stake out your territory, but I see that bringing us to Sully's signals something different. Something more. I see you."

My throat shuts down. I swallow. I glance here, there. Everywhere but at Connor. Of course he gets my gesture. Had I really thought he wouldn't? No. Still, I'm no more comfortable with emotional nudity than I am with physical. When I open my mouth to reply, nothing comes out.

"*From the death of each day's hope, another hope springs up to live,*" he says, using a late-night deejay voice. "I move we amend the agenda and see if this hotel has whipped cream on the a la carte menu."

There he goes again, rushing in to save me, my modern-day knight gallant.

Right. Time to shag him silly. And naked.

I grab his hand and stride in the direction of our hotel.

"Oh, are we suddenly in a hurry?"

"Shut it." I accelerate, pictures of whipped-cream-covered Connor dancing in my head until we're jogging. One more block, turn left, and… I stop short as we hit a police barricade. "Holy what the hell?"

"Flash mob?"

"Some kind of mob."

Blue cop-car lights strobe the mass of humanity rubbing up on each other as if their body friction alone powered the city's grid. A slow jam celebration of hot nights and midnight rain throbs in the air, dirty and demanding. Certain hollow parts within me throb in sympathy.

"That's our objective." I point to the entrance of the hotel where the swarm is densest.

"And our plan of attack, Generalissima?"

"Operation Dance, Dance Infiltration. Your mission, should you choose to accept it—and you better—is to sneak us through enemy territory and into the green zone of the hotel."

"Roger that, ma'am."

Eyes alight with equal parts humor and hunger, he drags my hands over his chest to rest on his shoulders. He begins to sway, his lean hips coaxing and seductive, until I match his rhythm. We bump, grind, and rub our frictional way through the mosh pit, laughing and sweating and snatching kisses.

By the time we get to the hotel entrance three songs later, I'm a slick, panting mess.

The controlled chaos from outside carries into the lobby. So many lanyards. So many tote bags. Any other time, I might enjoy people watching with Connor, the two of us coming up with ridiculous groups in need of a conference. The Society of Cream Pie Makers and Consumers. The Association of Ale-swilling Arachnophobes.

But not tonight. I've hit my limit on delayed gratification, and there will be no laughing until gratification is well and duly shagged.

"May I assist you?" the middle-aged dude behind the counter asks.

"Reservation for Tanner." I reel off the confirmation number, and the front-desk attendant starts tapping away at his keyboard.

"You smell like my favorite flavor of delicious." Connor nuzzles my hair.

My skin tingles. My nipples pinch tight. I press against his erection, more than ready to grab our keys and find our room.

"Looks like you're early for your reservation," the attendant says with a grin.

"How do you mean? I thought check-in was three o'clock."

"Our system shows your reservation isn't until next month."

"That's impossible." I retrieve my phone from boob valet and check the emailed confirmation. "Son of a mother."

"What can you get us into tonight?" Connor flashes a little change-your-mind green. "We'll take a no-view double if that's all you have."

"Hey, I'm as susceptible to bribes as the next guy, but no dice. We are booked with a capital B." The dude waves to the hoopla on the street. "Word got out that a certain band is staying here while they're in town. Cue a room sellout. Add the three conferences already scheduled, and we have a more-than-full house. As do the hotels within a five-block radius. Spillover effect." He shrugs with a sympathetic "whatcha gonna do" smile.

"This date is cursed, cursed, I tell you." My stomach seconds my opinion, taking the opportunity to growl loudly enough to wake the dead.

"Hangry? Now, that I can help with." The attendant returns to his clickety-clacking, determined stare burning holes into his monitor. "Since you're a valued rewards member, it's our pleasure to comp you to appetizers and drinks for two at Bar 360 on the fifty-first floor." The printer beside him spits out a sheet of paper.

"Thanks, buddy." Connor accepts the voucher and slips the man a gratuity. "Guac and a cold one will go a long way to resuscitating date night."

"You're very welcome. Enjoy, and we'll see you back here next month." The attendant beams with thanks and well-earned pride. I still want to hit him.

Not his fault. I want to hit everything right now.

We make our way through the crowds in the lobby.

"Being cock blocked is not good for my blood pressure."

"It'll be all right, promise." Connor guides me into an elevator with just the two of us, his hand a centering weight low on my back. As the doors shut behind us, he gathers me close, snuggling a fully awake Junior against my stomach.

"Pelvis is not a sexy word, so how come I like yours so much?" I ask, leaning into his embrace with a peeved sniff.

"Because you know the motion in that ocean is a cruise you want to use?"

"You mean your pestle in my vessel brings the fun so I can come?"

"They always say a tussle with my muscle triggers the scream when you cream." He tilts said pelvis, which slides said muscle not remotely near enough the entrance of said vessel.

Everything south of my belly button squeezes with anticipation, but I remain bummed.

"Thanks for trying to distract me." I pull away and attempt to fluff his wilting corsage. One of the roses comes off in my hand. Figures. "This really has to be the worst first date in the history of first dates."

"Nah, that award goes to my grandparents, Floyd and Barb."

"Of the dented brass bed?"

"The very ones. Their first date involved bad dumplings and a trip to the emergency room. Nana says she knew he was a keeper when he pulled her hair as she puked on his shoes. Sixty years later, they're still taking chances with dumplings, only now they're down in Florida."

"Why do you have their bed if they're still alive?"

"They upgraded their queen to a California king. With an adjustable base." He cocks a you-fill-in-the-dots eyebrow.

"You really do come by your perviliciousness naturally, don't you?"

"What can I say? I'm damn proud of my roots."

What would it be like to be proud of who I came from? To be worried about my father's health? To miss my mother instead of breathing easier in her absence? To have parents who value people over status, relationships over acquisitions?

The elevator doors slide open on a wide, near-empty mezzanine.

"This isn't the rooftop bar," I say, pointing out the obvious.

"Nope. Sad as I am to admit it, I think sex on a barstool will have to remain a failed drink name rather than a reality. But"—he continues, guiding us down a quiet side hall at a fast clip—"Grandpa Floyd did the structural redesign when this hotel decided to go after the conference market. One of his briefs was to increase the restroom capacity on the meeting room floors. He managed to tuck one off the beaten path in the final build-out. Possibly for this sort of emergency. He's always been a planner that way."

"Are you suggesting what I think you're suggesting? Connor Mack, I love your deviant brain."

"*A man is lucky if he is the first love of a woman.* My brain and I thank you."

We speed up, flat-out racing now, and I laugh, letting his latest addition to his collection of odd utterances pass without comment. His breathless chuckle twines with mine until we arrive at an alcove far from the meeting rooms with a discreetly marked bathroom door.

We tumble inside, grabby and greedy, slamming against the wall of the small lounge area and spinning across its length. Finally, we crash into a corner, my back to the textured wallpaper, our foreheads pressed together as our chests heave, searching for breath.

"This dress." He ghosts lightly over the silk, growling low in his throat.

The barely there touch melts my spine. My thighs part, and Connor accepts my invitation, sliding his thigh into the gap. Rocking against him, I chase sensation after sensation, building up an urgent, needy heat. Closing my eyes, plunging deeper into pleasure, I purr. He grips my hips and growls again, animal, ravenous. I move faster. And faster yet.

"Thumb my clit. Now, now, now."

Snaking an arm low around my waist, he dives into my panties, his right hand a heat-seeking missile locked on target. He cups me, palm rasping my sensitive flesh. I writhe, searching for more. More pressure, more friction. His thumb makes contact.

I go up in smoke.

Seconds, minutes, or hours later, I rouse enough to note that we aren't standing in a ring of ashes. Huh. Guess we didn't burn the building down around us after all.

"It was good for me. Was it good for you?" I ask, stretching like a well-satisfied cat.

"Not completely, thank fuck." A proud Junior tents his trousers.

"That's a nice look on you." Still plastered together, it's easy to graze my nails gently along the outline of his cock. Shuddering, he thrusts into my palm.

"It would look even better in you." He paints a gentle arc over the hood of my clit.

"I, uhhh-mmm."

"I haven't moved my hand." Another glide, light as a feather.

"I n-noticed."

"You haven't given me new orders. Figured the first set was still in effect." He presses his thumb more firmly against my clit. All the muscles in my body clamp tight as my desire reignites.

"New orders. Wrap Junior in a rubber, remove your tie, and take a seat on that bench."

As he complies, I slide my panties off and tamp them into the handkerchief pocket of his suit jacket, fluffing to display the pale-gray lace against the fabric.

"Your tie, ma'am, sir, ma'am."

Accepting his offering, I climb onto the bench, straddling him, sliding in close to where we both want me to be. I snap his tie, once, twice.

"Ready to go up in flames?"

"Start the countdown, baby."

"Hands." He presents them to me. I tie a loose bow around his wrists and lead his arms behind his head. "Okay?"

"Yes. Good." His eyes are slitted, cheekbones ruddy. His pulse thuds at the base of his neck. "Go. Now. Please?"

Using his shoulder for balance, I snuggle closer before seating myself on his cock in one, long plunge to the root.

My head falls back as I soak in every scintilla of each sensation. The heat, my wetness. The way he smells. How well we fit together.

I've had his cock before, dozens of times now. Why does inviting him into my body always feel like a revelation?

He grunts, hips raising, impatient for more. I take a firmer hold of his shoulders and rock. At first, our rhythm is uncoordinated, our grace nonexistent. But soon, we hit our stride. Against a soundtrack of bodies grinding together and murmured pleas of *yes, yes, yes,* we arrow straight to orgasm.

He hits the bull's-eye first, climax ripping through him. I arrive a beat after, exploding on impact.

After a moment or ten to catch our breath, we take turns cleaning up, the everyday intimacy of this post-sex ballet both unremarkable and profound. Different somehow from our previous encounters. Cozier, maybe.

I... like it.

With a mock growl, he bats away my attempt to repair his smushed flowers, so I move on to re-knotting his tie. My attention locks onto the blocks of writing inked on the silk, and I slow down, mouthing the words, brain catching up with all those peculiar statements he's dropped tonight.

"Charles Dickens? You've been quoting Dickens at me all evening?"

"Figured for naked sex, it was only fair I break out the Big Dickens Energy."

"I'm honored. Possibly horrified. Maybe both?"

"Let's stick with honored." With a wink, he adjusts the knot under his chin.

"I guess it would only be fair to suggest making a second attempt at the naked sex thing. Soonish," I say as he holds open the door for me. "I mean, with results like tonight, we could fail at this particular As If experiment indefinitely, and it wouldn't suck."

"Sounds like you're saying *from the death of each day's hope another hope springs up to live tomorrow?*"

"Whatever, geek boy." I rap my knuckles against his belly.

He captures my hand to press a soft kiss on the underside of my wrist. "I'll be more than happy to As If with you however many times it takes. And you're right. It will only suck when that's a direct order from your lips to my mouth."

Before I can reply, my stomach decides we've delayed sustenance long enough.

"Time to feed you, Seymour," he says over the plaintive roar.

"Wise plan, Audrey."

Revolving in circles in the bar atop the hotel, relaxed, laughing, we swap worst-client-ever stories and compare double-dog-dare-you scenarios over drinks and small plates. He shares more from his collection of Mack family stories, and I wallow in the warmth of borrowed family relations, trying them on for size, wishing they were mine.

And repress the growing itch pestering me to tell Connor about what's going on with my parents, my new business plans.

He falls quiet, twirling the stem of his wineglass in circles on the tablecloth.

"You're worried about your dad."

"Yeah." He pushes the half-empty glass away. "We've always been a tight family, but since Mom… He had trouble after she died. Grief, depression. Normal stuff, but my brothers and I weren't about to let him stiff-upper-lip it alone. So we pulled together even more."

I touch his wrist in sympathy.

"Dad rallied, and he's been good. We've been good. We'll get through this together, too, despite the fear monster yapping like a rabid Chihuahua in my ear every so often." He offers a "what can you do" shrug and smile. "Enough stewing. Your turn. Spill something so exquisitely personal it would be a high crime for me not to know. Bonus points if it includes erogenous zones."

"Feeling the call of the booty again so soon?"

"Does that siren song ever really die?"

We clink glasses—*long live, libidos*—and for the rest of the night I keep us in dirty banter territory.

With all he's going through, he doesn't need me dumping my burdens on his shoulders. Despite his express invitation, my *personal* stuff can wait.

The itch returns, sounding a lot like Helena, but I squash it like a bug.

My parents, my career turmoil, they don't get to intrude in my As If sciencing with Connor. He's mine. This time is ours.

The outside world can go jump in a lake.

CHAPTER 35

CONNOR

Midday Thursday, I bound up the steps of the gym's entrance to meet Mateo, still riding a high from the date with Keira. I can't even whip up anxiety about Dad's appointment tomorrow.

I wouldn't trade a moment from last night. Not the man corsage or the attempted Sully's dinner. Not the reservation oops that had us checking another bathroom off our-sex-in-public-places bingo card.

Not even the farting horse.

But it's the hours we spent together while the city spun in circles around us I keep returning to, freeze-frames of a closeness that has zero to do with body parts and everything to do with intimacy.

I need to work a few coffee dates into our lineup while Keira figures out what she'd like to As If for our next attempt at naked sex. I can be patient for *soonish* if waiting includes a steady diet of the kind of afternoon delight where we keep our clothes on and simply talk.

After kitting up in the locker room, I head to the squash courts. Mateo greets me with a chin nod while finishing up a hammie stretch. I plunge into my own quick warmup before we move into place.

"The Moms are threatening a family-wide boycott if we don't let them in on the party planning. And by let them in, I mean let them take over." He tosses the squash ball overhead and arcs his racquet for a wicked slice.

"You okay with that?" I return serve. The ball makes that peculiar hollow echo as it smacks off the high wall.

"Helena is." He lunges, swings, connects. "And it works for me if it works for her."

"Happy fiancée, happy life?"

"Something like that."

"You're not doing this because of Dad's cancer, are you?" Eye on the ball, I dance back a few feet then wail on the sucker. "He's legit happy to offer up the beach house for the party."

"Location isn't the question. Music isn't the question. Shit, even the color scheme meets with The Moms' approval." He fakes me out with a soft lob.

"What gives then?" I rush to save the point but whiff my backhand. "Damn it."

"Emotional economics, my friend. Helena figures we can leverage a concession this huge through at least the arrival of the first grand-child." We return to the service box where he bounces the ball in preparation for his next serve. "She's a strategic thinker that way."

"No wonder she and Keira are friends. I could see her coming to a similar calculation."

"We seem to have fallen for wily women." Preparing to serve, Mateo bounces the ball twice, grinning.

"Lucky for us." I settle into the ready position. "Now, are we playing or gossiping or what?"

"Oh, it's game on, my friend. And you're going down."

He serves again. I hustle to return it—like hell he's going to ace me —and we settle into a cutthroat match, cheerfully trash-talking each other over every point lost or won. By the end of a profanity-strewn forty minutes, our ribs flex like bellows and the air inside the closed court reeks of sports stank. Resting my hands on my knees, the burn in my muscles warns of a few sore hours in my future.

"Have you heard from Keira how the meeting with her parents

went?" Mateo's voice is muffled by the towel he's scrubbing over his face. "No, wait, I guess it's probably still going on, so probably not yet, eh?"

His words don't make sense, so I shake my head to clear my ears. "Come again?"

"What a fuck fest, right?" He throws the towel over his shoulder. "I mean, my parents get up in my business more than I like, but paying my boss to spy on me? For years? Can't wrap my head around that wrongness. No wonder she quit that rat bastard's company and has been hustling like hell to get her new agency launched."

Immobilized, I try to decode his words. Keira quit her job. To start her own agency. Because of her parents? The words still don't make sense. But the sick pit opening up in my stomach does, a kind of been-there, done-that sense.

"I didn't know."

For a nanosecond I want to hit control Z. Undo my confession. Pretend I'm in the loop.

Pretend I haven't been dumped back into chumptown, Sherry-style.

"Wait, she hasn't told you?"

"Nope." With jerky motions, I throw shit into my duffle before hefting it over my shoulder.

"But that was the plan Monday night. She came over to Helena's for dinner and strategizing. Keira promised she'd tell you what's been going on during your quote unquote test date."

"She didn't." The pit deepens, hollowing me out.

"I'm sure she had a good reason." My friend's doubt-filled eyes contradict his own reassurance.

"Yeah, you're probably right." I open the door to escape and get slapped by an onslaught of noise. The whine of mixers at the juice bar, the high-octane music of a Zumba class. None of it is louder than the static shrilling between my ears. "Listen, I need to bag on lunch. Got a crap ton to clear if I'm going to take tomorrow morning off to be with Dad."

"Con." He stops me with a hand on my elbow. "Don't turn this into something it's not."

"I don't know what you mean."

"Bullshit. You're about to jump to some douchey conclusion without hearing her side of things because it's easier than admitting she's not perfect. That was part of your problem with Sherry. She had hella major issues, not that you were willing to see them, but you had your own flaws."

"Is that right?"

"It damn well is. You placed her on a pedestal so high, by the end the only move she could make was to fall." He squeezes my arm. "Don't pull that mistake with Keira. She's not Sherry. Hell, she'd probably figure out how to impale you with the pedestal if you even try to hoist her up there. And that"—he thumps my chest—"makes her worth the trouble."

"I'll take that under advisement," I say, sounding as douchey as he claims. "Now if you'll excuse me."

I slam out of the gym, eager to put space between us. Mateo has my back, but he doesn't know the full story.

She lied.

Keira's self-proclaimed game ender.

I get the reason for the rule intimately now. Being on the receiving end of a lie is a kick in the teeth, ass, and balls.

Damn, I'm an idiot. The mix-up with the date on the room reservation last night. For a person as persnickety about details as she is? That *mistake* had to be deliberate. Hell, she couldn't even bring herself to call it a real date.

Guess she really does only see me as a convenient, goofball booty call.

CHAPTER 36

KEIRA

The restaurant my parents choose holds no surprises. Dark, clubby, high-end. A see and be seen *it* spot with fusion food and a celebrity chef. Walking from the sunshine into its stuffy dim reminds me of the poem about parlors and flies.

I don't like being the fly.

I rejected that role, and their whole world, when I graduated college. Today, I'll reject it again. The way I should have done when they showed up in the first place.

The hostess leads me to my parents' table, and I try to buck off the sense of the walls closing in on me. I check over my shoulder. Sun paints a narrow band of bright along the tiles near the door. The promise of escape.

Not trapped.

My parents are enthroned in a raised alcove with a view of the main dining area, elegant spiders on display. I wouldn't be surprised if they selected this place for the elevated seating alone. Nodding thanks to the hostess, I take my seat.

"You're late," Mother says while I lay my napkin across my lap.

"Yes."

"We ordered you a salad. Your hips." She tsks as though having hips is a sign of the apocalypse. "And that hair. Whatever possessed you to dye it gray? You look old."

"A salad is fine," I say, declining to pick up her bicker gauntlet.

Silence builds after that, as if they're waiting for something from me. But they forced this meeting. Let them blink first.

"You've outperformed expectations during your sojourn on the East Coast," Mother says when it's clear I'll outwait her.

"You make me sound like a stock option."

"Don't be flippant."

"How about direct? You paid my boss to spy on me. On what planet is that okay?"

"We invested heavily in your development. Naturally we required regular reports."

"It was a violation of my privacy." Out of sight under the table, I twist my napkin, holding tight, reliving that gut-punching reveal.

"Keeping tabs on rising talent is good business." With a delicate shrug, she dismisses my complaint. "As to why now, your father and I believe you're finally well-seasoned enough to become a significant asset. It's time for you to return home."

"New York is my home."

"Don't be silly." She waves my statement away. "Your future has always been at Tanner Enterprises. Your father is pleased with your mastery over the challenges we arranged for you through the years. Your drive bodes well for the company."

"Challenges?"

"A little strategic interference here and there designed to see how you would react to adversity." She smiles as though messing with my career, my life, is a gift, not sabotage.

A team of waiters descends on our table with the choreographed precision of the City Ballet. Covered trays are placed before us. Silver domes are whisked away on some silent cue. A mound of bare, spiky frisée stares up at me. I push the plate aside.

Father methodically debones his baked white fish. He hasn't spoken a word yet, hasn't so much as acknowledged my presence.

"As I was saying, you've shown remarkable resourcefulness, exactly the kind of ingenuity required to assist us in reaching the next level."

"I'm not interested in taking Tanner Enterprises to the next level."

"You'll apprentice to your father." Waving her soup spoon, she rolls over my objection, not listening. Never listening. "If all goes well, at some appropriate point we would begin discussing the prospect of you eventually taking over the company in full one day."

I don't miss the caveats in her patter. *If* all goes well. Some *appropriate* point. The *prospect* of. *Eventually*. Wiggle words hidden within a straightforward presentation.

Why are you so upset? We're *practically* promising you the company.

"You'll have to shut down operations here before returning to San Francisco. Two weeks should suffice. We've acquired a condo for you close to corporate headquarters, only three bedrooms, but it will be adequate in the short-term. We'll host a dinner in a month, introduce you to the right people. There are one or two gentlemen your father and I wish you to meet in particular. I'll set you up with my stylist and personal trainer to address your hair and hips before then."

"Let's back this train up." I toss my napkin onto the table, tired and sad and ready to end this farce. "My hair and hips don't need your meddling, and neither does the rest of my life. I'm not returning to San Francisco. I'm not going to work for you."

"I see you haven't outgrown your emotionalism. Regrettable," Father says.

I can't control my flinch—or my knee-jerk search for the things I've never found in his gaze. Approval, understanding. Love. His expression remains as opaque as ever.

"We've indulged your penchant for drama long enough," he continues. "It's time for you to accept your responsibilities like an adult, not a disrespectful child."

Temptation licks at me, burning, snapping, a banked fire suddenly given the air and fuel to grow wild as I slide into their mindset. I could marshal every lesson, every pain, every last hurt, into a no-holds-barred siege of Tanner Enterprises. Make everything a battle, everyone either an enemy or cannon fodder and, division by division, sector by sector, wrest their empire away. Dismantle their ability to interfere in my life ever again.

And prove once and for all that I'm just like them. Not a fly but a spider.

Capable of the same harm and destruction. Just like them.

And relishing it. Just. Like. Them.

My heart cracks. I ran and ran, but I didn't escape.

This is why it's safer to keep everyone at arm's length. Why I regiment my life into strict silos.

Because give me an inch, and I'll spin the same webs as my parents, feed off the same toxic power trips.

"No." I push from the table and the seductive pull of my scorched-earth fantasy. "I'm your daughter, not a chess piece. Find someone else to jump through your hoops and leave me the hell alone."

Forty-five minutes later, I dump the box of hair dye on the bathroom counter, still skittery about all that the meeting with my parents dredged up in me but unwilling to let them or the emotions they conjure squat any longer in my headspace. As tempting as hiding under the blankets with Camuel's stuffed comfort for the next decade sounds, it isn't the right move. No, I'm going to come clean with Connor.

The way I should have in the first place.

If I'm rejecting how my parents function—and I sure as hell am—then I need to commit to our As If arrangement fully. Finally own the hell out of that "official couple" label Helena brought up after the barbeque. Finally tell him what's going on.

As If he can handle my baggage. As If he won't use the knowledge to his advantage. As If I deserve happiness, not just existence.

I tie off the ends of my hair, planning my next steps as each band snaps into place.

I'll head to his office. If my big reveal goes well, maybe we can test out his desk. Not the naked smashing we're working toward, but a quickie in his office is bound to be more intimate than in a public restroom or a hotel. Progress. In fact, maybe we'll start with sex. I nod.

Even better. Lead with my strength then ease into the serious talky-talk stuff within the comforting bounds of aftercare.

"Operation Sexy Times with Full Confession. A brilliant plan, am I right?" I call out to Camuel, who's hanging out among the couch pillows today.

I take my companion's silence for agreement, and—with stomach settled and shoulders no longer jammed up to my ears—open the hair coloring.

CHAPTER 37

CONNOR

can't shake off Mateo's bombshell. I should call Keira, try to get to the bottom of why she'd tell everyone but me about what she's been going through. About her plans for the future.

Instead I hunker down in my project room, shuffling paperwork. By delaying, I can As If a little while longer. Pretend As If it's Wednesday morning and I'm looking forward to our first date with all the eagerness of a kid on his birthday. Pretend As If I wasn't gutted on a squash court a few hours ago.

Pretend As If it's normal to stare at nothing, to try to feel nothing, while doing absolutely nothing.

My assistant drops a file on top of one of my stacks. I add it to my unproductive rotation, moving the manila folder to a pile on my left.

"I parked a walk-in in the conference room," Devon says, adjusting his glasses.

"A walk-in? What are we, a hair salon? Tell 'em to make an appointment."

"I made noises, but they insisted." The expression behind his thick lenses tells me I can fight him, but I'll end up in the conference room anyway, so let's not waste time.

"Fine. But next time, no appointment, no meeting."

"Sure, boo. Next time. This time—" He shoos me off, probably happy to get my gloomy ass gone, even if only for a few minutes.

Walking down the hall, I try giving myself a pep talk to get into the right customer-service headspace. Test out a couple of smiles that don't fit and don't last. Terrific. Well, the walk-in will just have to deal with my uncooperative facial muscles. I take a deep breath, sweep into the conference room.

And stop in my tracks.

"Keira."

She pivots from her inspection of the skyline. Sunlight through the floor-to-ceiling windows catches the newly orange ends of her multishades of gray hair.

"You dyed your hair." Before this morning, I'd have dived straight into negotiating how to play with those flames. Now, I cross my arms over my chest and stick near the door.

"Connor, hey. Yeah. I gave into a sudden urge after lunch. Like it?" She takes a step toward me then stops, her smile turning uncertain. "Uh, how's your dad? Ready for his appointment tomorrow?"

"Practicing his invalid status in advance. Last update from David is he had a bowl of Rocky Road for lunch."

"Ice cream? I like his style."

"He's an original, all right. Thank you for asking." I sound stilted, like I'm making small talk with a stranger.

Her smile fizzles all the way out. "Why are you hanging all the way over there while I'm over here, wide open for a kiss hello?"

Pulled against my better judgment, I close the distance between us to land a light peck on her cheek.

The brief connection snares me in her scent, a tantalizing mix that signals intimacy and caring and trust to my reptile brain.

Too bad that scent is a liar.

Stuffing my hands into my pockets, I step back, but stubborn hope has me asking, "Why the unannounced drop-in? Something come up?"

"You could say that." She reclaims her smile and closes the gap between us to play with a button on my shirt. "Or rather, that I'm eager for something to come up."

Junior, the perpetual horndog, is instantly *cram the torpedo, full speed ahead*.

But Keira's lack of disclosure lands with the weight of a sledgehammer, and the muscle behind my chest wall and a little to the left stutter from the blow.

"Funny, I hoped you might be here to tell me about your parents. Or your new start-up. Or maybe that you could use a shoulder to vent on, and mine is your preferred shoulder of choice." I smooth my shirt away from her touch and take another few steps back. "But the joke's on me, right? Because it turns out you're here for a booty call."

CHAPTER 38

KEIRA

I stand in the space Connor deserted, the hand I raised to his chest hanging in midair.

"How'd you find out?" I lower my arm, cuddling it into my waist.

"Mateo." Connor gives a "does the answer really matter" shrug. "Why didn't you say anything?"

"At first, because it wasn't any of your business." I want to kick myself when he winces. "You know how skittish I've been about the whole trust-fall As If experiment. I have a lot more experience compartmentalizing my life than with sharing."

"And later?"

"You had a lot on your plate." My reasoning sounds thin even to my ears.

His expression agrees.

My palms grow damp. My heart begins to race. "Connor, I—"

"Lied. Guess I should have listened better when you said all you wanted was kinky sex with no weird emotions getting in the way."

"No. That's not..." My rebuttal turns to ash in my mouth.

I can't argue. I did lie. My reasoning doesn't matter. I broke his trust. No amount of good intentions buys me a pass on that.

Grappling with the weight of my mistake, I retreat. I bump into the wall of windows and turn to stare unseeing at the vast, sunbaked bustle of the city far below.

He approaches, standing close but not touching. The warmth of his body stirs the nerve endings up and down my backside. Old me would have been tempted to plant my butt in his junk and try to hula tease us into losing our place in this sad scene. New me wants to spin a one-eighty, and dive headlong into one of Connor's patented hugs. Reeling, I do neither.

"My best friend is getting married. I'll be an uncle in a few months. I'm turning thirty next week."

"I'm aware. Contrary to what you might think, I have been paying attention."

"My point is, I'm done with placeholders and passing the time. Being with you made me realize I've been sleepwalking since Mom died." Tone gruff yet tender, his confession makes my eyes prickle. Slipping an arm around my waist, he rests his forehead against the top of my head. "I want something more, and these last few weeks gave me hope that more would include you."

"That's what—"

"My mom used to say when someone shows you who they are, believe them." In the next raw heartbeat, he presses a kiss against my hair then loosens his embrace. I steady myself with a hand against the window as he moves away. "You want a just-sex deal. It took a while for me to get the memo, but I finally believe you. Believe me when I say I have feelings for you, and I can't turn them off to play the role of handy dial-a-bang."

No, no, this isn't happening.

Part of me detaches to float above the room, an observer to my own downfall. Helena warned me I had it coming. After a century of moments, his reflection in the window attempts a smile, but halfway into it, his mouth loses interest.

"I guess it's time to say goodbye."

"Goodbye?"

"What do you think is happening here?" He gestures to the unbridgeable gap between us.

My mouth opens, but I remain mute, unable to untangle my tongue.

"Let me frame it in terms you can relate to. Your lie voided our contract, and I'm not willing to revert to the original fuck-buddies deal. Playtime's over."

I blink against the sonic boom of his words, ears ringing.

"What about planning for the engagement party?" I could give two shits about the party. Why did I ask about the fucking party?

"The Moms are taking it over, Mateo says."

We stand there, a few feet and a thousand miles apart.

"Well, I—" I pause to clear my throat. "I guess I'll see you around."

Chin tucked down, I head toward the door and escape.

"You take care, now," he says, a generic farewell he'd offer any visitor.

No sexy grin, no goofy joke. No *us*.

My recategorization to distant social acquaintance slices like a knife.

The door closes behind me with a hushed, deafening click.

Operation Sexy Times with Full Confession is officially a colossal failure.

And it's all my own fault.

CHAPTER 39

CONNOR

An insistent ringing impels me from oblivious sleep to miserable hangover. Rude and well-timed. Must be David.

"Whaddaya want?" Swaying on my feet, I open the door to two Davids.

I blink, and the double image resolves into David and Felix. And Donut Queen. Snagging the bag, I stagger toward the kitchen and crawl onto the bench before my eyelids succumb to gravity, residual booze, and the early hour.

I wake up for the second time to the smell of coffee, eggs, and bacon, with a blanket tossed over me, and the hum of soft conversation. Groaning, I cycle through red, yellow, green on the alertness scale.

"Back in the land of the living?" Felix asks.

"Coffee," I croak, sitting up.

"Water first," David replies.

Too brain-fogged to argue, I gulp the glass down and peer at him expectantly, a baby bird looking for a worm from its mama. He pushes a mug into my hands. The coffee is hot and caffeinated. Nirvana.

"Devon said you left work yesterday looking like you'd been

mugged and muttering about falling into a vat of Kentucky's finest. Then you didn't answer your damn phone. What happened?"

"Hold off on the cross-examination until after breakfast." Felix sets a bowl of cut fruit on the table and takes a seat. "No use letting the eggs get cold because you're mad baby bro didn't call in a wingman before going on a bender."

"I can eat and interrogate at the same time," David says.

"But chewing and swallowing may be all he's capable of in this shape," Felix replies. I aim my middle finger at them with my left hand while shoveling cheesy eggs into my gullet using a fork with my right. "Correction. Make that chewing, swallowing, and simple caveman hand gestures."

I grunt. Felix chuckles. David sighs, foiled for the moment. The clink and clatter of eating becomes our early morning soundtrack until all that's left is a box of Donut Queen hangover absolution. Continuing my caveman ways, I drag a maple bacon carcass to my plate lair.

"Spill." David's brusque order sits at odds with the worry in his eyes.

"I thought things were moving in a good direction with Keira, but it turns out we're not on the same page. End of story."

They don't let it go and proceed to tag team me until I'm squeezed dry, with no detail from my crash and burn left unpoked.

"Stop. Enough. I gave her the opportunity to come clean, and she didn't take it."

"I don't know, man." Felix pops a sliver of mango into his mouth. "Sounds like you wrote a script for that scene and forgot to give her a copy."

"I don't follow."

"You gave her the opportunity to come clean." Felix makes air quotes around the repeated words. "Did she know her cue? Why not just come out and tell her what Mateo told you?"

"I did."

"No," David says. "You laid a gotcha trap then pushed her into it. When she floundered, you dug in."

"Wait a min—"

"Connie, you want to dwell in your butt hurt. Totally understandable. But when you're ready to get your head out of your ass, you might try looking at things from her perspective," he continues. "She's admitted she's no good with emotions, right?"

"Right."

"But she comes to your office, and instead of diving straight into sex, she asks about Dad? That's not a woman who doesn't care."

"She's running scared," Felix says. "Not running away. There's a difference. Figure out what you need to give her so you become the one she runs to. In the meantime, go shower or you'll stink up the hospital."

Dad's appointment. I bow my head. Damn it, I should be focused on him today, not my own drama.

"You can mope and scheme while we're in the taxi." David takes possession of the plate holding my maple bacon. "But no shower, no donut."

"Listen, you dickless weasel, if you touch—"

"Tough love, kid." Felix rubs a noogie into my head then dances back with a laugh, avoiding my swing. "That's what you get with brothers."

"Jerks. Mom and Dad should have skipped the two of you and gone straight to having me." I collect my toothbrush from the cupboard above the sink and point it at David. "When I get back, that donut better be pristine."

As I stomp off, my brothers' version of a coach's halftime pep talk echoes in my ears.

Their arguments sound good, but they weren't there. I finally matched Keira's words to her actions, and her message couldn't be clearer.

She wants me in a sliver of her life, not the whole.

It's better that I accept that and stop clinging to groundless hope.

CHAPTER 40

KEIRA

Sunday morning I force myself out of the safe confines of my cruddy apartment to meet Helena at the boutique of an up-and-coming wedding dress designer.

No text from Connor. Slipping my phone into my purse, I pause at the crosswalk to take a deep breath. No sense in being let down. Not when I'm the one who destroyed something amazing. Crushed someone amazing.

The light changes. The soles of my sandals clip against the sidewalk. Left, right, left, right. *My. Fault. My. Fault.*

My fault for keeping secrets. My fault for continuing on autopilot with my old patterns. My fault for being a scaredy-cat and running away when he called me on my behavior instead of sticking and fighting for us.

I stop outside the boutique. The shop window is draped with a lush variety of fabrics and textures, all in lighter shades of pale. Offensively pretty and full of promise. I stick my tongue out at the display, tempted to turn tail and head home. Slide back under the covers of my bed where I can hide with Camuel and lick my wounds and pretend the ache inside me is food poisoning, not a rent in my soul.

"Hey, sorry I'm late," Helena says, handing me an iced tea. "Matty woke up amorous and who was I to say no?"

The joy on her face is a lifeline, pulling me out of my spiral, reminding me of my friendship responsibility.

No more brooding. Nope, I'm one hundred percent here for my bridal bestie today.

"Who, indeed." I salute her with my drink. "Ready for our big game hunt?"

"We're gonna bag us the biggest, baddest, most-ferocious wedding dress this town has ever seen."

"Hell yes." I loop my arm through hers, and we troop up the steps to stalk our wily prey.

The shop assistant shows us to a private room where a dozen dresses from their fall collection, *Love from the Heart of the Ocean,* have been pulled for Helena's perusal.

"I'll be back to check on you in a bit. The bridal party in the main room has escalated from feisty to bickering."

"No worries," I say as Helena lets out with an *ooh* and scurries into a curtained-off alcove with her first pick. "We're good."

"Fantastic. Holler if you need anything."

I suspect she means if we need anything wedding-dress related, not a personality transplant or stupid-decision magic eraser, so I keep my mouth shut and wave her off to referee the brewing dress drama.

Helena exits the alcove with shoulders thrown back and cheeks sucked in, strutting to the mirror setup as if born to the catwalk. She's cinched into a gown the color of sad oysters that nips in tight at the waist and offers mounds of perky egret feathers at the shoulders. The angled mirror panels reveal other alarming aspects, including a décolletage cut low enough to threaten serious wardrobe malfunction during the first dance.

"You're rocking the hourglass figure. But that shade isn't doing you any favors."

"I was afraid of that." She spins in a half circle and shakes her booty in the mirror. "Also, it makes my butt look fat."

"On the plus side, it does miraculous things for your boobs."

She cups her rack and swishes through a half-dozen poses, a calculating gleam in her eye. With a sigh, she drops her hands. "As much fun as it would be to scandalize The Moms, I'm not buying a wedding dress that makes people think I'm wearing baby-ocean puke."

"Wise."

The next dresses greet us in a rainbow of ever more questionable off-white hues. Broken shell. Vintage whale bone. Sunbaked seafoam.

"Ugh, and I thought the first was bad," Helena says as I unzip her from the latest "yeah, no" option. "How is it they all make me look like the walking dead?"

"Maybe the designer raided Davy Jones's locker for inspiration." I rehang a reject while she chances another selection.

We cycle through a mermaid-tail train—complete with iridescent, plastic scales—a bustle that resembles a salacious pink clam, and some atrocity with coconuts and rayon.

"For these prices, I think the least you deserve is silk." I flick one of the coconuts on the skirt. It protests my disdain with a hollow thunk.

"I'm thinking this designer is a bust." Helena slumps onto the royal blue fainting couch. "My choices seem to be Three Day Floater or Porn Star Ariel."

"Or both." I settle into an overstuffed armchair and gesture toward the dress rack. "Better to go naked with a long blond wig then consign yourself to one of these shipwrecks."

"Aphrodite on the half shell?"

"Embody the goddess within. Can't get more real than that. You know Mateo would approve."

"Tempting. And if we were eloping, I'd say why the hell not? But." She scrunches her face.

"The Moms," I say.

"Navigating other people's expectations kinda blows."

"You could always take a page out of my book. Be a solitary island, hold the bridges." I pick at a loose thread on the arm of my chair, carefully not making eye contact.

"I knew it. I knew something was up. Mateo said Connor was clueless on Thursday, and you've spent the weekend avoiding my calls.

Last we talked, you decided to explain your current events to him on your date." She aims a beady, suspicious glare at me. "What the hell happened?"

"I changed the plan and somehow managed to accidentally on purpose break things off with Connor. Or purposefully on accident. I'm not sure which."

"Only you." She pinches the bridge of her nose. "Okay, cough it up. Tell me everything."

I detail the blow-by-blow from Wednesday on. When I'm done, the shelter of focusing on my maid of honor duties is toast, crushed under a new wave of misery.

"I hate to say you finally proved your I-am-a-rock shtick is bullshit."

"And by hate you mean can't wait to rub it in." I smear x's and o's on the glass top of the side table and lose to myself in tic-tac-toe.

"I am filled with exquisite pleasure by the prospect of saying I told you so. I'll pounce at some more appropriate point, when you least expect it." She stops my busyness with a gentle hand on my wrist. "That's not today. Today, I'm worried about you."

"I—" Pressure clogs my throat. I shake my head.

"Ah, honey, c'mere." Helena pulls me onto the couch and swathes me in a hug.

I let loose the full waterworks. I am Niagara. I am Victoria Falls. I am every dam whose barriers have failed utterly.

Throughout my collapse, my best friend strokes my hair, murmurs assurances, and holds me. Her care dredges up all my crap. The hurts and wounds and emotional injuries I've buried deep, year upon year, in order to keep on keeping on. I cry for all my fuckups, all the times I didn't deserve a raw deal but got one anyway, and every situation when I went out of my way to ensure sugar morphed into shit.

After who knows how long, I pull out of Helena's embrace, accept the napkin she offers, and mop my face.

"Why do you put up with me? I'm tedious."

"Hush. It's okay to make mistakes. It's okay to feel like shit. It's not okay to kick yourself when you're down." She drills her point home with a sharp red fingernail to my breastbone. "Don't make me beat you up."

"Ow. Okay." I hunch away. "No need to get stabby."

"I feel stabby every time I think about how hard you are on yourself and the shapes you twist into trying not to hurt other people."

"You've met me, right? Since when do I care about hurting people? I'm the original ice queen."

"Oh, please. The whole reason you attempt this very-not-successful impersonation of an island is because you're afraid you're too much for anyone to handle."

"Maybe I am."

"Bullshit. You aren't too much for me."

"Because you're stubborn."

"No, because you're good people. My kind of people. A broken, trying-your-best beautiful mess who accepts my beautiful mess and laughs with me over champagne cocktails and isn't going to let me wear seaweed on my wedding day."

"That's not—"

"Not finished," she says over me. "Your parents have the emotional intelligence of a pair of dried-up toadstools. They couldn't hack it when you grew into your own person. They still can't. That's on them. Not you. They don't get to keep you small and beholden. And you don't get to give into that."

"What do you mean?"

"I mean every time you repeat the patterns of the past, you let them eat a piece of your soul. Yeah, you're related to dicks. Wake up, girl, we all are. But it's on you if you dwell in the pain pit. Get some help. Reach out. Let your friends and lover be needed. We might surprise you."

"I don't know. I think if I reached a hand out to Connor, at this point I'd yank back a stump. What I did was pretty fucking shitty."

"True. And if you ever try that crap on me, I will add hair-removal tonic to your next box of dye. But maybe all isn't as lost as you imagine."

I raise a disbelieving brow.

"You've lectured me often enough about safe words. You didn't mention him using his."

"Thin reasoning." Magical thinking. A bump of hope-filled nerves sparks in my chest, speeding my heart.

"Worth contemplating, though. Unless you actually want to be done with him?"

"No. I'm not done. Not even close."

"Sounds like it's time for a new strategy. May I suggest Operation Connor Retrieval?"

"Two new strategies, I think," I say slowly, working my way into the idea. "Operation Connor Retrieval—"

"And?"

"Operation Find a Shrink. What you said about getting help? You're right. I need to clear some land mines if I'm going to undoom myself from constantly blowing my happiness to smithereens."

"Proud of you."

"Don't you make me cry again."

"You got it." She smacks my thigh then surveys the room, wrinkling her nose. "I'm done here."

"Scratch pirate booty off the wedding favors list?"

"And how."

"Get dressed." I return her thigh smack. "I'll see if Lola's Designs can fit us in earlier."

As Helena disappears behind the curtain, I handle the arrangements, lighter in spirit.

I'm done taking potshots at my heart because it's easier to give into my fears than go after my wants. My parents taught me there's always a winner and a loser in any deal. I'm calling bullshit and replacing their way of thinking with Connor's win-win philosophy.

He's the one that I want. He doesn't deserve to lose, and neither do I.

CHAPTER 41

CONNOR

After Dad's appointment, we spend the weekend at the beach house, letting water and food soothe everyone's edges. My brothers and I swap turns keeping eagle eyes on Dad and Celia. They do the same with me, if the sudden breaks in their conversations whenever I enter a room are a clue. I pretend not to notice. Pretend I don't have a slow, steady bleed in the area of my heart.

My confidence that I'm covering my pain well enough holds until Dad maneuvers me out to the pool deck on the pretext of firing up the grill.

"You've been walking around with a rain cloud over your head. What's up?"

"Should have known you had a motive other than food prep for getting us out here."

"I'll never understand why you and I find it so hard to stick a piece of meat on a flame and come out with something edible." He bypasses the unfathomable grill to duck behind the bar. "You're avoiding the question."

"Keira and I split up. Pardon me if I'm not the life of the party."

"No one's asking that of you."

I slide onto a barstool as he falls into a practiced rhythm prepping a couple of Old Fashioneds. Muddle the sugar, bitters, and water, add the whiskey. Drop a huge globe of ice into each glass.

"Want to talk about it?" He deftly slices an orange peel for garnish.

"Not really."

"Your mom and I broke up once." He hands me my drink, clicking the rim of my glass with his. "Worst three weeks of my life."

"Is this where you tell me an inspiring story with some pertinent lesson on human nature?"

"Nope. Just offering sympathy to my boy when he's down."

"Why'd you break up?"

"She was being a dumbass."

I cough as whiskey goes down the wrong pipe. "Excuse me, what?"

"She was being a dumbass." He looks into his drink as though the ice is a crystal ball showing him the past. "An immature, selfish, dumb bucket of ass rocks, and I was done putting up with it, so I walked. Of course, the way she recalled it, I was being a grade A, pompous wind-bag, and she kicked me out."

"Details, please."

"The details aren't important. I walked. Realized pretty fast I was more miserable without her than fighting with her and resolved to figure out a healthier, more-productive way to disagree. Thankfully she reached a similar conclusion." He lifts his glass in a salute.

"It's not that we fought. It's that she lied."

"Lies happen."

"Really, Dad? That's your wisdom? Lies happen?"

"What, you've never lied to be kind? Never lied to get out of trouble? Never lied to protect your vulnerable places?" He tilts his head to the side. "Never lied to yourself?"

"That's—"

"My pertinent lesson on human nature. People lie all the time for all kinds of reasons. Some suck. Some keep humanity from going insane. Why did Keira lie? And who was she really lying to—you or herself?"

CHAPTER 42

KEIRA

Leaving the office of my new therapist Wednesday, I aim for Central Park and a bench where I can regroup over a hotdog. Or maybe a pretzel. Definitely an ice cream confection. It's hot and hazy, and by rights I should be moving like a slug, but there's a bounce in my step and a hint of English in my hips.

When my phone rings, I finish squirting mustard on my dog and answer around my first bite. "'Lo."

"How'd it go?" Jessica asks.

I chew and consider. "Good. Weird. Good. I have another appointment next week and a couple books to read."

"Homework on the first day? That's hard core."

"Nah, it's cool. I have a lot to bone up on. In the meantime, I'm going to eat some of my feelings." I finish my first course and head toward a pretzel cart. "Thanks for recommending her."

"Hip, hip, hooray for the carb load. Remember, if she doesn't work out, there are plenty of other therapists in New York. There's no obligation to stick with the first one you see."

"Understood, thanks. Did the tie arrive?"

"Yep. It's a beauty. Midnight-blue silk with stars and a full moon shining above an outline of the Winstonian stitched in gold thread and its neighbor buildings in red. My cousins thank you for the marketing idea. Custom city block ties. They've already sold four more buyers on the concept. I sent you a pic."

I click over to her text and whistle.

"Oh yeah, now that's what I'm talking about. You'll courier it over?"

"The box is due to be picked up in ten. Your man should have it thirty minutes later."

"Thanks, Jess. For everything."

"No sweat. Now about Gigi and Bridget."

She leads us over a quick agenda as I make my way through a pretzel—more mustard—and a chicken kebab. Yes to hiring Gigi and Bridget, yes to the proposed logo design for our new company, no to the telecom contract—too-restrictive, keep looking—yes to cute promotional swag for the staff, but let's not go crazy before we make our first commission.

"May I say what a distinct pleasure it is to work with someone I don't have to manage with kid gloves?" Jessica asks as we wrap up.

"Tell me about it." I place a hand on my belly and debate between the ice cream cart and fries. "I've kissed enough overinflated egos to last a lifetime."

"Amen."

My woo campaign is in full march. Monday, I sent apology flowers to Connor from the shop where I ordered his man corsage. Okay, so I hid behind the name of my new business for the signature, *The TSB Group Wishes You a Happy Birthday Week,* and there wasn't an actual apology included, and, yeah, okay again, it's a stretch to think he'd remember the vendor name and connect it to me, but I'm still counting the baby steps as forward motion.

Yesterday, he received two novelty stress squishies as close to a side-boob shape and feel as I could get without drawing on nipples with a felt-tip marker. Again, signed from the business because baby steps.

Today, it's the tie. One last gift shielded behind the thin anonymity of the new company.

Tomorrow, my campaign starts marching out in the open. Transparent.

Naked.

My insides flutter, and it's not a reaction to the ketchup and curly fries I just shoveled into my squirrel cheeks.

The mini avatars represent all the big things Connor and I have shared. The intimacies we built a friendship on. The jokes and the trust and the caring that were always so much more than just two bodies banging.

Will he understand I get that now?

Maybe my realization needed prompting from my friends. Maybe without their support I wouldn't have given myself the chance to win him back. But Helena, Jessica, the rest of my work crew, even Mateo, not one of them thinks I deserve a life sentence as a lonely party of one.

So why should I?

"Lemon ice."

"Good choice, girlie," the ice cream guy says with a wide smile. "It's a scorcher."

"Sure is." I accept my treat, and—miracle of miracles—find a bench in the shade. Scraping a wooden spoon across the pale-yellow ice, the familiar pleasure of the scritch and tug calms my fluttering nerves.

A bit.

I could still lose everything on this gamble.

But it won't be because I gave up on myself.

CHAPTER 43

CONNOR

"Thanks, gentlemen." I smooth my new tie as I rise from the conference room table, ending a promising meeting with the owners of a start-up materials supplier. "You'll be hearing from us."

They're on the short list for the renovation. Their supply company may be new, but between them, the two guys have a couple decades each in the industry. Going with them will be a smart move.

And speaking of smart moves, wearing this tie isn't one. I adjust the knot at my throat for the millionth time. Adjust, smooth, adjust, smooth.

Flowers, silicone stress-relief boobs. This damned finger magnet of a tie.

Three days. Three deliveries. Will there be a fourth?

Keira's up to something. Despite the bland corporate name of the sender, no one else could be behind the parade of packages I've been receiving all week.

I drop the marketing materials from the supply guys on my desk and wake up my computer. One thirty. If she stays the course, her next move in whatever game she's playing should arrive soon.

Safe money is on a thong.

It's the next obvious choice. Another reminder pointing out what I'm missing and how big a mistake I made breaking things off.

The flowers, though. I tilt back in my chair, lacing my fingers behind my head. They're a mixed message that doesn't add up. Does she want a return to just sex? Does she want something more?

Trying to puzzle out their meaning has kept me tossing and turning in bed all week.

That and reliving the events of last Thursday on repeat.

Her secrets and lies sucked, hurt, and blew rotten fish chunks, but with a few days' perspective, I get what Dad was saying. What Mateo and my brothers were saying too.

None of us has a lock on perfection. We're all just trying the best we can with what we have. And while we're trying, we pull a lot of bull-shit moves to protect ourselves and sometimes to protect the ones we care for *from* ourselves.

Keira cares for me. In the logic-sapping depths of my initial hurt, it was scary easy to lose sight of that, to mix my past in with my present, and jump to a wrongheaded conclusion. It wouldn't have surprised me if, after my impersonation of a grade A, pompous, dumb bucket of ass rocks, she thought trusting me to be there for her was a fool's game and not worth her time.

But the gifts. The gifts, especially the flowers, open a door to possibility.

On Sunday as we headed back into the city, David asked a question. I couldn't answer then, but I can now. What do I want?

A life with her.

On any terms?

I frown at the ceiling, considering. We both have a lot of room to get better at this relationship thing, no question. But in order to be there for her, I kinda need to be there, so, yeah. Any terms. If the offer this gift cavalcade is leading up is a return to a no-strings arrangement, I'll say yes. Then work my ass off to convince her to turn the opportunity into a lifetime of more.

Because we both deserve another shot at forever.

Thursday, 1:47 p.m.

> Connor: [neck-down selfie of tie] Thank you.
> It's perfect.

I pick up a stress boob and toss it from hand to hand, too wired to settle. How quickly will she text back? And what color did she pick for the thong?

"How'd the meeting go? Celia's heard good things." David swings into my office a few minutes later holding a cardboard box with a newly familiar courier label.

My pulse kicks up a notch.

"I did a background check on their financials," Felix says, following a few steps behind. "No red flags."

"They knew their shit and didn't bother trying to impress me with their metaphoric dick size."

The box seems overlarge for a scrap of barely there underwear. Did she send me a thirty-sex pack? A dirty six-pack? I pinch my nose. A thirty-six pack?

"A rarity." David sits in one of my visitor chairs and bounces the package on his knee.

I bite back my demand for him to hand it over. I can be patient. Especially when it comes to not giving my brothers a peep show. They can source their own thongs.

"Saturday night." Felix leans against the doorjamb. "If you had plans, they're canceled now."

"Come again?" I ask.

"We took a family vote," David says. "It's been a hard couple of weeks. We all need a boost. Which means we're coopting, I mean celebrating, your thirtieth birthday—"

"By throwing you a party with cake and ice cream and candles."

Felix's expression crosses pity with amusement. "Fun and games for the whole family."

"I didn't vote."

"Celia voted your proxy."

"Uncool."

"Better than brooding alone in your boxers all weekend." David stands and sets the box on my desk. "If you're not feeling it for yourself, do it for Dad."

"Damn it. You always know the right button to push."

"Pushy is his superpower." Felix claps David on the shoulder. "Look, you know you're going to end up having a good time. That's your superpower. Also, do yourself a favor and invite Keira."

"All right. Fine. I'll come. And"—I smooth my tie—"we'll see about Keira. No promises."

They leave, and I sit down with the box in my lap. Heavier than lingerie would be. I shake the package. The weight shifts and thunks. Louder than lingerie would be.

So not a thirty-six pack?

I cut through the tape and open the flaps. An envelope with my name handwritten across the cream paper is tucked beside a cookie tin with the same Winstonian skyline that graces my tie. I pop the lid, and the scent of chocolate chip cookies fills my nose. I immediately cram one into my mouth.

Soft and chewy, the perfect balance between chip and cookie. Heaven. Nirvana. Paradise. These aren't mass-produced. I stuff another into my cookie hole. And they aren't from some gourmet boutique.

They're regular, plain old, homemade chocolate chip cookies.

No way these puppies are about sex.

I sniff my chocolaty manna. No, they definitely smell like affection.

And effort and… possibility.

I pluck the envelope from the box but hesitate over the flap. What if I'm reading her play wrong? What if this weeklong buildup is good-bye, not let's try?

Shaking my head, I inhale my third cookie, this time for courage, and tear open my fate.

. . .

Connor —

An honest tale speeds best, being plainly told.
(Richard III, Act 4, Scene 4)

I fucked up. I'd like to apologize in person. Can we
meet?

— Keira

P.S. You didn't safe word out. That better mean you
say yes.

I snort crumbs down my front. Classic Keira. Direct, vulnerable, vaguely threatening. Shaking my head for a whole different reason, I grin as I brush cookie bits from my tie.

There's my prickly lady.

Thursday, 2:02 p.m.

> Connor: Can we meet? Yeah, that'd be good.
> We have some unfinished business to
> attend to.

Some unfinished business that hopefully includes reaching a consensus about the status and nature of our relationship followed by a rousing round of kinky make up sex.

CHAPTER 44

KEIRA

S tanding in front of Connor's door Friday night, I mutter a rally-the-troops, pre-battle speech that sounds more like "Stop being a baby, you big coward" than "You've got this."

Add another item to the list of things to work on with the therapist. Kinder self-talk.

At least it's only muttering now. Not the manic pacing between columns I'd been doing down in the lobby where Felix, laden with bags of takeout, found me, his stern face relaxing into approval and knowing amusement.

"Good to see you," he said before pressing a key into my hand and chivvying me into the elevator. "Go get 'em, tiger."

Maybe it's not too late to slip into a parallel universe. One where I know in advance that Operation Connor Retrieval doesn't blow up in my face.

Because how ironic would it be to find we'd swapped ambitions and now he's the one who wants to exit stage left? Ironic and tragic and all the other icks.

I glare at the door's peephole. If that's the case, I'll have to continue my siege on his heart until he surrenders. Sneak attack, open engagement. I'll do whatever it takes to make Connor give me one more chance.

Releasing my death grip on the key, I take a centering breath, resettle the weight of my bag on my shoulder, and unlock the door. Probably I should have knocked. Probably I should have texted before coming over. Too late now.

A rug with bold colors and geometric shapes guides me down a short entry hall to the living room. Connor is sprawled on the couch, surfing through sports channels on the television. With a single throw pillow shoved behind his head and his bare feet hanging off the edge of a cushion, there's something vaguely lonely about him, like the balloon of optimism that inflates him sprang a leak.

My fault.

"Did you get the soup dumplings this time, or will I need to kill you?" he asks without looking up.

"Sorry, no dumplings. But maybe we could skip the killing and talk?"

"Keira." He jumps to his feet. "How'd you get in?"

"Felix took pity on me downstairs." I toss Connor the key ring. "Pretty sure this means no dim sum."

"I wasn't that hungry anyway." He motions to the coffee table where today's tin of woo—peanut butter chip brownies—has been reduced to rubble.

We stand there, taking each other in. His white T-shirt stretches over his shoulders and sets off his summer tan. His toes wiggle against the carpet, nibbleable and sexy. But it's his wary eyes that kick me in the heart.

Please, please let this go better than that day at his workplace.

"You look different." Squinting, he cocks his head. "What's up with your hair?"

I tug on a strand. "Part of my grand gesture to show I'm serious."

"By dyeing your hair brown?"

"By returning my hair to its natural color." I clear my throat. "Naked hair."

"Naked." He leans forward, posture shifting from guarded to intent. "Tell me more."

"Alligator," I blurt like cat vomit in the space between us. He blanches, and I race to him, dropping my bag to the floor. "Wait, it's not what you think."

"If you say so." He tries to turn away, but I grab hold and hang on for dear life.

"No games. No subterfuges. No hiding behind clever words or rules or role-playing. No lies. No contracts or clauses. Just me. Here to give you my truth, if you'll have it. Unvarnished and naked."

The moment stretches out with no response. Shit. I've lost him. I crumple, dropping my hands to my sides. In the next instant, I get a bellyful of shoulder as he hefts me off the floor and stalks down the hall. I land on his brass bed with a bounce before he scrambles over me, lowering his face so close to mine his hair tickles my forehead.

"What are you doing?" I ask, though the bed is a downy-soft clue.

One lights a small kernel of hope deep down inside.

"A naked conversation ought to occur in its natural environment."

"Are you turning my grand gesture into something goofy?" I level a beady-eyed glare at him.

"No." He loops a lock of hair behind my ear. I shiver from the trail of goose bumps he leaves behind. "Maybe." He grins. "We can be serious. We can be honest. But we also have to be true to who we are or this won't work. That skews us squarely over to the goofy side of the scale."

"I guess I can't argue that."

"It'd be wasted breath." He settles along my side, half on me, half on the mattress, his heat and weight two old friends I've missed more than I could ever have imagined.

Though it would be easy to slide into the distraction of his nearness, to put off my apology a little longer, it wouldn't be fair. Inhaling that breath I saved, I hold it for a long beat before slowly exhaling.

"I'm sorry I kept the full truth about my parents from you. That I lied with silence and secrets when I made us promise not to. I did it, I'm beginning to realize, out of a misplaced sense of shame that's keyed into a fear of rejection. But that doesn't absolve me."

"It gutted me." He glances up from watching his index finger paint a figure eight on my ribs, blue eyes swimming with ghosts. "Learning from Mateo all the bullshit they were slinging your way, and you never told me? Never gave me the chance to ride to your rescue? Crushing blow to my manhood, gotta tell you."

"Don't. Don't hide the pain I caused you behind a joke. And never think you weren't rescuing me this whole time with your As If chicanery. Every step you cajoled me into taking outside my comfort zone, every breath of freedom you wheedled me into making, what was that but a covert ambush to rescue me from my self-imposed fortress of solitude?"

"I really want to make a joke about watching you, but you nixed that idea."

"Like I could get you to stop joking for longer than a nanosecond." I place my hand on his chest over his heart. The heat from his body warms my palm and eases my soul. "Hurting you wasn't deliberate, but I did it, and I'm sorry."

"Apology accepted."

"As easy as that? No groveling?" He plops onto his back, leaving cold air to nip along my side. "Connor?"

"I have an apology to make too." He seeks my hand, threading our fingers together. "Then we can see who needs to grovel more."

"What apology?" I turn my head on the pillow.

He meets my gaze. "At the boathouse, you gave me a pretty good sense of how awful your parents are, and I'm sure that was just a glimpse of the full story. But instead of wondering how their sudden reappearance in your life might mess you up, I made the situation about me. When you came to my office, I don't think it mattered what you intended to say or do. I'd already made up my mind about how the meeting should go, and since I didn't let you in on the playbook, there was no way you weren't going to foul out."

"We're a mess," I whisper, turning onto my side.

"We sure are." He mirrors my position, bringing us nose to nose on our shared pillow. "I'm sorry I was a rigid dick."

"I like your rigid dick."

He raises an eyebrow, tacitly calling me on my own penchant for making jokes out of the serious stuff.

"Right. This intimacy thing is hard. Pun only kinda not intended. I accept your apology." I suck my lips in between my teeth before letting out a sigh. "My new business partner found me a shrink. I've seen her once already. I probably should have talked to one ages ago, but hey, here now."

"Therapy is good. We went to one after Mom died." He smiles briefly at the memory. "David made us."

"Your family continues to awe me." I pump our tangled fingers. "Where do we go from here?"

"A new contract."

"I'm listening."

"Our old contract was too limited in scope, and our addendums and amendments and codicils and subparagraphs muddied the waters. Time to swim in a fresh ocean."

"Oceans are saltwater."

"Work with me, here."

"Freshwater ocean contract. Got it. Continue."

"We'll keep the sexy times kinky stuff. That's a winner for both of us."

"Agreed."

"But we need to include a section about care and comfort and turning to each other first for help. And another where we're on the hook for encouraging each other to try things that scare us."

"And one that holds us accountable for lying."

"No."

"No?" I scrunch my face.

"Lies aren't good, don't get me wrong. But I don't think we can make them a dealbreaker. You ask me if a dress you're wearing makes your butt look fat, you think I'm ever going to say yes? When I ask whether my best man's speech at Mateo and Helena's wedding held the most erudite wisdom you ever heard, you're going to smile, pat my hand, and say, 'Yes, dear.'"

"So honesty isn't the best policy?"

"Honesty is a great policy. We should adhere to it as much as possible. But honesty without compassion is cruel, and sometimes a lie is the epitome of kindness. However misguided, you lied to shield me from the crazy in your life and to protect yourself from rejection."

"My motives didn't keep either of us from being hurt."

"Motive makes a lot of difference, though. Ask my brother the lawyer. So does remorse. If your intent was to inflict maximum damage before jumping ship, you wouldn't have spent a week sending me apology gifts." He traces a wet line trailing from the corner of my eye to my cheek. "You wouldn't be here now, eyes leaking, lips trembling, swinging for naked despite your fears because you want there to be an us."

"Do you have to be so damned romantic? You'll make my mascara run." I sniff and rub stray tears away with the crook of my elbow.

"You're not wearing mascara."

"Naked face to go with the hair," I mumble. "Don't move. I need my bag." I scramble off the mattress and stagger to the living room, my center of balance offline after his tender, practical, screwball acceptance of human nature. And me.

On my return, I find him propped up against the brass headboard, hands laced over his flat belly, legs crossed at the ankles. Intriguing dents and scars decorate some of the burnished slats.

Ah, yes. The infamous grandparent bed.

I can't wait to test it out. But later. After opening another door between me and true naked. I clamber my way to sit facing Connor and hug the bag safe in my lap.

"Whatcha got there?" His thigh bumps my hip.

"It's stupid."

Jackknifing up, he places a finger under my chin and turns my head until we're nose to nose again. "You're not saying it's stupid. You're saying you're stupid for thinking what you have in the bag is important. Don't. Please. Trust me. Trust yourself."

"Okay." I nod, squeezing the bag. I can keep acting As If brave if it means getting what I want.

Reaching inside, I close my fingers over the plush squishiness of my target and draw him out. "I'd like to formally introduce you to Camuel, my emotional-support animal. Outside of Helena, he's the only family I claim. He's been staunchly Team Connor since I first told him about you."

"Camuel, buddy, good to meet you in person, finally." He shakes one of Camuel's hooves, his gentle smile disintegrating another metric ton of walls between me and naked. "You have great taste."

"Figured you should be aware of all my operating system quirks before we go any further." I stroke Camuel from neck over hump to tail like the movement is rocket surgery and needs my utmost concentration.

"A support camel is the least of your quirks, but it may be the most endearing. Thank you for the introduction. I look forward to getting to know him better." He snakes an arm around my waist and tugs me to lie on top of him as he leans back into his pillow nest. I let Camuel drop to the mattress as Connor's mouth captures mine.

We kiss, slow and lazy and lilting. A dance of homecoming.

He pulls back a half inch. "Hi."

"Hi."

"I missed you."

"Same." I lick my lips. Mm, peanut butter and Connor. Two great tastes that taste great together.

"Maybe we need to add a time limit to fighting in our contract. Say, no more than two days before we start face-to-face remediation."

"What if one of us is traveling?"

"If we can't cut the trip short, we use vid chat." Junior stirs and stretches, called to full pervy attention. "Yeah, vid chat has distinct possibilities."

"Vid chat. Reasonable. Sure." Distracted by Junior's proximity, I trail kisses along Connor's throat. After being AWOL for a week and a half, General Hoo-ha reports in, willing and able to match Junior's readiness. I wriggle closer to the hot hardness underneath me. With a hungry groan, Connor arches up, shuddering.

"Think we've practiced enough emotional maturity for the time being?" he asks, panting.

"Hell yes." I work the other side of his throat, sucking little hickies into his tender skin.

"What would you say if we switch things up and practice some physical nakedism?"

CHAPTER 45

CONNOR

I try not to tense up waiting for Keira to reply. She's come so far, been so open, shared so many squishy feelings tonight, and here I am, still pushing for more. I blame the hella-hot vampire bites she's landing on my neck.

"Hey, I didn't mean to—"

"Shush." She lays her index finger over my mouth. "I'd say I'm not getting any younger."

My toes curl. My pulse pounds.

Game on.

"How do you want to do this?" I squeeze her hips. "His and hers striptease? Last one naked is a rotten egg? Yours to command? Whatever you want, as slow or as fast as you want it."

"I think my underwear disintegrated." She presses into a sitting position astride me, her lush heat beguiling my erection through our clothes.

"What color were they? You know, so I can properly mourn." I get my hands under her shirt and, oh, skin. Soft, warm belly skin. Belly skin that's only inches away from softer, warmer, private skin.

"Pink. With multicolored unicorns cavorting hither and yon."

"Hard to imagine there's enough yon in a thong to pull that off."

"They're briefs." Her cheeks turn bright red.

"Wait, is this more nakeding?" I sit up, bracing her back with my hands. "Why does mentioning briefs make you blush?"

"Because they're normal. The kind of undies I wear every day, not the cut-you-off-at-the-knees stuff I save for you." She huffs her bangs off her face. "The thongs were part of a carefully designed disinformation campaign intended to keep you distracted from seeing the real me."

"Didn't work." I beam at her, self-satisfaction oozing out my pores.

"None of my regular camouflage worked on you, you relentless, persistent nudge."

"You say that like it's a bad thing." I turn on the puppy dog eyes.

She jabs me with her finger.

"I'm on to you, buster, being all deep and schemey-scheme strategic while acting like sunny Mr. Innocent."

"Good." I kiss her nose. "Matching bullshit meters have got to be relationship gold, don't you think?"

"Relentlessly persistent and flabbergastingly positive. What am I going to do with you?"

"Short term? Tie me up and fuck me." I slide my fingers along either side of her spine, digging in that magic amount to make her writhe and push into the pressure. "Long term? I have some ideas."

"Save 'em," she says, working my T-shirt up my chest, "for after-nakedism practice."

I help her rid me of the shirt, falling like an obedient domino when she presses me flat. Looming over me, she examines my face, her naked brown hair framing us within a curtain of intimacy.

"Ready to play?"

"Ready to run the bases, Generalissima."

"Safe word?"

"Do you need to pick a new one since you used yours? Are they like a one-and-done thing? I'm good with crocodile, but you could go with monitor lizard, gecko, pterodactyl."

"Connor."

"Yeah?"

"It's okay that you're nervous." She scritches me behind the ear with affectionate reassurance. "I am too."

"Didn't know I was until you said it." Releasing a sigh, I lean into her pets. "Okay, I'm crocodile, and you are whatever reptile comes to mind. My vote is dragon. Is it time to take our pants off?"

"Impatience doesn't get rewarded, young man." Her stern tone is belied by the laughter crinkling her eyes. "Do you need to be spanked?"

"No ma'am, sir, ma'am. I need to be stripped, mounted, and ridden hard."

"That sounds like an ambitious, admirable agenda. Let's do it."

She takes a deep breath, then poof, there goes her shirt, dive-bombing the floor, followed quickly by a plain cotton bra. Wasting no time, she lies against me, skin to skin, the shape and weight of her breasts burning into my long-term memory.

"Halfway to naked," she whispers.

"Excellent progress," I whisper in return. Keeping our bodies locked together, I roll us onto our sides. "Definitely something to celebrate."

Our celebration kiss starts out soft, a light press of lips. With each touch of our tongues, the intensity builds, the need for more increases. The heat between our bodies grows until we're panting for air, straining for more pressure, a new angle. Our hands fan the flames, stoking our desire with every brush of fingertips, every teasing scrape of nails.

We stop breathing altogether when my hand discovers her breast.

Her hard nipple pokes my palm, demanding attention. I break the kiss and skim down her body until my mouth hovers over one sweetly pinched nipple.

"May I?"

"Yes, please."

With her consent, I pay homage to the delicate, sensitive curves, learning what touch makes her gasp, how much pressure coaxes forth a moan. I pull back to admire my work, blowing gently over the taut and shiny berry-red peaks. With a sound of frustration, she threads her fingers through my hair, tugging me back, and who am I to say no?

Humming with pleasure, I settle in to suck and nibble and drive us both wild, but she distracts me into stillness, sliding her slim hand past the boundary of my waistband. She explores the little she can reach. It's enough to lock my breath in my chest as I wait for the next touch. When she makes a circle in the wetness at my tip, I shake with glorious agony.

She prods me onto my back.

"Ready for three quarters of the way to naked?" Her hands hover over the placket of my cargo shorts.

"Yes to you undressing me all the way—which just pointing out would make me one-hundred-percent naked and you still only half naked—but yes, please open my damn shorts and haul my boxers to my ankles. I am ready to be naked in your sight."

She suits her actions to my babble, freeing Junior, who preens tall and proud.

"What a pretty boy." She cups my balls with one hand and grips the base of my cock in the other. I dig into the mattress, trying to ground myself so I don't come early. "Did you know there are five arteries that supply blood to the penis?"

"No."

"Yes, and boner is a misnomer." She strokes up my erection, ending with a twisty tug. "Human penises don't have bones keeping them stiff. It's all blood."

"Okay."

"But," she returns to teasing the tip, and helplessly I shove myself more firmly into her hand, "penises can break."

"Enough with the weird penis facts, please. My boy is gonna start taking them personally."

"We can't have that." She bats wide, innocent eyes my way. "Would a hand job improve his attitude?"

"No. A good hand job is nice—don't get us wrong—but right now he'd probably pout through it. You don't want that. Very disconcerting to rub one out of a mopey dick."

"How about a blow job?"

"Well, if nothing else comes to mind." I tug on the waistband of her denim shorts to ensure something else comes to mind.

"Wait, I know. What if I"—she swallows then forges on—"meet him where he's at? Naked and sticky with need?"

"I'd say the prospect is already reinflating his spirits."

"Connor." She shakes her head with the concerned frown of someone about to lay down a hard truth. "Your cock... it's a little easy."

CHAPTER 46

KEIRA

"Keira." He brushes my hair back and offers me a small, gentle smile. "We can keep bantering. We can trade banter and kisses and pets all night, if that's what you want. No pressure for more naked than you can handle. You're safe with me."

"Groan. Nerves are freaking annoying. Who invented them anyway? And why is naked so damned hard?" I knock my forehead against his shoulder a couple times. "I want this. With you. More than I can say."

"Maybe you're making it too complicated." He rubs comfort into my shoulder. "Giving naked too much leverage."

Laid out atop him, I rise and lower as he breathes and waits for my response. Our bare-skinned proximity both soothes and excites, keeping my nipples tight and General Hoo-ha wet and jonesing to ride.

Yet one final barrier exists, and dismantling it has nothing to do with clothes.

If I reveal my full self, will he still want me? That's the question.

No, that's the fear.

My parents never wanted the real me. Weren't capable of handling the odd and offbeat edges that made me different from their image of the ideal daughter. Little wonder I've kept myself safe from further rejection. And why, after so many years, changing the pattern is so damned difficult.

But from the beginning, Connor—pushy, persistent, bright-eyed, pervilicious—has prodded me to reveal more and more, and he's never judged me as less than. Not even when I kept trying to bulldoze us back into the buddies-with-bennies zone. All that hurt I inflicted, and his ultimate response is always compassion and acceptance.

He's not interested in my hip size or disapproving that I'm starting a business. He wants to support me emotionally and fuck me silly.

Put that way, my next step is a no-brainer.

"Right. Let's do this." I roll off him, shimmy out of my shorts and briefs, and roll back before I can chicken out. "And to prove I'm not going to push you away…"

I wind my briefs around our opposing wrists, cuffing us together.

"Connor Mack, we're going to have naked sex. On a bed. With the lights on while staring into each other's eyes. I'm going to ride you slow. I'm going to ride you filthy. And I'm going to make you come hard enough your eyeballs might pop their sockets. Are you okay with this agenda?"

"I was born for this agenda." His crooked smile puts a bow on my heart. "Bring it."

With my free hand, I reach for his cock then stop. "Shit. Condom."

"Under the pillow." He winks a smug wink. "Former Scout, remember?"

"Lucky you're cute." I retrieve the wrapper. "Also, it's possible I should have thought twice before tying our hands together. Talk about awkward."

But our chuckles fade away as our gazes lock, and we fumble through the sheathing. The intimacy of working together on this private task by touch alone ramps every little sensation up. It's not awkward. It's hot.

Hot and exactly right for us.

With a firm guiding hand, I play his head over my clit and struggle to keep my eyes from rolling to the back of my head. Maintain eye contact. What a stupid agenda item when all I want is to shut out the world and drink in this bliss.

But I'm not shutting out Connor. Not ever again.

I rock back and forth, a slow grind that teases hints of the ecstasy to come. Soon, I'm shivering, and airs saws in choppy gasps in and out of Connor's lungs. Taking him inside, I slide inch by inch down to his base, savoring the fullness and heat. Fully seated, I contract secret muscles to welcome this most-wanted return guest.

He moans, hips flexing in gratitude for my hospitality, his length rasping against that one spot.

Slow flies out the window. I flatten our hands, tied and free, to the pillow and set a rhythm that steals my sanity. Fast and faster, I strive to get us to the peak, keeping eye contact, straining to see into his soul. Letting him into mine.

No veils, no hidden agendas, no secrets or lies.

Ruddy lines flag his cheekbones. A drop of sweat trails from his temple.

So close, so close. Just… need…

A wicked, knowing light glints in Connor's gaze. He frees his hand, wets his thumb then strums my clit.

Right. There.

Every twanging nerve clamps tight for that endless second before climax.

One last, firm stroke, and I detonate, shimmying through an electric current of bliss.

I collapse into Connor's one-armed hug.

"All good?" He nuzzles the skin behind my ear. Too spent for speech, I nod. "Excellent. My turn."

He rolls me onto my back. The repositioning frets his still-hard cock against my sensitive walls, and I moan. Threading the fingers of our bound hands together, he thrusts, reigniting my need. I wrap my legs around his waist, feet digging into his butt, giving as good as I get.

I pull his face to mine until our lips brush and put everything into my eyes, all my hopes and promises.

"I love you, Connor Mack."

He comes with a shout, his body quivering in my embrace. His orgasm trips mine, and I convulse over my second peak, a drawn-out spin of mind-melting pleasure.

We're a tangle of sweaty limbs as I surface back to the present, somehow lying on top of him again. Sex perfumes the room, tangy and sweet. His heartbeat thuds in my ear. The AC cycles on, and I shiver. He yanks the duvet over us.

If I weren't already wrecked, his knee-jerk blend of courtesy and protection would have knocked me flat.

"So," he says.

I grunt.

Riding his silent laughter, I snuggle into our nest. Who needs words? Words are overrated. He tugs the ends of my hair.

"What?" I grouch mumble.

"I didn't quite catch what you said back there. Think you're going to have to repeat it." He clears his throat. "A few million times. Preferably over several decades. You know, to make sure the message sticks the landing."

Bracing for a barrage of my old fears, I stay huddled and safe in his arms. But the expected hordes of doubt don't arrive. My interior landscape remains quiet on all fronts. At peace.

Giddy with dreams of the future, dreams I've never allowed myself, I push up until we're eye to eye. "I said I love you. I meant it. I'll mean it every time I say it. And I'll gladly say it a few million times over several decades, if you'll have me."

"If I'll have you." He issues a dismissive grunt. "Have you been asleep this whole time? I've been going full-court press to win your heart since I first saw you at Sully's."

"I'm awake. I swear. And I'm promising decades, so I'd say your campaign is a success."

"Good." He kisses me, no tongue, a simple, sweet punctuation to his approval.

I pull back. "What about you?"

"What about me?"

"Dude." I poke him.

"I love you too." Smiling, he tucks a strand of hair behind my ear.

I attack him, kissing every square inch of his face.

My exuberance dislodges Junior, and we stop to deal with the practicalities—our undie-cuffed wrists, condom disposal, private parts cleanup. I imagine us in the future, gray-haired and creaky, still eager to get busy with each other while coping with the mundane moments in life.

The picture makes my heart skip with little-kid joy and big-kid excitement.

Back in his room, I scoop my bag off the floor and search its depths while he plumps pillows into a more-pleasing arrangement. My breath catches when he settles Camuel on his own fluffy throne.

"Oh boy. Are you in for it now." Target acquired, I drop the bag.

"What? What'd I do?" He looks over each shoulder, down at the pillow nest, back at me.

Instead of answering, I point. "On the bed."

A half smile of bewilderment tugs at his mouth as he obeys. Lying back, he stretches his arms along the brass slats of the headboard, grabbing hold of the two with the most dents. Taunting me with the flex and play of his broad, muscled chest.

"You can stop trying to lure me with your wiles. We're totally going to usher in your birthday by adding our own dents to that headboard after the clock strikes midnight. But first…"

I settle beside his hip and open my fist to reveal a small, square, black-velvet box. He goes statue still.

"What's this?"

"Good faith on our new long-term contract."

With unsteady hands, he snaps open the lid. Inside, an antique signet ring nestles within silk folds, glinting with dreams and promises.

"It dates back to the year the Winstonian first opened. If you don't like it, we can get something else. That is, if you want." I clamp down on my verbal diarrhea and start again, "What I mean to say is, Connor, will you wear my ring? Go steady with me? Maybe marry me one day?"

"Hell yes, I want." He plucks the ring from the box and presses it into my hand. "And none of this going-steady nonsense. We're engaged. You've claimed me fair and square."

He wiggles his ring finger, an impatient demand I step up the pace.

Grinning like a loon, I slide the ring into place and turn our As If experiment into Happily Ever After.

ABOUT THE AUTHOR

IF YOU enjoyed Connor and Keira's story, please show it some love with a review! Reader support makes all the difference—and helps others fall in love, too.

———

J. KEELY THRALL writes contemporary and paranormal romance filled with heart, heat, and sass. She believes romance—writing it and reading it—invites us to practice the art of building healthy relationships. In fact, romance just might be the secret key to answering the age-old question: *"How do I human better?"*

Founder and president of the Stays Up Too Late Society of Book Addicts, Keely has been known to mutter "just one more chapter" until sunrise. When she's not emotionally torturing fictional people, she's nerding out with friends about books and travel—or admiring her inexplicably large collection of camel figurines. Her motto: Write with joy. Read with abandon. Say "yes" to the nap.

Want a *free* steamy contemporary romance ebook? Sign up for Keely's thrilling, enthralling newsletter: **https://jkeelythrall.kit.com/**

———

Want more of the Mack family?
You're in luck! Keep reading for a sneak peek at David and Celia's spicy Christmas adventure in *The One That I Need* and their seductive Thanksgiving shenanigans in *The One That I Miss*…

SNEAK PEEK OF THAT ONE THAT I NEED

D A V I D

'Tis the season for making merry… and keeping secrets.

FOR MARRIED couple Celia and David, Christmas is a time for the spicy romantic role-playing that deepens their connection—especially this year, when they're dreaming about the future they hope to create together.

But when perfectionist Celia begins hiding something big, it threatens more than her work. It cracks the foundation of the deep trust they've built though love, laughter, and just the right amount of kink.

Reeling from her silence, David engineers a seductive intervention to remind his wife that no matter how much life changes, the one thing they'll always need… is each other.

———

CHAPTER ONE

My Responsibility

March 21, Present Day

"It's not like Celia to flake on the important stuff. Is she okay?" my youngest brother, Connor, asks. Voice on speaker, his concern bounces off the walls of my office to lodge at the base of my skull.

"She coming down with a late-winter bug?" Felix, my middle brother, guesses.

"Does she need help?" Dad asks. "Do you need help?"

I pinch the bridge of my nose. Connor set me up for a classic Mack family tag team of support. I should never have answered his call.

On the other hand, it's good to have confirmation that Celia's erratic behavior lately hasn't been a figment of my imagination.

"No, thanks. We're going to talk in a few minutes. Clear the air. I'll brief you on whatever's going on over the weekend."

"Sooner if you need us," Felix says.

"Sooner if I need you."

Clicking the red end button, I preempt what would likely be a million follow-up questions from Connor. Hell, from all of them. It's not that I don't appreciate my family's support. Right now, though, I need to focus on addressing Celia's spin cycle, not their concern.

Perched on the bookshelf beside my desk is one of the Christmas cacti she decorated all the firm's cubicles, offices, and meeting rooms with back in December. Before she started spiraling. I touch the orange-red blossom, fragile and out of season.

Is she doing it on purpose? Belly flopping in big and small ways because she wants my attention?

It's true I've been distracted. Slack in my care. Dad and I have been immersed in wrapping up the final blueprints for Platinum Harbor, the luxe retirement community slated to begin construction this summer. My focus has been on work, not Celia.

A mistake.

She needs a refresher in asking for help.

A slow, hungry smile pulls across my face. I lean back in my chair, something deep inside me stretching with anticipation.

The beast I keep locked down and muzzled.

He's not suitable for civilized company, but there are times when it's necessary to let him free. Times when acting like a plain vanilla businessman won't cut it.

I adjust my half chub. If I hadn't answered the damn phone, I'd have cleared my little head so my big head can stay in charge of calling the shots. Too late now.

No matter.

Celia is lost.

And it's my responsibility to help her find her way again.

What kind of sugar and spice surprise does David have planned? Unwrap this swoony, sexy Christmas story and see how one night changes everything —
*get **The One That I Need** now!*
www.jkeelythrall.com/books

SNEAK PEEK OF THE ONE THAT I MISS

There's nothing like becoming a first-time parent to dish up all your deepest fears.

HAUNTED BY a tragedy in his past, new dad David worries he won't be enough to protect his infant daughter. Determined to ease his fears, his wife Celia cooks up a Thanksgiving holiday chock full of hope, love, and heartwarming family support—and some spicy alone time guaranteed to reignite their intimate connection.

Though most of the week goes according to plan, a series of interruptions foils Celia's attempts to turn up the heat on their love life and her seduction becomes a comedy of errors. Still, Celia won't give up—not until the two rediscover the flame of their love.

———

CHAPTER 1

David Mack

"THIS STRETCH of beach was Paul's favorite place in the world. Mine too." I lift my gaze from my jotted notes, eyes too full of sting to read the words or see the people fanned out before me. "Some of my first memories are of the two of us sneaking out at night to run races in the sand. Some of my second memories are of getting caught. Punishment was swift—no playdates for a month." I pause for a beat. "Some of my third memories are of the two of us learning how to sneak better."

The crowd chuckles.

"I think—no, I know he'd be thrilled that his beloved beach will now, finally, be enjoyed by the community for years to come. On behalf of the Kosmos family, thank you all for your support through the years and especially for being here today to help us dedicate this new park. You'll find coffee, hot cider, and fixings for s'mores on the tables behind you. Let's honor Paul's memory by getting sick to our stomachs eating his favorite treat in his favorite place."

With a click and a whoosh, the kindling catches and Paul's memorial bonfire roars into greedy life. I step back from the flames, making a quarter turn away from the attendees.

Friends, my brothers, neighbors. The old guard who grew up with Paul and the newcomers, here out of curiosity or compassion or whatever the hell reason. He'd laugh at the crowd size, say something cynical about his parents' presence. Be over the moon at seeing his sister.

If he were here.

The wind off Long Island Sound carries the cold snap of November and the brine of salt water.

Surely that combo is what's making my nose run.

For fifteen years, we've gathered to remember a life snuffed out too soon. Another three years and my best friend will have been dead for as long as he was alive.

Damn it, Paul.

My fingers curl into impotent fists. It wasn't supposed to play out this way. Why couldn't you hang on? Send out an S.O.S.?

Do something, anything to show... I would have helped if I'd known you were in trouble.

How did I not know? How could I have been so fucking blind?

Like the pound of the surf, the questions crash in my heart, an unceasing riptide of regret.

Regret and guilt and helplessness.

"Head's up. Daddy Kosmos is incoming," Celia says, pretending to straighten the collar of my black wool coat. She gives me a pat of reassurance. "Luckily, you have a built-in exit strategy this year."

"A cute one."

"Utterly adorable, one hundred percent. But also kind of a tyrant."

"Oh?"

"If my boobs are anything to go by, cute Holly Amaryllis is going to start demanding her afternoon tea soon."

"So noted." I kiss her temple, tucking her into my side, and meet the outstretched hand out of Paul's father. "Mr. Kosmos, sir."

"David." As usual, he tries to squeeze my palm into submission.

He lets go after a beat too long when I give him no reaction, disguising his annoyance in the clearing of his throat.

I don't give into bullies. Especially not this one.

"The benches are lovely, Mr. Kosmos," Celia says when it's clear neither of us is going to speak. "Visitors will enjoy being able to look out over the water without having to worry about getting sand in their shoes."

"The wife's idea." Grimacing, he issues a quick grunt. "Make that wife and daughter. Me, I'd have sold out to a developer long ago if the property hadn't been in the wife's family. Better to turn this land into something profitable over creating this—" His dismissive wave encompasses the half circle of wooden benches surrounding the firepit and the short flight of steps down to the beach. "—this shrine to my son's weakness."

"You take that back. He wasn't weak," Mrs. Kosmos says in tear roughened protest, stepping from behind his shadow. "My baby was a beautiful soul. A beautiful, lost soul, too misunderstood to withstand this cruel world."

"That is a load of crap, Maria. The truth is, he took the coward's way out when he hit his first taste of real life pressure. There's nothing beautiful about being spineless."

———

CELIA extricates me before I give into the impulse to deck Paul's father. It's good that my brothers drove over in their own vehicle, because we take off as soon as our seat belts are fastened. I use the short ride to calm down until I can see details out the passenger window instead of an angry red mist.

Back at the family beach house, we collect a fretful Holly from Dad —who volunteered to miss the memorial so he could babysit—and retreat to her bedroom. Shrugging out of my coat, jacket, and tie, I press play on the sound machine, already set to Holly's favorite "spring forest rainfall". At eleven weeks, she's very definite in her preferences.

Like—having both her parents with her when she feeds.

Dislike—the overhead light's glare.

"Hold her a sec, will you?" Celia asks.

I secure Holly in the crook of my arm while my wife performs a similar shedding of outerwear. I make a circuit of the room and flip switches on or off according to our baby's will. Snagging a blanket, I sit in the glider, welcoming Celia's weight as she plops herself in my lap.

Yanking up her top, she frees a nipple from her ingeniously engineered bra and guides Holly into latching on. The whole sequence is utterly prosaic and sexy as fuck.

"I feel that bone growing." She wiggles her butt over my semi.

"Autonomous response. It too shall pass."

"The doctor says we don't have to let it go to waste anymore."

"Let's concentrate on milking and napping this afternoon, Princess." I swathe us in the heavy fleece, creating a cozy, just-right nest to lure my wife into resting. Celia's go-go-go energy needs more frequent pit stops these days. "We can revisit the question of what to do with my bone another time."

"Spoilsport," she says around a yawn.

"That's me. Spoiling you rotten, like a good sport."

She sniffs her disagreement, but can't quite suppress her small grin. Chuckling, I set the glider in motion. We drift, listening to gentle, out-of-season rain and the amusingly robust grunts of our daughter.

When Holly finishes, we do the burping thing. Celia shifts into a more comfortable position along my side for snoozing. I nestle our baby on my chest, grateful to serve for the next hour or so as their mattress.

"You sleep too." Celia pokes my side.

"I will, I will."

If I can.

If my brain will stop.

It races from Thanksgiving logistics to the suspect soil test data on the Dyson project to that weird ping that sounds whenever the SUV makes a left turn.

Cycling through any and all of the solvable problems on my list.

Avoiding the one I can't do anything about.

The day of Paul's bonfire each year is always rough, bringing up bad, sad memories.

Regret and loss and a recurring phantom limb syndrome-style reflexive action where I wake up and reach for the phone first thing, only to realize that I can't coordinate a time to meet Paul later at the bonfire.

Because the damn thing is for him.

If it weren't for Petra, Paul's sister, I'd have stopped attending the memorials long ago.

But shared guilt is powerful glue.

Once she hit eighteen, she escaped her parents' thumb and rarely returned to check on her ten-years-younger brother. Her sense of failure comes from being absent. Mine from being right there, *right there,* and never noticing how much pressure Mr. and Mrs. Kosmos put on their son to conform to their competing expectations.

Neither of us recognized the toll it was taking as he tried to comply.

Neither of us had a clue how desperate Paul was until it was too late.

Too late.

I tuck the weighted fleece a little tighter around Celia. Since Holly's birth, a swirling cocktail of post-pregnancy hormones has played havoc with her brain.

Almost leaving the house without pants. Almost flooding the bathroom because she forgot she wanted a soak and left the water running. Ordering yet another ice cream scoop—I count on my fingers, we're at seven now—because that ad in her feed was adorable and she was sure we needed a good one. I smile. They are good scoops. They'll make great stocking stuffers next month.

Instead of crying in frustration each time she realizes she's been zapped by chemistry, she laughs. She laughs, I laugh with her, and I do a final loop of the apartment each night to make sure everything is on, off, locked or otherwise in its intended place.

In the past week, the hormones seem to have piped down, but I would remain watchful, make sure I'm on hand any time my princess needs an assist. Make sure she can continue settling into motherhood with more ease and joy than either of us anticipated after all her early doubts.

Pressing a kiss to the top of her head, I linger, taking in Celia's scent. Still delicate, with that hint of citrus from her shampoo, but there's something more now, an added layer that smells like our daughter. Like family and home.

Holly smacks her lips and punches herself in the chin. I lift her a little higher, reassuring us both that she's okay.

I could sit here until I'm one hundred and twelve, with her sweet, solid weight against my heart and Celia curled in beside us. Taking in a deep breath, I try to seal the moment into my long-term memory, this moment when they are here with me. Here and safe.

Never.

The promise surges from the depths of my soul, flooding my system until my hands shake.

"Never," I whisper into the tiny shell of Holly's ear. "Never will you feel for one second like you aren't well, full and wholly loved."

Every last inch of you.

"You'll never need to doubt that I'm in your corner, good times and bad. Whoever, however, and whatever you want to be. Not like Paul. Your story won't end like his. I will protect you. I swear."

Don't miss out on Celia's heart-stopping reaction to David's declaration —
*read **The One That I Miss** now! https://jkeelythrall.com/books/*

www.ingramcontent.com/pod-product-compliance
Lightning Source LLC
Chambersburg PA
CBHW051528260626
47170CB00003B/830